Joanna Lumley

Stare Back and Smile

Memoirs

VIKING

For my family and for Stephen

VIKING
Published by the Penguin Group
27 Wrights Lane, London W8 5TZ, England
Viking Penguin Inc., 40 West 23rd Street, New York, New York 10010, USA
Penguin Books Australia Ltd, Ringwood, Victoria, Australia
Penguin Books Canada Ltd, 2801 John Street, Markham, Ontario, Canada L3R 1B4
Penguin Books (NZ) Ltd, 182–190 Wairau Road, Auckland 10, New Zealand

Penguin Books Ltd, Registered Offices: Harmondsworth, Middlesex, England

First published 1989
1 3 5 7 9 10 8 6 4 2

Copyright © Joanna Lumley, 1989

Printed in Great Britain by Richard Clay Ltd, Bungay, Suffolk
Typeset in 12/15pt Lasercomp Garamond

A CIP catalogue record for this book is available from the British Library
ISBN 0-670-82174-8

Acknowledgements

———

Photographs by the following appear in this book and on the jacket. To all of them, and to anyone I have inadvertently left off the list, my warmest thanks.

John Adriaan

H. Albert

David Appleby

Brian Aris

Celia Armitage

Micheal J. Barrett

Carl Bruin, *Sunday Mirror*

Michael Claydon

John Garrett

Ray Green

Barbara Kleiner

Patrick Lichfield

Beatrice Lumley

James Lumley

John Neman, Susan Griggs Agency Ltd

Terry O'Neill

Robert Penn

Roy Round

SKR Photos International Ltd

Peter Shirley, *Daily Express*

Peter Smith

David Steen, Scope Features

Peter Tanlie

Thames Television

Chapter One

Sometimes I wake up just before dawn, when the wind is blowing and the sky is grey and I think I am on board ship again. The breeze clamours down the chameleon-eye air duct, the port-hole is open. All around us for days is the sea, and we are crawling across its wrinkled surface to Hong Kong. I can hear the slap and hiss of the waves, the drone of the ship's engine: above are bleached decks, tilting with the swell of the sea, metal edges and rivets covered with thick paint, everything tasting of salt. Then I see the tops of English trees, and rooks, or hear a car in the street and I am back on dry land.

So much journeying. It took five weeks from Southampton to Hong Kong, four weeks from Singapore to Southampton via the Suez Canal. 'Were you an Army brat?' asked a reporter, and although I'd never heard the term before, that was what I was.

My father was with his regiment, the 2nd 6th Gurkha Rifles, in sweltering Madras when I was born. My mother left Abbottabad with my sister Ælene, who was two years old, and travelled to Srinagar in Kashmir to spend the summer in the cool hills. Her great friend Helen Stavrides lived there. Helen was Ælene's godmother and gave her the Greek name Eleni, but spelt it in a rare and beautiful way which has caused difficulty with pronunciation ever since.

My mother had been Thyra Beatrice Rose Weir, younger daughter of Leslie and Thyra Weir. Thyra was a Danish name, Granny being half-Danish and from New Zealand. Leslie Weir was a Scot, in the Indian Political Service. When I was born, they too were in Srinagar, staying at Nedou's Hotel. My mother's married name was Lumley, Mrs James Rutherford Lumley, which at the time she thought a clumsy and difficult surname, not nearly as graceful as Weir. My father's father, Charles Chester Lumley, had been a banker in Lahore, my father the only boy amongst four children. On both sides of the family, India had been home for several generations. It seems the most normal thing in the world to have been born in Kashmir, surrounded by the Himalayas, kingfishers speeding over the lily-covered lakes, blue irises in wide swathes under pale green poplar trees. I was born in the early evening of 1 May 1946, arriving promptly and rather hairily. The doctor was pleased, as he was off to have dinner with my grandparents.

Ælene had been a particularly pretty baby, with platinum hair and porcelain skin. My hair was quite black when I was born, and my nose seemed to have been forgotten, just two holes poked in by an orange stick while the clay was still damp. My mouth went half-way round my head: my father, seeing me for the first time, said I looked like a hammer-headed shark.

Even Srinagar gets hot in the summer, too hot for a small baby and a fair-skinned toddler, so my mother went on up to Gulmarg, which stands at about 9,000 feet. There we spent the summer in the Hut. They were called Huts but in fact they were spacious, long low wooden bungalows, with wide verandas tumbling with flowers. Hut 206 looked out over a marg, an alp, across to Sunset Peak and Ferozepur peak. It was a kind of paradise, with fir trees, butterflies, shady mountain paths, streams, meadows and rocks. There was a golf club, and neat paths edged with flowers led from hut to hut. There were no vehicles up there: you had to ride up on a pony through the steep forests, the air getting cooler at every step.

I almost think I remember Gulmarg, but I must be influenced by seeing photographs as I was only a few weeks old when we were there. And yet in dreams I can see from my wicker basket the tops of the pine trees and hear the distant roar of a waterfall and feel the warm sun on my face. Would I be the same person if I had been born in Alabama, say, or New South Wales? Are we affected by our surroundings or only by the people who bring us up? Yes, yes, rich, poor, healthy, handicapped, I understand those arguments: but the shape of a tree, the heat of a desert wind or cold rain in a back alley – are these things instrumental in the way our minds form and characters grow; or are we pressed into genetic moulds long before we take our first breath?

In the high alpine air of Gulmarg I caught whooping cough at six weeks old. We had to rush down to hot Srinagar for me to recover. That winter we spent at Miss O'Connor's Boarding House. Now Srinagar is shackled with huge luxury hotels, but then there was only Nedou's, and a few modest boarding-houses – and, of course, the houseboats, carved from stem to stern, made of deodar and walnut, moored on the Dal and Nagin Lakes and down the canals, near the Residency, by the Bund. They never moved from their moorings, rocking gently in storms, visited daily by a swarm of tiny shikaras, gondolas propelled by heart-shaped paddles, bearing fruit, vegetables, cloth, live chickens, jewellery and embroidery. They were broad and long, with four or five large bedrooms, drawing-room, dining-room, verandas and, instead of servant's quarters, a small dunga moored close by, on which the attendant family lived. The city is laced with waterways, all interconnecting, coiling and creeping between tall lattice-fronted wooden houses, under Mogul bridges, between vegetable gardens and lotus swamps. The huge fertile valley is ringed by the Himalayas, which feed the paddy-fields and fruit orchards with melted snow and hide emeralds, amethysts, garnets and fossilized coral in their stony sides.

The Partition of India was being prepared; it had been brought forward with precipitate speed. We must be gone, everyone must be gone by August 1947. We travelled down to

Bombay by train in March and boarded the *Franconia*. We arrived in Tilbury to be met by my Uncle David Gamble, who was married to my father's eldest sister, Rosa. We travelled by train with him to Bedford, eating on the way the lunch specially packed for us before we left the ship; envious eyes watched our soft white rolls, as in Britain they were still chewing through wholesome but cheerless National Loaf.

We stayed in Bedford for a few weeks, then travelled down to Emsworth where my mother and a friend, Joan Barber, rented a small house called Sherwood. I cannot remember any of this: there are photographs of me and Jane Barber in a pram, looking like two furious old men, of me pushing a toy wheelbarrow, and being held close to whiskery tweed lapels. We stayed in England for a year; then in December 1948 we set sail again, this time on the *Empire Windrush*, a Strength Through Joy ship requisitioned from the Germans after the last war, with the taps marked *Heiss* and *Kalt*. There were storms all round the English coast as we set off, and Queen Alexandra's Nurses looked after us as we chopped down through the Bay of Biscay, through the Mediterranean, where they disembarked at Malta. Malta was a shell, flattened almost beyond recognition by the wartime bombs, flattened but indomitable. We were not allowed off: instead my mother bought almonds from a bumboat and she bent the steel doors trying to crack them in the hinges.

We arrived in Hong Kong and stayed for a short time with my Uncle Alastair Panton who had married my father's youngest sister, Isabel. We then moved into an Army flat in Chatham Road, Kowloon, overlooking Lyemun Gap between Hong Kong and the New Territories. Our flat was rather like a Kensington apartment: from it, looking out over the road, you could see the railways and beyond them the harbour, filled with ships and junks. We bought two guinea pigs, Sammy and Michael, who lived on the narrow balcony and whistled back at the sailors in the streets below. There were two amahs, Ah Geng and Ah Kwong. Their black long hair was pulled tightly back into thick buns and lacquered into position with some sort of gum, boiled in a saucepan and applied while the hair was still wet. As was the custom, they wore shiny black trousers and blue overshirts which fastened diagonally at the neck.

The flat I remember as tall and dark, with glass inner doors, a warm kitchen which smelt of garlic and ginger, and some terrifying hot water-pipes which juddered 'gudduh-gudduh' at night-time, scaring me so much that I would be taken into the kitchen to sit with the amahs, listening to their peaceful chatter and eating salted melon seeds. We were taken out on 'boiling hot shoppings', through the busy market stalls and thronging pavements. Once, sitting in my pushchair outside a shop, I was approached by two young Chinese boys. They bent down and looked into my face, laughing and talking. One of them took a lump of grey, shiny, well-chewed gum from his cheek and pushed it into my mouth. I can feel it now, the horrifying warm smoothness and me without the necessary skill or strength to spit it out.

Ælene and I learned from the amahs how to sing Happy Birthday in Cantonese and it went something like this:

> *Juni kwai lawdi tun-shun*
> *Juni kwai lawdi tun-shun*
> *Juni see fu woo serch-ee*
> *Syunna hy-yung kun sun.*

(Twenty-eight years later, when we were filming *The New Avengers* at Pinewood Studios, we were asked to make a small broadcast to Hong Kong Television, which was in its infancy, congratulating them from *The New Avengers*, whose shows they watched with such loyalty. I'm pleased to say Purdey was able to sing this to them, although it may have furrowed some brows, having been learned only phonetically.)

My father taught us to swim; we started off balancing on

our tummies on coffee tables, making frog-like movements. We swam in the sea, and walked in the hills where the roads petered out. There was a song in my head, 'Oh what a beautiful morning', so *Oklahoma* must have opened half-way across the world. Mozart's *Eine Kleine Nachtmusik* was on the wind-up gramophone, and my mother sat on our beds and read us *Bambi* at night-time; she wept when he lost his mother, but our hands plucked relentlessly at her skirt, 'Do go O N!'

I made up a poem.

> *The cat sat on the road*
> *Suddenly came a car and runned it over;*
> *Up jumped the bandage and the plaster*
> *And popped it on.*

At Christmas I was given a strange-looking doll dressed in a sailor-suit; made of felt, he had a big Doctor Dolittle nose and flat brown eyes. I thought he was good enough to be called Peter Pan (my repertory of names was small), but Ælene pointed out that he pinched the other toys when we weren't looking, and he was called Pinchy Pan. I also received a little brown-grey kangaroo with a joey in her pouch. I have Kanga to this day but Roo fell off the roof of the flat, a tiny helpless cream-coloured button, far into the street below.

During this time, the British frigate H M S *Amethyst* had been driven aground half-way up the Yangtze river by the Chinese. No one knew how to get her out, as she baked in the hot sun under the Chinese guns. Then one night, after the hot weather broke, when the moon was hidden in a bank of clouds, she slipped free, tucking herself in the cover of a Chinese ferry. Commander Kerans steered her into the open sea and freedom. When she arrived in Hong Kong harbour, all the ships whooped and clamoured and set their fire-hoses spraying up into the air. A typhoon came, tearing and scream-ing through the water and islands to the harbour. All night long the little *Amethyst* had to go at full steam ahead to prevent herself from being ripped off her anchor and thrown into the city, where shutters were nailed closed and everything was ducked under battens to ride the storm.

We sailed back to England again on home leave on the *Empire Orwell*, stayed for nine months and set off again for the Far East on my fifth birthday on the *Dilwara*. By the time we got to the Red Sea, the baking climate had brought out prickly heat in many of the children, and the hot scratchy spots which were not prickly heat turned out to be measles. When we got to Singapore, we were scarlet and our eyes watered in the bright sunlight. Scratching madly, we were put into a dark room in Joan and Dickie Barber's flat and were given lovely plastic dark glasses to wear. The Emergency had started in Malaya in 1948, and now in 1951 travelling about was undertaken with caution as there had been many Communist ambushes. My father brought down an armoured three-tonner to drive us from Singapore up to Kluang in the Malay peninsula. We stayed in Kluang for a few months, then caught a train which delivered us at midnight at the grand white station in Kuala Lumpur. In pitch darkness, we drove to the bungalow, 16, HQ, Malaya, where we were to live for the next three years. Square-eyed with fatigue we looked out of black windows into the night beyond the veranda.

'But what's it LIKE?'

'Wait until tomorrow.'

In the morning, as the light and even greater heat arrived, we leapt up and looked out. A flattish plain stretched away in front of us, dotted with palm trees and low bushes. There was a jungle in the distance, a light air-strip made from red laterite mud to the left, upon which Austers buzzed to a halt and zoomed off, like dragonflies. The garden didn't exist: just an area fenced off from the wild lalang, the saw-edged grass that was everywhere. In the years that followed, my father made flower-beds and planted trees. He and Ælene planted a pomelo tree and a moonflower, a huge white flower of the Morning

Glory family, whose snowy furled-umbrella bud would open before your eyes into a flower the size of a soup plate, smelling of lemons, lasting one night; spreading like bindweed. There would be the ubiquitous canna lilies and zinnias and hibiscus, and the lawn would gradually be tamed and cut by our scythe-swinging Tamil gardener, the Caboon. He chewed betel-nut and spat crimson ploops like lizards as he slowly and rhythmically swung the bright curved blade inches above his bare feet.

We were enrolled at the Army school. My mother was given a piece of paper with the three recommended styles for school dresses shown on it; these could be made up in any material as long as it was blue and white cotton. In a land where clothes could be run up so cheaply there was no need for a school shop. My mother sewed our dresses herself on a black and gold Singer sewing machine which had belonged to Granny Weir and which now sits in my attic. I was put in a class presided over by Mrs N. F. Cuddy, Nancy Fancy Cuddy as she became at once. All the school buildings were on stilts, to keep the white ants away and to cool the wood which became oven-hot as the day wore on. School started at eight o'clock in the morning and finished completely at half-past twelve, when sweat was pouring through our hair. We started with a general assembly, each class trotting in line from its black wooden bungalow, down the veranda steps and across the hard road to the airy school hall. We sang, 'New every morning is the love' but 'New every morning' is what stuck in my head because that is just how it was in Malaya. Before the heat came whamming down on you, the dawn was fresh, the roads were cool and you could look without screwed-up eyes. Things were washed and fresh and vigorous early in the day, but as that fat tropical steam started, so did the sweat and the dust, always bright red from the laterite.

I remember the first morning at break, looking out as browny-yellowy British children yelled round footballs and skipped, all knowing where they were and who the others were. 'I shall know all this soon, so I shan't worry now,' I thought. What milk would we like to drink at break? (What did they mean?) White milk, pink milk, chocolate milk; all powdered and flavoured, there was no fresh milk in Malaya. Children brand new from England chose white milk, saying the words with disbelief, but most of us drank chocolate milk. Pink milk was for weeds and for Kenneth Nip-Hard.

His name wasn't really Nip-Hard, but as people introduced him they would pinch him with their nails, 'Here's Kenneth NIP-hard!' I felt sorry for poor Kenneth and watched him covertly. He didn't seem to mind what was done to him as long as he was included. Once he owned up in the class to Nancy Fancy Cuddy for something he hadn't done (we knew the culprit) and when he was given a punishment the teasing petered out altogether as he settled down to his lines, his face shining with joy. Graham Kennedy was in my class too, with dark blue eyes and black hair. When he chased me round the playground it was exciting, but when he caught and kissed me my ardour cooled at once. How dark the classrooms were, shadowed black compared with the brilliant light outside beyond the shadowy verandas, where cleaners in saris swiped with desultory brooms, padding in paper-thin bare feet, Tamils far away from their native India. There were big ceiling fans turning in the classrooms, papers fluttering slightly on the desks, lizards darting and peering on the window sills, the soft scratch of chalk on blackboard.

The lizards, chee-chaks, were tiny house geckos who were part of every room at home. If trapped, they could release their tails, detach them and leave them squiggling distractingly on their own while they slipped free and grew another. There were scorpions and millipedes and when the monsoon came the ground seethed with a billion new froglets. There were snakes, but in the three years we were there I saw only one, a cobra quickly crossing our path in the rough ground by the tin mine. 'Always make a noise and the snakes will keep clear of you,' said my mother. 'They don't want to have anything to do with us if they can help it.' Once a python got into the monsoon drain and neighbours and caboons blocked one end and fixed a tube from the exhaust pipe of a car to the other end. But once the lethal fumes had stopped and the tunnel was peered down again, the python had gone, having escaped through the house. I can see the look of triumph on my mother's face even now.

She was, is, a champion of all animals, and indeed anything that needs protection from bullies. Once, after staying with friends at Kluang, we were on the platform waiting for the train when my mother saw some day-old ducklings packed as tight as berries in a wicker basket. In a trice she had bought three, to ease the pressure within; an enamel bowl was found and filled with water, and we spent the journey to Kuala Lumpur balancing the little pond on our laps, the water slip-slopping and the three baby ducks floating like corks. One yellow, one black, one brown: when we got home a cage was made for them at the kitchen end of the bungalow, and they grew up quickly.

About this time, when Ælene and I were playing one afternoon on the veranda with our toy farm animals, my mother squatted down beside us and said, 'What is the biggest lizard you've ever seen?' Prone to exaggeration I stretched my fingers to indicate about ten inches, but when she led us out to the kitchen veranda the iguana lying there was about three feet long. I don't know how he got there but he was my mother's pride and joy. One dreadful day, our Chinese cook discovered that the iguana had been stealing the duck eggs and he clubbed it to death. He was fired on the spot, and Mummy took the poor iguana's body away in a sack to bury it. Apart from Bambi, and once when she spoke to Aunt Joan Mary in England on the telephone, we'd never seen her cry, and it was an awful thing. Grown-ups should run the world, have drinks parties and dress up, drive cars, stay up late and generally

behave invulnerably. (When we grow up we want govern-
ments to behave similarly; incorruptible, tireless, all-knowing,
and benevolent.)

When the Chinese male cook had gone, Ah Feng looked
after the house. Although my parents conversed fluently in
Urdu and Gurkhali, Malay and Chinese became pidgin-
tongues, with Ah Feng replying in pidgin-English. When
breakfast was served, Ah Feng would announce: 'Belly-foot
syup-la.' Same clothes as Ah Geng and Ah Kwong, same
delicious garlic cooking in the kitchen. Ah Feng's chow fan
was our favourite, rice fried with garlic, ginger, prawns, peas,
strips of lettuce and raw egg in soy sauce. Ælene didn't eat
very much, still craving English apples. Sometimes at night
she would only eat a saucer of condensed milk. I ate anything,
everything. Our hair, cut short like page boys when we
arrived, grew into long plaits, gradually getting blonder in the
sun as the tropical heat sucked the colour from our cheeks,
turning us yellow at first, then brown as sparrows. There was
no autumn, no spring: every day there was heavy rain, muggy
thick air, brilliant sunsets, green leaves; every night darkness
fell with no evening, the temperature dropping a little, but
seldom cool enough to put even a sheet over you in bed.

Few things are as thrilling as a pure white mosquito net.
Suspended round the bed from a frame like a meagre iron
four-poster, the net was of the finest, most opaque gauze.
During the day it was hitched up high above the canopy; at
night it descended and was tucked in all round to prevent even
one mosquito from sneaking in. Inside you were in a tiny
white cloth room, with the white mattress as the floor. The cat
would sometimes sleep on the canopy, his ginger fur bristling
through under the bulge of his body. He had been rescued, as
had Judy our pi-dog. My father brought golden Judy back on
Christmas Eve: she had been looked after by the Officers'
Mess but there was no one to feed her over the holiday. She
was a good sweet dog, always laughing and enthusiastic. We

took her out for a walk every afternoon at about four o'clock when the heat of the day was dying. Because of rabies, dogs had to wear inoculation discs round their necks, which changed colour and shape every year – green triangle, yellow circle, blue square. Any dog not wearing one was shot on sight, and when there was a rabies epidemic, dogs were not allowed off their leads. My mother made a lead for Judy from a washing line that was about fifty yards long; one day when we heard a mewing sound from a huge drum-sided water tank, she lowered the end of the washing line and pulled up a tiny soaked ginger and white kitten. He had a kink in his tail, like most Malayan cats, and was called Kinky. Never roused to anger, he would allow us to dress him in dolls' clothes and put him upside down in a cot.

Far across the ground in front of our house was a prison camp: at night the search lights would flick through our bedroom, through the dark green shutters, sending sudden stripes across the black room. Very occasionally, there was gunfire in the distant hills, or there would be talk of an ambush up-country. We heard that the Batu Caves were shut, or had been taken over by bandits as a stronghold. Certainly we never went there, although you could just see the mouth of the caves far across the plain, a Hindu shrine filled with monkeys, reached by 300 steps. I dreamt that the Batu Caves was the opening of a witch's mouth and I would fly screaming towards her as she yawned her slavering toothless jaws at me. She was the witch from *Snow White*, last seen clawing her way up rain-lashed rocks with a wart on her nose. How much she weighed on my mind! I dreamt that she was sitting by the road disguised as a beggar, that she was creeping around the verandas, always a heartbeat away from my staring eyes, suddenly springing out with her gaping mouth and the Batu Caves between her bloodless lips.

At night the tock-tock bird tocked away: three tocks, seven, twenty-three, fourteen, four, and down in the town the Chinese gambled on how many tocks and clattered their Mah Jong tablets and laughed and talked into the night. The night round our bungalow was peaceful; chee-chaks clicking on the ceiling, my mother writing letters in the drawing-room in a pool of light, or sewing party dresses for us to wear with broderie Anglaise round the hem. On the wireless, late at night, the dreamy music of *Desert Island Discs* was followed by popular music, 'Sugar Bush' or 'Moon above Malaya', which sounded, the way they sang it, like 'Moon a Burma-laya'. 'Some Enchanted Evening' rings in my head, so *South Pacific* had opened by then in the United States, where one day I planned to sip martinis in evening gloves on a terrace high above Manhattan. We had dollars and cents in Malaya, American comics which we weren't allowed to read and fat pink bubble gum, completely forbidden, which contained a waxed strip cartoon of a plump duffer in Ohio.

Every afternoon, we would drive to the Selangor Golf Club to swim. Ælene swam and dived far better than I did, and I only once jumped off the top board, hitting the water so hard that my hand was snatched from my nose and the water seemed to shoot into my brain, in the deep burbling gash of heavy chlorine when for a moment you are at the bottom and feel you may never rise to float again. There was a thick hibiscus hedge round the pool, with dark green shiny leaves and scarlet flowers proffering hairy long stamens.

Sometimes we drove to Kinrara Hospital to visit the Gurkha soldiers. By one bedside, the sick Gurkha took my hand and put into it a little bottle of cheap Indian scent which he'd bought for his daughter. 'No, no,' I said, looking to my mother for help, but she nodded to show I could take it instead of the little Nepalese girl far away, whom he may never have seen again.

Every week, we went to Mrs Calvert's dancing class. We took wicker baskets with bottles of orange squash, a towel and our dancing shoes, and before every visit we had to take salt pills. One afternoon, with Offenbach being hammered out on the piano and the storm clouds gathering, making the hall darker than usual, the news came that there was a rabid dog under the building. Each child must wait until its own car came right to the foot of the veranda steps, then run down and leap in, peering through the pillars that held the house up to see the poor dog in the shadows. (In Spain I saw a rabid dog, tumbling and snarling in the baking midday sun in Torremolinos, but everyone stood by the side of the street and stared; no one brought a gun.)

In the summer holidays in a country where it is eternal summer, you search out the cool places. We would drive up to Fraser's Hill, north of Kuala Lumpur, through kampongs, villages, where palm-leaf huts stood on bamboo poles high above the ground, through the endless grey-green rubber plantations, each tree slashed to release the latex pouring sticky-slow into a wooden cup, past feathery oil palms squatting in regimented lines, past banana palms and chickens, wayside stalls, along a wide rocky river and up into the jungly hills. Fraser's Hill had a unique one-way road with a lodge at each end. At each hour the direction changed, up or down, with twenty minutes grace for the cars caught in between. The road zig-zagged and rose steeply, the trees as tall as the sky, their primeval splendour laced with long vines and orchids, monkeys whooping softly to each other. Up and up, the bends getting tighter and tighter, glimpses to the left over lofty tree tops to the soft folds of the jungle in the valleys far below. Then it all flattened out in a high clearing, where an immaculately tailored golf course meandered through clumps of trees and Surrey stockbrokers' bungalows teetered on steep cliffs above the close green grass. There was a dispensary, where, coiled in formaldehyde, were snakes, bats and toads, a two-headed chicken and a pale innocent baby, claws of eagles and scorpions' tails, all suspended from good or evil or pity, floating forever in yellowing dignity. There was a lime tree and we filled my small opened umbrella with limes and walked home with the heavy limey smell hanging around us. The umbrella never regained its shape and I've never smelt limes without seeing the Fraser's Hill Golf Course, and its steep path back up to the Governor's Lodge.

My father was an honorary ADC to General Sir Gerald Templer, the High Commissioner in Malaya during part of the Emergency. Once we were lent the Governor's Lodge, which stood at the end of a road on a steep triangle of hill with vast views across the faraway villages and jungles.

Early on the first morning (sleeping with a blanket! and a real fire downstairs, and the house had an upstairs *and* a downstairs and wood-panelled rooms), we got up and went out into the garden, with cardigans on, an excitement in itself. What we saw was the most beautiful world I have ever seen. From the edge of the garden where the ground sloped steeply, sharply down for a hundred feet, were clouds, nudging up to the very flower-beds and billowing away, fat and clean and clear as far as the eye could see. The garden was drenched with dew, the sun sparkled in every drop, sighing and dripping from a tangle of scented roses and dahlias, runner beans and vines, zinnias and lantana, morning glory twining through every dense, moist, leafy, fruity thicket. Birds unseen screeched and chirped, monkeys hooted and crashed below the clouds and the morning sun was warm and everything glittered and glinted and hissed with life. In the distance, tree tops appeared above the clouds, making willow-pattern islands. The trees were enmeshed in spiders' webs and pitcher plants, all spangled with dew, and the garden itself was an island floating in a cloudy sea.

One day in Kuala Lumpur we didn't go to the swimming pool. My father came home in the afternoon unexpectedly, was wearing his proper uniform, not khaki shorts as usual. 'The King is dead,' he said, and his face was grave and sad.

The King! How awful. A shadowy figure in a forgotten country had died and made our father sad and stern. 'Home' was where people from school went, swanking as they collected their pencil boxes, 'We're going home to England.' England had fat sheep and sleek cows and Ælene's apples, but the essence of England had evaporated and I could only think of it as remote as the pictures of the Holy Land we were given at Sunday School. I had managed to get hold of a picture of St Peter being crucified upside-down, which my mother took away as soon as she saw it. 'What do you say in your prayers?' she asked me once. 'God bless Mummy and Daddy and Ælene, Judy, Kinky and Ah Feng, and please make us win the Lottery,' I answered, but she said, 'Oh darling, you must never pray for money,' and I felt aggrieved and cheated.

We walked with Judy to the tin mine, a spindly collection of tall chutes and tiny huts, where water could rush down delivering tin ore, full of puddles and low ponds and smooth milk chocolate mud flats. We walked up through HQ Malaya, a new development of bungalows built for the Army, into the hills where there was the grave of Loke Wan Tho's father, a beautiful broad flat orange circular grave with low walls, far prettier and more exciting than dull old gravestones. The Chinese Grave was a favourite walk; on the way I noticed a sign saying, TO THE CIRCUS! 'Oh please let's go!' but it turned out to be a circular road, a dreary round of tarmac which brought you back to where you began, no tents or high-wire acrobats.

Ælene and I walked to school, which was only about half a mile away over a hill. The path that led up the hill, past a Chinese tea house (where they could see us but we couldn't see them in the dense shadow of the veranda), was made of crystal quartz. We were walking, it seemed, over diamonds the size of rocks, all crystal shaped and glittering in the sun, some tiny, some as big as a treacle tin. When we walked back after school, sweat dripped from the ends of our plaits, particularly after PT at midday in the padang, the open games field where the Coronation celebrations were to take place.

There was a huge fancy dress competition, real clothes, not paper ones like the Poppy Fairy dresses my mother made us on the ship from crêpe paper. Ælene and I went as Norwegian girls with our plaits round our heads, but I had a temperature that day and a bad headache and looked like a thundercloud in the photographs. We all were given Coronation medals to wear, and I had a Coronation pencil box and a bone china mug. We saw the film of the Coronation several times. When in doubt, the school would show us the film again, twice in black and white, once in colour. There were extended celebrations, my parents dining and dancing at King's House where the Templers lived, looking immaculate and evening-y, with long gloves and jewellery, and on my father a dazzling white uniform.

When the time came to go, it was exciting in the way that change is exciting, even when you can't imagine what's coming next. Carpets were rolled up and stitched into sacking with curved needles, our toys were carefully packed into baskets and all the black leather cases and trunks had 'Lumley' stencilled on them, and their reinforced corners were painted red. Sometimes 'Not wanted on Voyage' was added, or 'Hold'. The bungalow grew emptier until the day came to go – Judy and Kinky were to be adopted by the incoming family, for whom Ah Feng would work; we went down to the station in our pyjamas to catch the night train to Singapore. People came to wave us off and there was a thrill and a pang in my heart as we left again – would we be always leaving? ('Heaven is goodbye forever, it's time for me to go.')

By the next morning we had crossed over from Johore Bahru, over the causeway to Singapore Island and were to spend one night in the Federated Malay States Railway Station Hotel before embarkation. The station was tall and shady; the hotel was within the station itself, above the booking offices, up flat stone stairs to an echoey internal gallery where you could see people from a bird's-eye view, milling about in the concourse, and hear the whistle and clang of departing trains. There were black and green tiles and high on the station walls were plaques showing scenes from Malay life; oxen pulling carts, tin mining, rubber plantations, ships and trains, paddy-fields. That evening, echoing out from a guest's room, I heard Purcell's Trumpet Voluntary.

We went to Tang's and I was given a pottery Chinese horse. We went to lunch in a restaurant ('Will the waiter be angry if I can't finish all this?') where the band, at my request, played 'Moon a Burma-laya' (it was my birthday). We went down to the harbour, up the gangplank on to the familiar, if shrunken, *Dilwara*, and nosed out of Singapore harbour between a thousand islands, facing north-west and heading for Ceylon.

Dream journey, where my dreams begin and end. Smelling land before you see it, watching land creep into view over the horizon, the jostle of small boats selling things, bringing the Gully-gully men conjuring with live chicks and red ping-pong balls; the dark blue sea, 'As blue as a sapphire', said my mother, spreading out her hand so we could compare the water with her engagement ring. Eating oranges on deck after supper, fire drill every day, film shows once a week, a school of porpoises suddenly appearing and a huge shout of 'Porpoises!' as the whole ship rushed to the rails to watch them bullet and plunge beside us with effortless speed and strength, keeping up mile after mile then, as suddenly as they came, disappearing. We saw flying fish skimming over the crests of the waves and camels trudging beside us in the Suez Canal – which fitted the ship so tightly we had to take a pilot on board, and we had the impression we were sailing through sand-dunes.

My father was travelling with us. We had done well at the Army School and were allowed to skip the school on ship, but every day we had to do some work set for us by my father:

sums, essays, geography questions. Every Sunday we went to church in the rearranged dining-room and sang for those in peril on the sea. Colombo, Aden, Suez, Port Said, Malta, Gibraltar, the awful Bay of Biscay where my mother and I were sick and my father and Ælene remained quite unaffected, continuing their game of chess. We bathed every night in sea water in tin tubs on duckboards, with a quick freshwater shower at the end to rinse off the salt. We had Imperial Leather soap Disney characters, Donald Duck and Mickey Mouse; now I can bring back the ship by smelling that soap and sniffing a tin of Vaseline, of which the whole ship smelt. Then we were out of the hot weather, and there was no more salt in a teaspoon, 'Eat up your nemuk!' from the ship's nurse.

Would England ever come? Here it was, run on deck, watch that whale shape turn into land, it's home, it's Southampton! Oh, how dreadful Southampton was: my heart nearly broke at the great grey mess of it, cold, untidy, noisy, no green fields and apples and milkmaids, just clanging cranes and hawsers strangling capstans, railway tracks and filthy trucks full of sludge and slurry, clocks and customs men, thin grey light coming through tall grimy windows. Gone were the coral strands and coconut beaches, gone Afric's sunny fountains and Quinquereme of Nineveh's sunny Palestine, with apes, ivory and peacocks, gone the palm green shores (in my sorrow everything I'd read became everything I'd seen and knew) – here was brutish England, friendless, chilly and made of metal.

But it was June 2nd 1954, and as the train trundled towards Ashford in Kent we saw fields full of fat sheep and shiny cows, hedges blowing with honeysuckle and roses, cow parsley and nettles, and when we got to Court Lodge Farm with Aunt Joan Mary (my mother crying again), and our strange little freckly cousin Maybe, we heard a cuckoo calling in the evening, and all the roses smelt exactly as they had done in Fraser's Hill.

Chapter Two

Mickledene School was divided into two houses, the boarders' house and the school. The boarders' house had three dormitories called Early Lights, Middle Lights and Late Lights. In Late Lights, as eleven year olds we had to be in bed by seven-thirty. There were, at most, sixteen boarders: sometimes as few as eleven. There was one bathroom: in the mornings Miss Bentley would take a bath, and before we went down to breakfast we would knock on the bathroom door and the following ritual exchange would take place:

Us: '*Puis-je descendre?*'
Miss Bentley: '*Avez-vous un mouchoir?*'
Us: '*Oui, Mademoiselle*' (waving unseen handkerchief).
Miss Bentley: '*Descendez maintenant!*'
Us: '*Merci.*'

I learnt this dialogue parrot-fashion but, never having heard French before, the meaning only became clear after a year. We wore pinafores at mealtimes – smart cotton aprons kept in the 'pinny cupboard'. Food was heralded by the cry 'Pinnies on!' We were allowed three sweets a day after tea – six smarties counted as one sweet.

The floors were polished wood and lino. Grey-haired Mrs Judge came to clean and if you were ill in bed, you listened to her whistling under her breath as she mopped around the bed legs. Windows were kept open, even on cold days. School lunch smells wafted upstairs – alien, hairy dark beetroot, boiled potatoes, cold meat which sometimes our puny childish hands couldn't cut. You had to finish what was on your plate. People became adept at concealing gobbets of gristle and fat in hamster cheeks to be spat out into the low box hedge on the way back to the school house.

The school itself was in two oast houses – four classrooms in the roundels; and the hall, full of beams and always dark and shiny, must once have been the barn. We assembled there for morning prayers and the register, to which we answered 'Present!' Present! So I went up to collect mine, and found, as with the word 'circus', the dull reverse of the coin. Mrs Kedward would play the *Marche Militaire* and we marched back to our classrooms.

Kindergarten, Transition, First, Second and Third Forms: boys stopped at Transition, when they were sent to prep schools. After lunch, we would have Rest, all lying on the bare floorboards in neat rows like sardines while we were read a story. Those with colds 'hung', lying on tummies on desks and tables with heads hanging over the edge, and great nose-blowings when Rest was over. I longed for a cold, but never had one. I also longed for a plate, a brace to go round my teeth, which could be clacked in and out and gave one an air of superior intelligence – but my teeth were straight, and I had to make do with bent kirbigrips twisted round my back teeth. Crazes came and went – skipping games, conkers, diabolos and jacks, and collecting inn-signs. Whitbread made playing-card sized pictures of their pubs and wrote their histories on the back. They were lovely: The Hop Poles, The Black Horse, Castletons Oak with the old man sitting on his coffin waiting to die, The Green Man, The Chequers, all swapped and gloated over. In singing lessons we would try to sing 'Blow the Wind Southerly' like Kathleen Ferrier, and 'Three Gypsies Stood at the Castle Gate', 'Dashing Away with a Smoothing Iron' and 'Green Grow the Rushes-O' from the schools' songbook. When the end-of-school bell rang, cars would queue up in the lane to collect day-children while the boarders went back to change into home clothes. Then, in the summer, to the Village.

Over successive years the boarders had swept around the roots of trees and laid stones marking out Houses: we would bring little jugs and cups and tin boxes, the paths between the stones were kept spotless, and it was called the Village. We would spend hours there, making nettle tea and twig stews and fashioning plates and dishes from clay taken from the Dip, a wide ditch which you could just jump. Pine Corner, three pine trees at the end of the field, was where important boarders' conferences were held.

In the winter we would sit inside with our oddment boxes, small collections of tiny things kept in toffee tins. These were stamps, marbles, china ornaments, little dolls, hair clips and the ubiquitous manicure sets. Once a week we could be called for hair washing – Miss Stanford, long fingers red from the water, plunged our heads into boiling basins and scrubbed our scalps with Coal Tar Soap to keep nits at bay. Then we roasted in front of an electric bar fire till the hair was dry and our faces scarlet. In the summer we would play in the garden and listen to the gramophone – Miss Bentley had the record of Danny Kaye singing Hans Christian Andersen, and *Salad Days* and there were a couple of swoony numbers – 'Isle of Capri' and 'Dreamboat'. There was a border under an old wall, filled with poppies and delphiniums, lilies and wallflowers, buzzing with bees. The smell of silage sometimes drifted towards us on the evening air from the neighbouring farm. In Hole Park opposite, all the horse-chestnuts were covered in candles, their lower branches eaten off neatly in a straight line by the cows.

We read *The Carved Cartoon* about Grinling Gibbons and the great plague, and I cried all one night because I thought I could feel a lump in my armpit, the first sign of the Black Death. We were cold in bed, but not allowed hot-water bottles. We would wear our socks under the bedclothes for warmth and have beauty competitions in our dressing gowns. Nikki Barker and I usually set these up, and usually won. Nikki, Vicky and I: Vicky was double-jointed and had a dip in her breastbone which she could fill with water in the bath. Nikki had ponies at home. We took our ballet exam, Cecchetti Grade II, together in London. Miss Crusoe taught us dancing, provided us with Grecian tunics and took us on a train to Charing Cross on a hot summer day. We danced in a stifling wooden room with barres and mirrors, to a gramophone playing on a table, and passed. I was offered a place at the Sadler's Wells Ballet School but I didn't want it, I wanted to ride, and riding turned knees in, toes up, while ballet did the exact opposite.

Nikki was chosen as the May Queen, not I. 'She has such a lovely smile,' I heard the staff saying to each other. 'Come on, Joanna, try not to scowl!' and I bared my teeth in a jealous leer. On Mickledene Sports' Days the sun always shone. All the day-children brought flowers to the hall on Friday, and the school was filled with scent from a hundred flower-filled jam jars and vases on windows and mantelpieces. There would be races on the games field. Egg-and-spoon, wheelbarrow, the Gentlemen's race (Miss Cheeseman, eagle eyes on their toe-caps as they lined up, calling, 'Be-HOIND the line!') and the Ladies' race which always involved some maths to trap Mummy, who would stand there last ('Oh dear, I can't do this,') with Mrs Shaw, who being Swedish didn't understand our mathematical terms. Then there would be the school play. When Veronica Shaw was head girl we did *Robin Hood*. Veronica was Robin and Ælene King Richard. Felicity was a Merryman and I was Will Scarlett.

'Can you fire a bow and arrow?'

'Oh YES, Mrs Kedward,' I swanked, but on the day my arrow fell with a dismal thwonk at my feet as we sang a hearty song:

Let life go unforbidden
Straight limbed among the green,
Let laughter be unchidden
And charity unseen.
They're grey men, are the town men,
With crooked legs to run,
But we're the jolly brown men
Carousing in the sun!

And we strode and slapped our jolly brown men's thighs and laughed in deep chappish voices. There was a breeze that Sports Day, and the parents sat in rows on the recently run race-track and watched us mouthing words that the wind snatched away. The Kindergarten children were usually rabbits and had to be herded on and off.

Mrs Kedward taught us elocution. Because of playing Portia, I learned Act IV Scene i of *The Merchant of Venice* in its entirety. We learned a great deal of poetry by heart. 'Diction and vowel sounds are very important,' said Mrs Kedward, who had kind blue eyes (and a soft Kentish voice), and we would copy her in the last line of the first verse of 'The Lake Isle of Innisfree': 'And LIVE a-LONE in a BEE-LOUD GLADE!' opening our mouths like fishes. In French lessons we learned of a girl who, to make her mouth more beautiful, was advised to say '*Petit pomme, petit pomme,*' but forgot her fruit and said, '*Petit POIRE, petit POIRE,*' and her mouth stretched instead of pursed. There was a picture of her with her new big mouth but as she now looked rather like Leslie Caron in *Gigi* we felt she'd done the right thing.

We read *Girl* comic which was sent every week from home. We wrote letters on Sunday: mine began every time, 'Darling Mummy and Daddy, thank you very much for your letter and the *Girl*.' After letter-writing we walked in crocodile to Rolvenden Church, a mile away, and sat in the Mickledene Pews. After the service the local garage owner, Mr Tonbridge, would drive us back in his small bus, and as we hopped out we each said with ingratiating sincerity. '*Hank*-you, Mr Tonbridge!' My father had returned to Malaya on his own – two letters must be written each week, Daddy's on a beige Forces' Air Letter, sent for 2½d to Depot, the Brigade of Gurkhas, Sungei Patani, Kedah, Malaya. My letters to my father still exist – they are full of drawings of ponies and descriptions of the latest craze (' – the craze at the moment is handstands . . .' 'Ratatat is the craze now it is a bat with a ball attached to a piece of elastic, all joined up it comes like this [drawing] you hit the ball with the bat like in tennis . . .').

Day-girls were sometimes kind enough to invite us out to tea – Patricia de Kraft, Rosemary Lane and, several times, Mary Steele, whose mother made unforgettable cakes with blobs of chocolate in them. Mary lived in Rolvenden and her garden had a soft tennis court and was always filled with flowers. Patricia de Kraft lived in a very big house near Tenterden (a longer bus ride) which had an echoey squash court and dark spreading cedar trees. These excursions were thrilling interludes in the humdrum routine of pinnies-on and homework. I still have locked in my memory the Saturday I spent with Rosemary Lane because it was the first time I had smelt sweet peas – the tiny kitchen garden in Newenden in high summer was a mass of colour and scent, a narrow path with runner beans and roses, all jostling for space – inside there was dark polished beeswaxed wood and low beamed ceilings, and outside the bright glare of the midday sun, strawberries and forget-me-nots and, everywhere, sweet peas.

Sometimes I was homesick at Mickledene, homesick for Malaya, dusty roads, the muezzin calling in the evening; homesick for heat and monsoons and our bungalow. When my parents took a short holiday in Scotland I couldn't think where Scotland was and thought they'd gone back to the Far East without us. I had a dream that Scotland was full of tiny intensely steep hills and bridges like a willow-pattern plate filled with rushy glens where we daren't go a-hunting for fear of little men. This became blended with 'Down Yonder Green Valley' and 'Piping Down the Valleys Wild', with buddhas on every hillock and the air filled with the sound of waterfalls. Scotland seemed a good place in my dream, and though I've since discovered how different it is, I have always thought of it as a good and special place. I can remember sitting in the downstairs lavatory in the boarders' house where the juniors had their lockers, with my blue summer skirt over my face humming, 'What a friend I have in Jesus,' and wishing I was at home. But homesickness drifted quickly away from me and the feeling has returned only once or twice in my life, experienced now as stage fright. Both produce an almost overwhelming desire to be somewhere else, with a doctor's note saying you must never go back.

Holidays were divided up between three houses – Belgar, where the Shaws lived, Epsom (91 West Hill Avenue) which we nicknamed Pokey Hole although it was a perfectly decent small house in a row of others; and Court Lodge Farm. Court Lodge at Woodchurch in Kent belonged to my Aunt Joan Mary and Uncle Ivor Jehu. Apart from the twins and Reay and Maybe, it usually had a quota of other children whose parents were stationed abroad. Hugh and Chris Drake were there often; the Drakes and Reay slept in the attic in a kind of *Just William* chaos. Ælene, Maybe and I slept together in Maybe's room. The beginnings of the holidays were always the same: two or three days of studied indifference, when we hardly spoke to each other; then some vague taunts in the Molesworth vein ('you're an utter weed and wet and hav a face like a baboon'); followed by a week or two of collaboration on how to outwit the Grown-ups. We built a pontoon in the pond near the Top field, a ramshackle arrangement of planks and barrels which we code-named Nootnopski ('pontoon' backwards, 'ski' attached to fool the casual listener).

There was never any evidence that the Grown-ups understood or minded what we were up to, but we treated them as if they were foreign spies. The neighbouring farmer, Mr Douglas, had a barn, and we would climb out of our bedroom windows to visit Dougie's Barn in the long summer evenings. Dougie was a real threat. We built him into a fearsome figure bent on revenge with a big stick or even a gun, but apart from once shouting, 'Clear off,' he seemed remarkably unconcerned about us.

We helped to harvest and plant potatoes for 6d a day, and had potato fights with the vicar's son and two village boys, Snazzy Tie and Red Socks. We went to the cinema in Tenterden to see *Moby Dick*, *Gunfight at the OK Corrall*, *Pinocchio*, *The Battle of the River Plate*; and sometimes Uncle Ivor bought tickets for shows in London, *The Yeoman of the Guard*, *Cinderella* and *My Fair Lady*. We travelled by train: on one journey back the carriage was full of Hungarian refugees. An old man took my hands while tears ran down his face – I reminded him of his granddaughter left behind in Hungary. 'Poor, poor people,' said my mother and like a well-trained dog I sat and allowed my hair to be stroked.

The twins were six years older than me and were so frightening that it took several days to dare even to look at them. They had red hair and freckles and were first-class sportsmen and scholars at Wellington. They were identical: although I could just tell them apart. They would swop jerseys and Michael became Gordon to all but their closest family. I admired and feared them greatly. Sometimes they would address us directly and we quaked before them. Usually it was a request to make their beds or to field while they batted and bowled.

In a letter to Daddy the day after Easter I wrote:

Yesterday, when we went to Church we picked flowers and put them in our hats. It was wizard eating sweets again [given up for Lent] except they seemed very sweet. Maybe, Ælene and I gave Michael and Gordon each a cravat [it was their birthday]. Reay, Hugh and Chris gave them a record each. One was 'Banana Boat Song' another 'See You Later, Alligator'. Their cake had 34 candles on: two 17s. I am hoping for a bit of cricket coaching from the boys. I have got a wizard style of bowling now [drawings of pin men, a bat and a ball]. Longing to see you. Tons of Love.

As a reward for menial tasks the twins would give us piggyback rides round the house, at high speed, up the back stairs, across the landing, down the front stairs, two at a time with us clinging on and screeching at the thrill and the privilege. Afterwards we would resume our former roles of ticks to be ignored. It took me very many years to address them as equals.

The twins' father, Brook Neale, had died in India when they were two so they were half-brothers to Reay and Maybe. Maybe, whose real name is Myfanwy, was called Maybe because she was born after Joan Mary had had three boys, and people said, 'Maybe this time it will be a girl.' She was smaller than I was, had very blue eyes and dead straight hair. We became, and remained, like sisters. Reay was a brainy, scruffy boy a year older than me. The attic where he and Hugh and Chris Drake lived was a chaotic mass of clothes and books and comics. Once every holiday there would be a competition for the tidiest bed. It was incredible to see their idea of order: everything crammed under mattresses and forced into cupboards. Chris Drake didn't like bacon, so instead of throwing it away at school, he kept it in a tin and brought it back in his suitcase, where it grew green mould and stank. The ends of holidays were marked by the arrival of the Carter Patterson van to collect school trunks, haircuts which suddenly revealed necks, ears and foreheads, and, for the girls, helping to sew on nametapes.

Peter and Monica Shaw lived at Belgar, a fine Elizabethan farm just outside Tenterden in Kent. They had three girls: Christine, Veronica, who was Ælene's age, and Felicity, who was a month younger than me. The house was approached down a long drive with very wide grass verges upon which rabbits appeared and disappeared depending on the spread of dreadful myxamatosis. There was a huge barn where the ponies were stabled, a pond covered with duckweed which I believed so strongly was mossy grass that I walked on it and fell in, and the Oast House which we had rented on home leave when I was four. From the early days, the Oast House meant the smell of apples, owls roosting in the roundel, marmite toast on winter evenings and *Listen with Mother* after lunch. Felicity and I found a pair of scissors and cut our fringes right off so we had tufts at the tops of our foreheads like tiny G Is. My bottom was smacked but Felicity's wasn't. At four we had to be put on to the ponies, and we would trundle off down the drive, Felicity on Brownface and I on Squirrel, who at just over twelve hands seemed to be a heavyweight hunter. The ponies would shamble to the long grass and graze peacefully while we flapped and tugged and wailed, 'SquirrE L! Brownfa-a-a-ce!' until my father came to rescue us. Felicity and I ate raw rhubarb and had stomach aches and were ticked off. After that we sailed off to Malaya and I almost forgot Belgar Farm.

When we returned it was high summer. The closely cut lawn was speckled with sun through the pear trees and the smell of cut grass and roses hung in the air. The house was white weatherboard, rose-coloured brick and timber. At the back the great tile roof swooped from the high attic right down to the Back of the Back, a few feet from the ground.

Orchards stood all round; the Home Orchard, the Bramleys, the Pears, the Plums, the Ten Acre, the Kentish Cobnuts and the Cherries. There were woods and spinneys, streams and ponds, marshy bits, nettles and the bridle-path.

After three years the girls had overtaken us in height and strength, and we had all forgotten almost completely about each other. Veronica and Felicity had very blonde, almost white hair. Felicity and I shared a bedroom. We were never bored, never had time to be. There were ponies to ride and muck out, tack to clean, tables to be laid and cleared, shoes to be polished, fires to be laid. We filched cigarettes and smoked them in the woods, singeing our hair with matches as we lit up. We played horses when we weren't actually riding, galloping about on bamboo-stick steeds. We dressed up, stole lipsticks and painted our faces red. We made little houses in tree roots and a big house in the straw in the barn, into which we unbelievably took a hurricane lamp to sit around. We sabotaged the Grown-ups' dinner parties, hiding behind curtains and in cupboards in the dining-room. We went swimming at Jury's Gap on the shingle; I dived out to sea from a breakwater straight on to another hidden in the water, and scratched myself from stem to stern on the barnacles. There was a gymkhana at Tenterden, a mile away across the fields. The elder Shaw girls competed, the loudspeakers blaring a Swedish Rhapsody in a distorted echo. The children of Tenterden put on a pageant at Hales Place; Christine Shaw was the Pied Piper, Ælene and Veronica were anxious Hamelin parents, and Felicity and I were rats or children, I forget which. There was a grand woman in a wide-brimmed hat, Vita Sackville-West from Sissinghurst Castle, who smiled and waved approval as we gambolled rat-like or child-like behind Christine miming on her recorder.

We weren't allowed to ride till we could groom the ponies properly and knew how to put the tack together. My father taught us how to ride with stirrups crossed, arms crossed, over low jumps, to lie back on the pony's rump, to steer with our knees and weight. We were taught to hum and sing if we were nervous as this fooled the pony into thinking you were relaxed, and we had to walk the last half mile home to cool the ponies down, and reward them with an apple at the end of each ride. Felicity and I would collect windfalls and feed them till they foamed and lathered at the mouth and we clutched our sides with suppressed laughter. Tresca, too fiery a pony for me to ride, was as placid as a bishop in the stable, but Harlequin – Quinny – would back you into a corner with his fat piebald hindquarters and would kick even when in the open. When we rode across ploughed fields, Quinny would gradually bend his knees and feeble riders would have to leap off and stand despairingly holding the reins while he rolled and grunted in the mud. Sometimes he gave you a kick for good measure as you tried to remount. In the autumn, ground mist lay over the Ten Acre as we rode home. There was a piece of corrugated iron making a bridge over a stream, and every time we galloped over this most familiar piece of path the ponies would shy and leap and pretend to be frightened out of their wits, while we whooped like cowboys waving imaginary stetsons above our heads. We rode in 'dungs' – dungarees – and laced-up walking shoes and windaks. We learned from Christine how to make ash whistles, and how to squawk on grass blades squashed between our thumbs. We were summoned to meals by a bell rung outside the back of the house where there was a wooden bench amongst the wallflowers, bearing the verse:

> *The kiss of the sun for pardon*
> *The song of the birds for mirth*
> *One is nearer God's heart in a Garden*
> *Than anywhere else on earth.*

When my father went to the War Office we moved to 91 West Hill Avenue, Epsom, Surrey. After the two farms and Mickledene, it felt very townified, although the avenue, a cul-de-sac, was planted with all sorts of shrubs, pink flowering cherry trees and laburnums. Our garden had golden rod, some apple trees, a clumpy little rock garden and a place to make a bonfire. There were stained-glass windows in the hall, and a piano in the drawing-room. The next-door neighbours, the Downings, had a television set on which we watched *Muffin the Mule* and the ob-glob-de-glob-glob *Flower Pot Men*. A family of hedgehogs adopted us and every day my mother bought extra milk and brown bread to put in their dishes in the evening. The big hedgehogs ate politely from one dish while the two babies climbed right into their dish lapping and snuffling like tiny pigs. We listened to the *Goon Show* on the wireless and sometimes in the evening my father would play the piano: 'Time on my hands' and 'These Foolish Things'. He played by ear, and taught us how to pick out 'Jesu, Joy of Man's Desiring' and 'Solveig's Song' with one finger. Very occasionally we got up early and went up to Epsom Downs to watch the horses gallop by in the mist. We went to a race meeting and I put half a crown on Gypsy Lady who led most of the way but came in third out of three. One summer night I heard a boy's voice in the alley between our garden and the next. It was a very still evening, not quite dark, and the husky voice sang a popular song, ending '. . . and oi will love yew evah-mo-ah'. It sounded, still sounds in my memory, thrilling.

Chapter Three

Ælene left Mickledene and went to St Mary's, an Anglican Convent on the outskirts of Hastings. Letters arrived full of descriptions of food and I became impatient to join her. I left at the end of the summer term in 1957, and during the holidays shopped at Daniel Neal's for my new school uniform. Navy-blue tunic, saxe-blue great coat and velour hat, lacrosse stick and games shorts, Sunday dress (known as the Sunday Sack), grey socks, striped blue and red tie. My hair was cut quite short: it had already become unruly ('It wants to curl,' said my mother, enviously twining it round a finger while I scowled and yearned for dead straight Chinese hair), and now it looked as if it had been grazed away by wildebeest. They used to cut hair with thinning scissors and razors, and setting lotion crisped the strands wound tightly round small rollers before they went under a too-hot drier. Why more of us are not bald now I can't imagine. The twins had gone back to Wellington, Reay to Marlborough, Maybe to her brown-uniformed school, Brampton Down; and I stood in the driveway at Court Lodge to be photographed before we went off to St Mary's.

The traveller and writer Augustus Hare had once owned St Mary's, when it was called Holmhurst. Standing on a south-facing hill in Baldslow, it was a grey stone, rather gothic-looking building with a grey stone terrace, sweeping lawns and a view across fields and woods to the sea three miles away. Augustus Hare had sold it to the Community of the Holy Family on the proviso that they kept his treasures intact –

stuffed owls and eagles, drawers full of birds' eggs and the original sandstone statue of Queen Anne, the copy of which stands outside St Paul's Cathedral. The school had built on wings and corridors, and the first impression was of a rabbit warren. Wooden corridors wound on for ever, lit by gas lamps to dormitories with biblical and Greek names: Hebron, Siloam, Salem, Alpha, Beta, Gamma, Delta. My first dormitory was called Kappa and was so far from the front door that my mother said goodbye to me by my bed, where I sat in my coat beside my trunk, speechless with excitement.

The two senior girls in charge of our dormitory, Angela Savage and Katie Galbraith, were only sixteen and fifteen, but with their rustling petticoats and jingling bangles they seemed to be wise and old beyond their years. I've often thought there are few people as grown up and responsible as school prefects, few people as powerful and frightening. They knew everything, what every bell was for, where to go, what was done and not done, and to whom you may or may not speak. I committed an unforgivable gaffe on my very first night. Dressed in pyjamas and carrying my sponge bag, I asked a senior girl who was only my height where I should clean my teeth. But this was Imogen Newbatt! And she was Head Girl! And I had spoken to her! The word got round at once that I was bumptious and very cheeky and to be squashed. Far from depressing me, this was music to my ears and started a tremendously enjoyable skirmish with Authority that lasted several years.

Kappa had three bathrooms, Kappa One, Two and Three. Kappa Three echoed like an engine room. The bath stood in the middle of the floor, with duckboards to stand on (like on the *Dilwara* or *Windrush*). We were allowed four inches of water to wash in, and a quarter of an hour to have a bath. Juniors bathed first, having checked on the bath list if they were Tuesday, Thursday and Saturday or Monday, Wednesday and Friday. No one bathed on Sundays. The nuns slept in the nuns' hospice down another long brown corridor, far beyond the New Classrooms (built during the war) and the Chapel. We were patrolled and ruled by prefects and seniors, and the housemistress, Mrs Beer. There were eight of us in Kappa, each with a narrow iron bed, a chest of drawers, and curtains on iron bars dividing each bed, which we were supposed to draw for modesty's sake. Instead, we hung from them by our knees, hooting like monkeys.

Although I had asked if Mary Steele – a new girl with me – and I could be in the same dormitory, she was at the other end of the school in Salem. My companions were new 4Bs like me – Alison, Jackie, Rosemary, Rosalind (who had a senior older sister) and Elizabeth Neylan who we nicknamed Spokey because she had sharp elbows. Spokey had dreadful colds and thick glasses and seemed too thin for words. Only when her bony little fingers clamped around an outsize fountain pen did her talent emerge. She wrote in enormous stabbing italics, covering page after page with imaginative stories, illustrated with spikey blotched pictures which even then I could tell were exceptional. Spokey didn't stay long. I hope she went on writing.

St Mary's was on such a huge scale compared with Mickledene that it was bewildering to know where to go when bells rang. At least two bells a day meant Chapel veils on. Chapel veils were like large rectangular handkerchiefs which you tied over your hair with two bits of tape. New girls always tied them on as advised by the nuns, tightly down over the forehead covering as much hair as possible, with the face peering out like a water rat from his hole. As one got older and more worldly they were attached further and further back, until sometimes they clung on the back of the head and were quite invisible from the front. Bells summoned us to rise, to eat, to assemble, begin and end lessons, eat again, do prep, go to Chapel. The Angelus would be rung at midday, and in the evening bells called the nuns to Compline and us to bed.

The junior common room was called Utopia and had hand-painted original William Morris wallpaper which I am afraid we thought was rather dreadful. Wide windows looked over the terrace to the lawn on which Queen Anne stood and crumbled: her hand holding the orb had fallen off, and some of the seated figures had moulted pieces into the surrounding brambles. There was a soft tennis court, and rhododendrons of every kind and colour and a curved path which led past the sacred turf of Pilgrim's Progress lawn. To tread on PP lawn was an instant blowing up: the sixth-formers, whose common room PP was, would lean and leer from the windows to see we didn't set so much as a shoelace on it. Huge beech trees shaded a pond called Typhoid because of its unappetizing appearance; beyond, past the bamboos whose shoots we would grub up and eat, were the Boarders' Gardens. Partly protected by trees on one side and the school vegetable garden on the other, the Boarders' Gardens had once been a small formal garden where geometrically shaped beds circled a round central flower-bed, all surrounded by low box hedges. Mary Steele and I applied for a garden, and were given one at the bottom of the slope. Mary had inherited her mother's green fingers but even so we could only claim real success with pale Michaelmas daisies and the odd primula.

Beyond the vegetable gardens, where we dug up small potatoes and ate them raw, was the Nuns' Graveyard. The nuns had a splendid approach to death, and when an old Sister died, Sister Barbara would announce it in prayers, adding, 'We must all rejoice for her Soul.' The funeral was attended by sixth-formers, nuns and the priest who would lead the procession with cross and incense-burner followed by the coffin draped in a blue bedspread with a cross on it. I went back to the school quite recently. There were many more graves and, unlike the old days, I now recognize and remember all the names on the crosses.

My parents chose the school for two reasons. First, my

mother wanted us to be taught to sew well (it was too bad that our nuns were no seamstresses) and second, when they arrived to meet the old Headmistress, Sister Elizabeth, she arrived breathless and late, a scurrying Tiggywinkle figure. 'Do forgive me. I had to catch the cricket scores,' which my parents felt boded well. In the summer holidays, legend had it, the nuns tucked their habits up and played cricket on the games field. The games field sloped, like an exhausted sigh, from top to bottom. Our lacrosse pitch went across it so the goals were even but left and right wings were steeply divided. At the end, tall pine trees allowed the gales through from the Channel. In winter, mottled purple and orange in our games shorts and aertex shirts, we had to keep moving to stay alive. In summer, with daisies mown down, running tracks marked, and the tock-tock of tennis balls hanging in the air, it was a far more agreeable place. Sometimes we would practise tennis in gumboots and hit balls over into the patch where they grew peas and beans. Retrieving the balls we would fill our boots with pods and shuffle back to eat them in the shade. We were always hungry: at high tea we would eat bread and jam until the bell went for prep. Anthea Warman ate a whole sliced loaf once.

Anthea played the cello, always had inky hands and was incredibly untidy. In seconds, a clean shirt and reasonable-looking socks crumpled when she wore them; her hair escaped in wisps, her tie turned to string, her blazer looked like a flak jacket filled with rocks. She was the absolute opposite of Sarah Rushbrook-Williams, whose socks stayed loyally grasping her calves, whose hat was crisp, whose chapel veil was always neatly ironed and folded. We three became close friends. We would choose desks together at the back of the class, out of the eye of the mistress where we could pass notes and do drawings and become convulsed with laughter at almost anything. We laughed till we wept, in Chapel, at choir practice, after lights out and during prep, with silently heaving shoulders and tear-stained faces. Nothing was too stupid or unamusing not to set us off into spasms of mirth. We had nicknames: 'Antipas' Warman and 'Rushbrook-Williams-bug' (not a very snappy label, that). Mine seemed only to be Jo, but irate seniors called me 'That Jo Lumley' through clenched teeth.

Not all the nuns taught: the Community was headed by the Reverend Mother, first Mother Mildred, then Mother Gwendoline. The headmistress Sister Lizzie was succeeded by Sister Barbara Allen, and we only dared hum under our breath, 'In Scarlet Town where I was born . . . cruel Barbara Allen!' Some of the nuns, like Sister Elsie, tended the garden; Sister Eileen used to be in charge of food. Sister Kathleen Mary was a nurse. Tall Sister Veronica was a remote smiling shadow and tiny old Sister Margaret was in charge of the newest boarders for evening prayers in the Stable Chapel. Her husband had been killed in the First World War; she was the only nun to have been married. She was four foot ten inches high and so ancient and frail that the hulking great eleven year olds in her care felt like cuckoos in a wren's nest. It was her task to help us to fill our hot-water bottles, considered too dangerous for us. She would stand on tip-toe on a chair, hitch back her long grey sleeve and, with her little sparrow's claw, fish into a scalding tank with an enormous enamel jug and tip the boiling water into our bottles. 'Oh Sister take care, oh look out Sister,' we would squeak as she teetered in the steam in the stone-floored pantry. Our dormitories were unheated and uncarpeted. On very cold nights our flannels would freeze on the washstand. We were allowed to bring back our own eiderdowns, and if you were really cold you put on games jerseys and socks as well.

One summer we kept mice, provided by a thoughtful daygirl. Mine, a beautiful brown female, was called Reepicheep after C. S. Lewis's mouse. We made homes for them amongst our socks and pants in the drawers, and kept them in our blazer pockets during lessons. One summer evening I put Reepicheep into the big oak tree by Queen Anne's statue for a run. The bed bell went and she wouldn't come down. So I went upstairs and changed into pyjamas and sneaked out over the terrace, down the steps in the moonlight across the lawn and there, waiting for me where I had put her, was Reepicheep. We were later banned from keeping mice and there was ghoulish talk that Sister Mary Frances ('MFB') would gas them over a bunsen burner in the chemistry lab; so we let them free in the school kitchens where they multiplied and flourished.

MFB taught Biology and Chemistry. Mr Mills, who had assisted Logie Baird in inventing television, taught us Physics. My favourite lessons were languages – French, Latin, German, Italian and English – and Art. English was taught by 'Hooter', Miss Hortin-Smith, an eccentric woman and first-rate teacher. 'John Gil-pin was a citi-zen,' she chanted, smacking the back of a chair to make the stresses, '. . . of cre-dit and re-nown.' When it got to the galloping bit, she turned the chair round, mounted it and galloped out of the classroom. She was never peeved by my questions, that others found cheeky or impertinent, and she had great humour and imagination.

Sister Olive, who came from the North Country, hadn't been blacked out, hadn't taken her final vows and so still wore a white veil. She took us for Maths: as she came swishing into the room she would call out, 'One to ten in y'rough books,' and before we had scribbled down the numbers, she was off: 'One: seventy-four divided by six . . . Two: thirteen multiplied by nine . . . Three: . . .' On bad days it was, 'One to forty in y'rough books.' After three years it was suggested that I should give up maths, although I had just come first in the exam. It seemed that I had the wrong approach: I often came up with the right answer but had no workings to show for it. Once I realized they would rather have workings and no answer than my right answer with no workings, I was pleased to see the last of the subject. I still have an elastic approach to mathematics and can get roughly the right answer using my own methods, which is invaluable when cash registers go wrong.

French, with Sister Joan, I loved. Latin I enjoyed so much that I wrote an extra twelve sentences relating to the *porcus parvus* wandering in the *silva magna*. By the time I got to Cicero's speeches my interest had waned but not before Virgil had made such an impact on me that I was to call my son Æneas as a second name. Art was our favourite lesson. Before the new classrooms were built on Miss Kennedy's lawn, we had art classes in the attic, stepping over wooden beams, and sacks of 'pom', a fearful powdered potato that we reckoned the nuns had been hoarding since the war.

Food at school grew steadily better. Margarine was replaced by butter, and the nearby farm provided creamy milk for the boarders' tea. We had the usual run of mince on Monday, green mince on Tuesday (called 'curry') and fish on Friday. On Sunday the pudding was Sunday Special, leftovers from every pudding during the week topped with pink custard ('face cream') and served in a glass bowl, so you could study the layers as in a geological survey. Tea was served in thick shatterproof glasses, and on Ascension Day we had tinned grapefruit for breakfast. The nuns always ate heartily when they ate with the girls: we found out that the rations in the nuns' half were very meagre, often only butterless bread with green jam.

Being an Anglo-Catholic Anglican Community, our chapel services were full of incense, bells, genuflections and plainsong. On Sundays there was an early Communion service, sung Eucharist and Evensong. The nuns of course went to chapel far more often than we did, starting the day with Contemplation.

'But Sister, what do you contemplate?'

'Anything at all,' answered Sister Lizzie, who used to keep sweets in her deep pockets. 'This morning I found I had put my shoes on the wrong feet so I contemplated that.' She used to take choir practice, her arthritic fingers skipping about on the piano. 'Sing the note from here – Baaa!' she would cry, tapping her forehead with her hand, and we took deep breaths and sang 'Baaa!' from our throats like Buddy Holly and Connie Francis.

Every Saturday night there was a dance in the gym: a Dansette gramophone was loaded up with 45s and we jived to Richie Valens and Cliff Richard. With my hair wet from washing, I would slick it forward and strum a tennis racket: 'Got muh-self uh cryin' talkin' sleepin' walkin' livin' dull,' and it was agreed that I bore a striking resemblance to Cliff. Anthea did a drawing of Dirk Bogarde, after we had seen him in *Song Without End*, and sent it off to him for a signature. Long after she had given up hope, it came back in the post with 'I think this is very good – Dirk Bogarde' written on it and we all squealed and fell on the ground with swooning appreciation. We swooned at the White Rock Pavilion in Hastings, at the musicians in concerts given by the Hallé and the LPO, falling in love with trumpeters and cellists and the conductors.

I wrote letters to Peter Cooper who was at Harrow, where Anthea's father was Classics Master, and kept his replies in my bulging blazer pocket. Anthea wrote to Titch Beresford and once we walked round the school gardens on a misty summer evening discussing whether we would marry them or not. Our letters were mostly full of match-scores and the trials of our particularly gruelling lives and the unfairness and madness of many of the staff.

With a few astonishing exceptions, we were an unprepossessing bunch to look at. I had spots and frizzy hair, and there was much in the way of greasy rats' tails, National Health glasses and bitten nails. Smart clothes still meant looking like our mothers (who in turn looked like theirs) and when we graduated from long socks to stockings, they were 40-denier bulletproofs worn with a roll-on. But we were good-natured

and chaste and uncomplicated, with high ideals and a firm
sense of duty.

We were cut off from the outside world to a large degree:
only at the end of my time at school did the wireless relay the
news, and newspapers begin to appear beside *History Today* on
the landing, which was also the library. Our excursions to
Hastings were rare; only once was a television brought into
the school and that was to watch the dedication of the newly
built Guildford Cathedral. Every other Wednesday there were
films in the gym: *Galilee Revisited*, *The Potter and his Wheel* and
Woody Woodpecker. There was a school lantern-slide contraption
called an epidaioscope, operated by Miss Edwards the History
mistress. Visiting lecturers would bring their sepia slides and
give talks on recent visits to the Holy Land, while we sat in
ranks in semi-darkness on chairs collected from the neighbouring classrooms, black-out curtains up on the high windows,
long stick tapping the screen and distant Arabs gazing at us
across dusty roads in the Middle East.

Every Michaelmas term we did a school play. I played
Aaron in Christopher Fry's *The Firstborn* and the mighty
Imogen Newbatt, who had already been obliged to give me
chunks of Bunyan to learn as a punishment, played Moses.
Rehearsals were strange – as a fourth-former I was not entitled
to speak to anyone in a higher form. 'The news runs like
wildfire, like an ostrich,' I said, moving an arm woodenly to
and fro to indicate the velocity of flames and ostrich legs.
Drama was taught by Mrs Curran, whose handsome head and
battleship bosom belied her lightness of touch. Once she read
me a speech from *Romeo and Juliet* and in front of my eyes she
turned into a starry-eyed fourteen year old. When I had to
open *Little Women* as Jo, leaning on my elbows and gazing at
the audience as if they were a fireplace, curtain just about to go
up, I turned my head to her in the wings. 'I can't remember
any of my lines,' I whispered. 'Christmas won't be Christmas
without any presents,' she whispered back, 'and you'll know

the rest.' We did *The Taming of the Shrew* and I was Petruchio; I sat nonchalantly moustachioed on a table and addressed the audience. 'As with the meat, some undeserved fault I'll find about the making of the bed,' I drawled, gnawing on what was supposed to be a chicken bone. The school couldn't run to a chicken bone, so I sucked a finger bone detached from the school skeleton which was kept in the sick bay.

The terms were enlivened by fire practices, midnight feasts and visiting days. When the bell rang in the middle of the night, we would assemble, thick with sleep, at our nearest fire-assembly point, in the front drive or outside the Barrow-way where the lacrosse sticks and tennis rackets hung, on the sandy drive where syringa covered the bicycle shed. There we would answer to a roll-call and blink at the nuns in their dressing-gowns and nightcaps. Without their habits and wimples, they looked more like ordinary people; we could see the shape of their heads, and, if a wisp escaped, the colour of their hair. Their habits were magisterial and graceful: long grey robes made of some kind of light wool or linen with a free-floating panel at the front, a girdle round the waist, knotted three times for poverty, chastity and obedience, a white wimple, square across the forehead and close to the cheeks, concealing the throat and opening into a wide yoke neck, over which hung the Crucifix. Long inner sleeves were worn under wider outer sleeves, which had to be pinned up, when dishing out food, with safety pins fished out of deep pockets that hung like windsocks under their skirts. They wore veils, too, white for a novice, black for nuns who had taken their final vows. Sometimes in the summer they would wear hot prickly stockings and in frosty midwinter we would glimpse cold bare ankles above sturdy lace-up shoes.

The clothes made the wearer at once anonymous and individual. We could tell from half a field away, in the twilight, with their backs to us, whether it was Sister Jesse and Sister Jean, or MFB and Plus Babs (so called because when the

Sisters wrote their names, the word 'Sister' was replaced by the sign of the cross). We would sometimes daringly refer to them as 'the Crows', the birds they most resembled as their black veils billowed and flapped behind them. Like all people of a religious order whose clothes identify them as such (monks, lamas, bishops), they inspired confusion and sometimes embarrassment in people who didn't know them well. Fathers on fête days would shuffle their feet, fingering packets of cigarettes in their pockets. New girls sometimes found them frightening, but after half a term the strangeness wore off.

I liked them all at once, as was my custom (having been born, it seemed, without any critical faculties). As their kindness and affection for me grew, so did mine for them, even though I was given tickings off and B order marks (the worst: A order marks were for less serious crimes). They forgave us for breaking bounds, passing notes, smoking cigarettes, missing History and filching food from the school kitchens. They also forgave me, I think, for not living up to my earlier scholastic abilities. When I arrived I was usually near or at the top in each subject – but because of the size of our year's intake (baby-boom eleven year olds, forty of us instead of the usual twenty), eight of us were peeled off, crammed for a term and, jumping a year, pushed into the form above. From then on my marks began to go downhill, principally because I was idle and inattentive, though my photographic memory served me well at exam times – I could recall paragraphs and maps on pages and read them in my mind's eye, scrutinizing and studying them in detail. The photographs faded after a few days (like lines in a play once you've finished with it) and I was left with almost no recollection of the question or answer. Only the things I learned by heart, by rote (so condemned now), have stuck, and I can now dredge up the definition of osmosis, Archimedes' principle and prepositions taking the ablative in German, and examine them at leisure. Poems I learned as a child have stuck; but nothing remains of the play I finished three months ago.

Where the school grounds met the road there was a high stone wall and a shrubbery of dark laurels, beeches and rhododendrons on which shone the street lamps. When the leaves were wet and darkness came early on winter evenings, we kept away from the shrubbery. It was the part of the school where the safe oblivion of our ordered life met the hiss of a passing bus and the world outside. It always made me uneasy. I liked things in their appointed place: holidays at home, prep at school, Chapel on Sundays, letters arriving on Monday morning. When in 1963 there came a great snow, only A level sixth-formers were expected back at the beginning of Lent term and rules were relaxed and informal. It unnerved me completely – aggravated by the fact that we were allowed to wear trousers, but only as well as and underneath skirts, so we wandered about like Muslim girls in a Christian convent. It was a relief to see the other younger girls, usually reviled, arrive, and normality return.

We were never given holiday work: when our terms ended, we tore down our timetables, monitor lists, team lists, packed our trunks and left. The next term would bring different dormitories and different desks. Lacrosse sticks were exchanged for tennis rackets and rounders' bats, scarves and gloves for tennis whites and bathing dresses. We swam at the White Rock Baths, reeking of chlorine and echoing skiddy tiles. A coach would collect us once a week; I soon stopped putting my name on the swimming list as I found the water too cold. From the dormitories at the front of the school – Salem, Hebron and Siloam – you could see the last rays of light on summer evenings on distant Hastings, so indistinct that it could be mistaken for Capri.

Sophia Loren and Brigitte Bardot and Gina Lollabrigida wore chiffon headscarves, gingham dresses and wide belts, and so did we. A favourite lipstick was Pink Sorrento, pointed high heels arrived in the shops, hair began to be backcombed, nylon petticoats were dipped in sugary water and dried into stiff umbrellas over radiators. We read *Doctor Zhivago* and Jane Austen, *War and Peace*, *Gone with the Wind*, *The Robe*, and listened to Wagner and the Everly Brothers, Beethoven and Billy Fury. We read at night with torches and tuned in to Radio Luxembourg on forbidden transistors with Horace Batchelor spelling out 'K-e-y-n-s-h-a-m' to help us win the football pools.

When my father came back from Malaya for good in 1958, I hadn't seen him for eighteen months. I had a dream that I went to Southampton Docks to meet him but I had forgotten his face. No matter how I stared at his photograph, I couldn't put the fear out of my mind that I wouldn't know him again. My mother had gone to join him for the last six months so Ælene and I spent the Lent holidays staying with godparents.

Joan Barber, widow of my godfather, Dickie Barber, lived in St John's Wood. Her daughter, Jane, and I had shared a pram as babies. Her son Peter was nine when I was twelve. We rowed boats in Regent's Park, climbed to the top of the Monument of the Great Fire, and walked round the Whispering Gallery at St Paul's. At the Monument I crawled out at the top and could hardly look out, let alone over. At St Paul's, I merely wanted to throw myself off at once. Vertigo is an odd thing and can, like all phobias, be conquered, and I have now nearly conquered mine. But the odd photograph looking down a skyscraper can send me off in a second, palms tingling, eyes stiffening in their sockets. At Madame Tussaud's I became transfixed with terror in the Chamber of Horrors, literally petrified and unable to move. Ælene had to walk me out, past those dreadful murderers standing in a silent row, their dead eyes fixed on nothing.

When my parents came home that summer (my father's face was even more familiar than I had dared hope), we moved into

Walnut Tree Cottage in Rolvenden Layne, which we rented for a year. My room had ivy wallpaper. On the first night of the Christmas holidays I was taken to hospital to have my appendix taken out. Arriving at two a.m. I was put into an old women's ward. All night long I listened to the soft moans and clank of bedpans and hoarse cries of 'Sister! My tube's come loose.' The next time I woke up I was in a huge children's ward; in the distance was a television set showing Popeye cackling. My parents stood by my bed but I couldn't speak so they went away and, overwhelmed with self-pity, I struggled out, bent double, to shuffle off to the lavatory. The Salvation Army came to sing carols and give us oranges and I made a remarkable recovery and grew an inch and a half in six days. I came out the day before Christmas, with a neat scar like a little worm, to presents of Narnia books and Chopin records. Keen as I was on human company, no relief was as thrilling as escaping from the kind-hearted Christmas-decorated children's ward.

A year later my parents bought Sparkeswood, a large white Victorian house with a mock Breton tower at one end and a garden of lawns and huge lime, chestnut and pine trees. When they came to collect us from school there was a small black labrador puppy sitting in the car. He was called Hugo and displayed throughout his long life unswerving affection and patience. When things seem a bit churned up, I often think of the nature of a dog and try to copy his enthusiasm, forgiving nature and loyalty.

Sparkeswood was the first house we owned, all the others having been Army or rented. We used packing cases as bedside tables and dressing-tables and it seemed better than ordinary furniture. Familiar pictures and rugs appeared – wherever you spread your carpet is home. Wistaria grew on the south face, and virginia creeper on the west side. There was a large fruit-bearing fig tree and a great magnolia grandiflora whose creamy flowers you could pick while leaning from an upstairs window.

Nearby were the Romney Marshes, and cornfields and hop gardens and bluebell woods, where we walked every day of the holidays, with Hugo putting up hares and plunging into dewponds. Rooks nested in the tall trees, and in the summer the air was filled with the cooing of woodpigeons and the distant sounds of harvesting.

There were parties in the holidays – occasionally tennis and swimming parties with barbecues and picnics but mostly rather formal occasions when boys wore dinner jackets and Mrs Pullen would be booked to play. Mrs Pullen and her drummer and double-bass player turned up everywhere. She smoked constantly with a cigarette holder clamped between her teeth, plump arms shuddering as she embarked on 'These Foolish Things' and 'A Nightingale Sang in Berkeley Square'. Dances ended at twelve-thirty, after 'God Save the Queen' when all the dimmed lights were brightened and we stood to tousled attention. Days of parties and the preparations were exciting. Hair was washed and dresses ironed, and we had an afternoon rest, like Southern belles in *Gone with the Wind*, wondering who would ask us to dance. The Benenden Tennis Tournament, held at the girls' school, culminated in the Benenden Ball, a very grand affair where grown-ups appeared in quantities to Strip the Willow and do Highland reels. Once, Patrick Millet partnered me in the Tennis Tournament, an English-speaking French boy of dazzling appearance, good humoured and immaculately lazy on the court. We lost every match but congratulated ourselves on our style. The thing was not to be seen to be trying; as we were both profoundly uncompetitive, it was most enjoyable.

Games were just that: games. The idea of being keen on anything was beneath our dignity: at school this lost us many matches. Our neighbouring schools were our competitors – Hollington Park, Lillesden and Bedgebury Park were our constant adversaries, and so too was Battle Abbey: but the Battle Abbey girls, roosting in their historic castellated school, with the ancient Abbey their daily neighbourhood, were as casual as we were, and provided the most agreeable matches. Afterwards there would be a match tea and a walk round the school, a sudden glimpse of another world, so similar and so different, with different bits of garden out of bounds and other school heroes. To admire someone slavishly was called having a 'pash' on someone – the devoted follower was called a pashite and could be used to clean tennis shoes and wash socks. Too much encouragement was called 'cultivating pashites' and was frowned on. This harmless hero-worship evaporated in a few terms, and the small offerings of Smarties hidden in your gumboots stopped.

O level exams were one thing; for A levels I was as unprepared then as I am now. Although I longed to copy my sister and take English Literature in one year and leave, I was encouraged instead to study French, German and Latin. As sixth-formers, we were expected to work on our own – we were moved into single rooms (Beta, Mu, Pi) with a bed and a desk and our prep times were unsupervised. I must have been more immature than most as I found it impossible to contemplate work unless a frowning adjudicator presided over a silent room of scribbling pens. These three languages had many set books, none of which I read more than once: I would lean instead on my window sill, sniffing the garlic flowers on the bank by the games-field path and dream of being free and wearing lipstick and nail varnish as I drove my open sports car through Rome, dark glasses and chiffon scarf in place. Nina Nesbitt-Dufort, whose home had been in Beirut, told us of the elegance of the women there, in simple black linen dresses and high-heeled gold sandals, when that troubled city was the Paris of the Middle East. (Nina also claimed that she could recognize any plane by its silhouette, and for years fooled us by peering at a dot in the sky and remarking, 'Boeing, of course.')

I was sent on a bus to Hastings to meet the careers' adviser in Warrior Square. I told her I wanted to be an actress, which was true in a sense. The idea of supporting myself in a real job was so odd and terrifying, and the pamphlets she pressed on me listing colleges of further education and even universities were so terrible to contemplate, that acting seemed to be the only work that I could understand. Mrs Curran promised me some private tuition to prepare for an audition to the Royal Academy of Dramatic Art in the autumn, and I left school with colours for lacrosse, netball and tennis, and the coveted Byers Cup which was given to me, rather unexpectedly, for All-round Achievement. This was a prize indeed, never to be touched or seen by me again.

For the first time ever, I caught a train on my own to London, and from there flew out to Italy, where my family was on holiday. As the train took me past back gardens and high streets and fields and stations I could feel school sliding out of my mind, slipping off my skin, like a suntan fading in a homeward-bound jet. By the time I reached Rome (attached to an ancient Turk, who had been clamped to my arm at London Airport by his niece, 'Take my onkel to Turkey!' 'I'm not going to Turkey!' 'Pliz! He spik no Inglis!'), by the time I stood in the huge unsupported arch of Leonardo da Vinci Airport, trying to locate a plane to Ankara for my Turkish uncle in faltering Italian, by the time I had been addressed by beady-eyed '*Bella Signorina*' officials, England in general and school in particular were almost forgotten.

Chapter Four

Autumn is my favourite time of year. The sudden crisp air in September, the smell and sight of bonfires, smoke climbing straight up on still afternoons, dahlias and green beans: everything is exciting. New jobs begin, new terms start, new fashions appear in shop windows, towns lose their tired summer filth and glimmer with attractive lights. By the autumn of 1963 the Beatles had taken the country – and us – by storm. Not a day passed without some reference to them in the newspapers, and their Englishness (notwithstanding that they were from Liverpool, at that time as remote to us as Zagreb), their town-ee identity, coffee bar, Cavern and Cilla and Gerry and the Mersey, for heaven's sake . . . their *ordinariness* made us feel that they belonged to us. (So had Cliff and Billy and Marty – so, of course, had Elvis, and the Everlys, but this was different: the Fab Four came from a real city and had real names, and looked nothing like Dion or Bobby Vee.) So it was 'I Wanna Hold Your Hand', 'Midnight in Moscow', 'Telstar' and 'From Russia With Love', that we played on our gramophones. Not being at school was strange – it took months to shake off the feeling that you hadn't handed in a German essay and I still have deep depressions on Sunday evenings until I realize that there are no more Latin unseens in my life. Leaving school means no more exams, I thought (but what else are first nights but exams in public?).

I was taken on as a shop assistant in the nearby town of Tenterden. Mike and Pauline Marriott had set up a shop called Argosy, painted the outside black, white and rust and filled it with Swedish Orrefors glass, modern lights, Portmeirion pottery, chrome and leather chairs. It sold trays and designer cooking utensils, stainless-steel teapots and was, all in all, the swishest place to shop in Kent. They also sold furniture, carpets and materials. I travelled in on the 97 bus with a packed lunch and learned from Janet how to gift-wrap a parcel and from Doreen how to charm customers into a sale by offering them something much cheaper. I was very happy there – I received £5 a week, and sometimes was given chipped things to take home. Once we went on an outing to East Anglia to meet one of our suppliers, an up-and-coming Terence Conran. At eleven o'clock I would go out to buy the doughnuts to have with coffee. With chunky homemade sand-wiches and no games lessons every day, I became larger. My father said I moved about the house. The fashion was for bouclé tweed skirts and chunky jerseys and I looked like a well-lagged water tank.

On an autumn day as I polished the back-lit glass shelf and thought of the filling in the homemade sandwich, the door opened and into the shop came a pale, pale woman. She was so thin that her legs could scarcely support her enormous fur coat. She had a white face and fair hair with heavily made-up weary eyes: long scarlet fingernails grew off her twig-like fingers. She moved listlessly about supported by a dark-haired man in a city overcoat, her hands indicating one or two things which we took away and wrapped up – then with a sigh she teetered away to the waiting car, leaving a trail of expensive scent hanging in the air. I decided at once to be thin, svelte, gaunt and to teeter rather than march. After the Christmas rush, I left the friendly Argosy, and it was arranged that I should stay with my Aunt Joan Mary Jehu, who had moved to London after the farm in Woodchurch had been sold.

London was still a complete mystery to me. I had travelled up to Gower Street to audition for the Royal Academy of Dramatic Art the year before. This involved getting off a train and into a taxi, queuing with other candidates, horror mounting at their confidence and the thought of competition; delivering a speech by Joan of Arc in gaol (which I made sound like Joyce Grenfell temporarily locked in a broom cupboard), being waved off half-way through my *Lady Windemere's Fan* piece, and going straight back to Kent.

I have always found auditions agonizing. Once I have the part there are no problems, but when I stand in the wings and hear other people declaiming, all the stuffing goes out of me and I just want to get away without being noticed. From early days at the Hastings Music Festival I began to dislike public speaking competitions. When I was eleven, I had to recite a poem which started:

> *The gardener's cat's called Mignonette*
> *She hates the cold, she hates the wet!*
> *She sits among the hothouse flowers*
> *And sleeps for hours and hours and hours.*

I didn't care for it much as a poem anyway, so I uttered it in my most matter-of-fact tones. Listening to fourteen children reciting the same poem is not the most enthralling way of spending a morning, but I was shocked when the judges gave the first prize to a simpering girl, who bridled and smirked and wagged her finger and actually put her two folded hands to her cheek to indicate the depth of the slumber achieved by the cat. In retrospect it was far more entertaining than my curt weather-forecast delivery, but it stunned me slightly to see how far wide I was of the mark.

My Aunt Joan Mary's flat was in Bramham Gardens in Earl's Court. It was on the fourth floor of a large Victorian mansion block, with balconies facing the square garden on the south, and long corridors with large rooms. Uncle Ivor had died very suddenly four years before, and my aunt with quixotic generosity had filled the flat with a shifting population of friends, family and the occasional paying guest. Many of us were complete strangers to each other, the central pivot being

Joan Mary. Most of us, however, knew the sometimes tenuous route which had brought us there: we were nieces, but there were schoolfriends of the boys, children of friends from India, and friends of friends who came for two nights and stayed six months. At mealtimes people would appear and a general shuffling around went on: some were in for supper, some were just going out, some would eat later, some decided to bring in fish and chips. A kind of anarchic splendour reigned in Bramham Gardens: so many people felt they belonged that it became a cross between a lost property office and the Russian Tea Rooms in New York.

My grandmother Thyra Weir stayed sometimes with Joan Mary, sometimes with my parents in Kent. She had become rather forgetful after an attack of mumps in her seventies and had to be brought back from South Africa, whence she had moved from Kenya, by my mother. She was extremely amusing and elegant and had great charm. When she was young, a traveller in a train had told her that the colour of her eyes reminded him of a speckled trout. Her favourite colours were rust red and mustard, black and mauve. She had never had her waist-length hair cut and wore it in a coil held by combs. She had tiny feet and slim legs ('Good Straight Legs' was one of the highest compliments she would pay) and her large hats she wore tilted rakishly, mixing costume jewellery with the real stuff with abandon. In her later years, she became a keen admirer of electricity pylons.

Her great artistic talent had started and ended in Tibet and Sikkim. Travelling with my grandfather to Lhasa had triggered her off. She drew quickly and astonishingly well in pastels. The first European woman to visit the Potala, the Dalai Lama's palace in Lhasa, she said conversationally to His Holiness that Amy Johnson had just flown to Australia in twenty-seven hours. The thirteenth Dalai Lama reflected for a bit, then said, 'What was the hurry?' She enjoyed amateur dramatics: of one of her performances in India it was whispered that she was 'better than Mrs Patrick Campbell'. After the Partition of India, when my grandfather had retired from the Indian Political Service, they moved to Kenya. Granny had never cooked in her life, but this in no way dimmed her enthusiasm for the kitchen. Putting on an apron, to which she attached a diamond brooch, she would plug the electric kettle in, put it on the gas cooker and call out, 'Kettle's boiling!' She had an infectious sense of fun and would often execute little tappy dance steps to the wireless, catching you up, if you were near, as a partner. From her I have inherited undiluted a love of scissors, hats, bolts of cloth which are never made into anything, and acting. Pylons are bound to come later.

The flat at Bramham Gardens was huge – the hall had mullioned windows and terracotta black and white tiles and was big enough to use as a dining-room when Granny Weir was using the long balconied dining-room as a bedroom. Two corridors led away from the hall: one to the kitchen and laundry room where the washing machine would occasionally break loose and come chuntering out of its kennel, dripping and digesting clothes as it came. The kitchen was large, with an Aga and a pulley to dry clothes hanging over it. Behind the kitchen was a bedroom, originally for a maid, where you could sometimes find a Dutch girl or someone's brother-in-law. The second corridor led down to five more bedrooms and two bathrooms. The end bedrooms looked out over the mews at the back, four floors beneath us. One of the mews cottages had a determined couple of party-givers – Trini Lopez was a great favourite. They played 'If I Had a Hammer' again and again, the guests joining in at the tops of their voices, the sound echoing down past the dustbins on hot summer nights to mingle with more mews dwellers playing 'Hit the Road Jack'.

I had left school. I had come to London. Now what? I had failed to get into RADA and was too ashamed and afraid to try another school. I couldn't think of anything that I could do: there were things I loved doing, anything to do with drawing, acting, reading, translating – good heavens, just helping; but I couldn't type. When I went to J. Walter Thompson for an interview, they couldn't think what to do with me and sent me away. It may have been something to do with the attitude at school – the nuns were mostly blue stockings and if you didn't go to university or have a plan for your future you would probably get married and, terrifying phrase, 'settle down'. Work was something you did until you got married. The uneasy spectre lurking in the background (money and how to get it) stepped closer when you weren't looking, like grandmother's footsteps. I would become like that pale blonde in the Argosy and be a model.

Lucie Clayton was then in Bond Street in a tall narrow building occupying three or four floors. It was a sort of finishing school (the Charm Course) and model agency (for which you enrolled in the Modelling Course). Mr Kark, the Principal, looked me up and down, weighed me ('too fat'), measured me ('five feet eight in stockinged feet and your back's too hollow') and accepted me for the Modelling Course, twelve guineas for a month of mornings. In great excitement I went to Etam in Oxford Street and bought a black and white linen dress, 49s 11d, with a white collar and some black patent-leather shoes from Russell & Bromley, 79s 11d.

That summer, I remember, was hot and full of thunderstorms. In the mornings I would catch the underground train from Earl's Court ('Stand clear of the gates') and learn at Lucie Clayton how to apply eye make-up, how to get in and out of an E-type Jaguar with your knees together ('smile, swivel, sink into the seat with your bottom first, then knees and ankles together – in – and smile'), and how to do the Model Walk: 'Your hip-bones should be the first things to come into the room, the ball of your foot goes down FIRST: cross left foot over right to turn, spin smoothly – wrong way, Susan, get up and stop giggling.' I would practise the Model

Walk on my way back down the Earl's Court Road, my body a yard behind my feet, awkward as a mule until suddenly it clicked and we could glide like swans. There was an end-of-course fashion show – we all wore our own clothes, and parents and friends were invited. My grand finale get-up was a safari outfit: khaki shorts and socks, Joan Mary's co-respondent golf shoes (too large) and, from the recesses of the flat, a rifle of some sort. A policeman stopped me as I came down from Bond Street station: 'Have you got a licence for that gun?' 'Oh no, it's only for a fashion show.' I passed out of the Modelling Course and was formally accepted on to the books of the Modelling Agency.

Mary Quant's Ginger Group, Tuffin and Foale, Jane and Jane, *Queen* magazine, David Bailey and Jean Shrimpton – these were the names of the world of fashion. It was a bit disappointing therefore to hear that my first job was to be a house model for Debenham and Freebody in Wigmore Street. I was engaged for £8 a week in the Model Suit Department, a quiet backwater of the store where the clothes were expensive and rather stuffy. One of my jobs was to make sure they all had labels on and weren't hanging too close together. There was one other person almost as humble as me: Robbie, a diminutive hedgehog person of about fifty, who would always be pushed aside when there was a sale to be made. She was so gentle and small that it made me angry to see the grey-haired vultures treating her disdainfully.

At lunchtime I would put on one of the suits, secretly rolling the waistband to make the skirt a bit shorter, and set off, with a glassy smile and my model walk, to the restaurant. We didn't have to wear numbers on our wrists, and as we tucked in all the labels, it was probably difficult to tell what we were up to, in all our red lipstick and eyelashes, moving in a creepy smiling way between the tables. At coffee breaks I found that the girls who worked behind the counters on the ground floor got only £5 for a five and half day week. We all had to clock in at eight-thirty a.m. in the basement, giving us half an hour to make absolutely sure that the suits weren't hanging too close together and no labels had imploded during the night. One morning I was five minutes late – Personnel called me in the next day, where a fish-eyed woman questioned me about loyalty to the firm and asked how I imagined I'd deserve a pension if I was so untrustworthy. This was my second black mark – the first had come on my first day when Fish Eyes asked for my cards and I said I hadn't had any printed yet. (Another thing we weren't told about at school – National Insurance cards.)

I plodded back to our silent carpeted department, wondering if modelling and I were cut out for each other. Robbie said, 'Someone's looking for you,' and an elegant Frenchwoman appeared, drew me aside and said in a stage whisper, 'Do you sink you would like to work for Jane and Jane?' She was called Lucienne Phillips, and in those days Jean Muir was still called Jane and Jane. Lucienne was a clothes-buyer: through my bulky tweed suit, spots and puppy-fat she could detect a possibility. In my lunch hour I walked to 19 Great Portland Street and climbed to the fourth floor. There was a small showroom with two chairs and a cheval glass. Miss Muir came in, tiny, ruler-straight hair, formidable. 'Mmm,' she said, looking me up and down. 'Mmm, mmm, a bit, you know, mmm, yes, good,' and went back behind her curtains. I gave in my notice to Fish Eyes, begged Robbie to leave, told the counter girls to go on strike, clocked out of Debenham and Freebody and started working at Jane and Jane.

This was how it was. Ælene and Nina ('it's a D C8') Nesbitt-Dufort, Dinx Sawday and I had moved into a flat on the third floor of 24 Trebovir Road, Earl's Court. Dinx was from the flat in Bramham Gardens. Her parents had put her there for safekeeping while she completed her ballet training. The new flat was £9 a week between four of us, and we each put a pound in the kitty for food, light bulbs and washing powder.

My mother.

My father.

With Ælene and my mother's Kerry Blue, Satan, in Gulmarg.

My father taught us to swim.

On board the *Dilwara*, 1951.

Sitting fatly in the shallows.

With Sammy and Michael on the
balcony in Hong Kong.

Norwegian girls at the Coronation Fancy Dress Parade. My temperature was 103°.

With my Coronation medal in the garden at K.L.

My first acting part: a princess at the Army School in K.L. My mother made the blue satin dress.

My mother with Kinky and Judy on the verandah.
Judy wears the mandatory dog-vaccination tag.

With Ah Feng at 16, H.Q. Malaya, wearing our school dresses. Our hair was unplaited for the photograph, making it wavy.

On the verandah in K.L. with Kinky between us. These were our party dresses – I am wearing a new watch.

Self as Will Scarlett, Æ. as King Richard, Veronica in a hat as Robin Hood, Alice Higginbottom as Maid Marian and Felicity, possibly as a Merry Man.

A Mickledene rounders match. *Front row left*: self and Nikki Barker. Miss Bentley, *centre*, with Vicki on the left and Mary Steele on the right.

The cousins at Court Lodge. Michael and Gordon,
Maybe, Ælene, me, Reay.

In the drive at Woodchurch, showing gnawed-off hair.

Anthea, Sarah and self, summer term, St Mary's, 1958.
The tennis racquet doubled as Cliff's guitar.

The school lacrosse team. I am looking sullen on the
left-hand side of the back row.

There was no refrigerator, no radiators: we put milk bottles on the window sill to keep cool and on really cold days we'd walk round to the huge Air Terminal on Gloucester Road where there were sofas and warmth. The flat faced east and west. The drawing-room, with generous window sills, a fireplace and stripped floor, caught all the evening sun. Next door was Nina's small bedroom which she had somehow persuaded us that she should have to herself; the hall which we painted terracotta and covered with rush matting; the kitchen, bright yellow gloss paint; and our bedroom which looked like a nursery with the three beds and as many chests of drawers. The bathroom, squashed between kitchen and nursery, was tall and narrow, and filled with dripping stockings and underclothes. The nursery faced due east over the roofs of the Earl's Court underground.

I was usually up first, creeping about in the darkness so as not to disturb Ælene and Dinx, lighting a candle by the mirror to do my make-up, hearing an echoey disembodied voice outside: 'The train now standin' at Platform 4 is for High Street Kensin'ton, Nottin' Hill Gate, Bayswater, Paddin'ton, Edgware R O A D train on Platform 4. Mind de doors.'

From Earl's Court I travelled to Oxford Circus, ran across Oxford Street and up to Great Portland Street. It was, still is, the rag-trade world: all kinds of wholesale and retail stores, fabric suppliers, belt makers, and across in Soho, trimming and buttons. Vans would disgorge rails of blue nylon dresses at street level and high above in glassed attics women would stitch and cut and machine; fake fur collar, half belt, deep gusset, hidden plaquet, concealed zip, toile, French seam, petersham tape, interfacing, peplum, pad and press stud. Clothes were called garments, the next season was six months ahead and house models like me would sew on labels and hooks, pack and deliver, as well as collect silk from Tissus de France and smoked salmon sandwiches from Foubert's Place. The sandwiches would be for grand buyers or magazine editors. Jane and Jane wasn't a shop, so the only place to see the clothes was in the showroom (on me); then the *Vogue* editor would decide on the yellow wool smock and the silk dress and jacket, to be photographed on Celia Hammond by Terence Donovan, and Geraldine Stutz would order twenty-four black wool harem pants for Henri Bendels in New York.

Miss Muir was Miss Muir to us all: I don't know why everyone was rather scared of her, but we were. She would not tolerate the second rate even if it fooled everyone else. Once I stood in front of the cheval glass being pinned into something, a jacket of some kind. 'What do you think, Joanna?' she said, peering over my shoulder at the reflection. I said I thought it looked wonderful and indeed it did to my unskilled eyes, but: 'That sleeve's awful,' said Miss Muir, yanking it out by the roots. 'All crooked, all wrong.' Sometimes she would examine a dart or seam intently, running her fine thin fingers over it murmuring, 'A whisker off here, Sylvia dear, a natz, a whisper, mmm?' You didn't have to be very clever to see that she was far out in front in the field of dressmaking. She used the very finest cloths – silk, satin, wool, suede, muslin, the most extraordinary buttons, some solid silver, some brass, pearl or perspex, overstitching in different colours, asymmetrical fastenings. Her clothes were, are, immediately recognizable, her high standards contagious, her energy infectious. She loved Danny la Rue and Judi Dench, Lena Horne and Henry Moore, hard work, craftmanship, vigour, bezazz, the city, the country, the people . . . she competed with no one and since the day that I put on my first Jean Muir dress, I have been ensnared by her witty elegant clothes. When we showed her dresses she liked us not to look like snooty models: we had scraped-away hair, heavy make-up like ballerinas, and inky black legs. Once she designed some shoes in Liberty silk to match her dresses: they were made up by Rayne and three of us put on black Jean Muir dresses, black tights and stepped about on a catwalk with spotlights on our feet. The models' names were up in the showroom window of Rayne. 'Look! Your name in lights for the first time!' But when I looked up my name was spelt wrong and I was Joanne Lumley.

At lunchtime I used to go to a café beside the Palladium Theatre behind Oxford Circus. There I would have one saveloy sausage for 5d. The sandwiches weren't a great success and quite often customers would leave them half-eaten on plates. When they left I would gather them up smoothly into my bag and take them home to eat later. Although I was now getting £10 a week, free food was always appreciated. Whenever any of us in the flat was asked out to dinner, we would collect bread rolls and butter pats to bulk up our fairly measly diet at home. We shared dresses and tights. Biba had just opened its first branch in a tiny corner shop in Abingdon Road, filled with feather boas and dresses for £3. We sometimes made our own clothes, in Liberty lawn print, sewing them by hand as we had no machine. We didn't have a hairdrier or heated rollers: in those days it was the mark of a photographic model to go about with a headscarf tied over huge high rollers. We did, however, have a telephone (Fremantle 9935) which rang constantly; there was a list beside it of people each of us wanted to avoid. If a bore said, 'Give me your number,' we would give them the number of the local plumbing firm who had once overcharged us.

After three months I left Jane and Jane to try to become a photographic model. This was extraordinarily difficult, a kind of Catch-22 set-up. You couldn't work unless you had experience, and you couldn't get experience unless you worked. (Later on I found that Equity, the actors' union, have much the same entrance test: you can't work without a card, but you can't get a card unless you have worked.) I had my hair cut by Vidal Sassoon, packed a bag of jerseys and skirts and a gaberdine suit from Jane and Jane, and went to John Adriaan's studio in St John's Wood to have some test shots taken by his assistant, Ray Green. And now a dilemma: what do you actually do in a picture? I half sat on things, half smiled, looked vaguely left and right, trying to remember the way professional models looked in magazines. I had by this time bought a huge wig, which cost £30, causing the bank to write stern letters for the next year, and I'd borrowed Dinx's black PVC mackintosh. The finished pictures I took anxiously to Doreen at Lucie Clayton. We put four aside for a card, had some blown up for my empty model book and she gave me a long list of photographers to visit.

I walked back from Bond Street, along to Marble Arch, and across Hyde Park. A great squall of spring rain suddenly drenched down – I found myself sheltering near the Round Pond with several people. We chatted amiably as the storm poured down – one person from Singapore, a tall Chinese youth called Jerome, said he was a keen artist. How lovely, I cried, Singapore! And an artist! The rain stopped, the sun came out and we all dispersed, all but Jerome who said it would mean a lot to him if I would look at his sketches (I don't think he said etchings) as his family was so far away. Blithely I followed him to Bayswater, and puffed up five flights of stairs behind him to his attic flat. As he opened the door, something in his face made me change my mind about his sketches and as he grabbed my arm I slithered free, hurled myself down the stairs, feet going like pistons, and burst out into the street, across the road at Lancaster Gate and flew across the park. I paused gasping just beyond the Spirit of Energy and peered back fearfully. There, running like a ghost in the bright sunlight, with flying cloak and striding legs, came Jerome from Singapore. I tore on, round the pond past the Broadwalk to Kensington High Street and hurled myself on to a bus which was just moving off. My heart was crashing so much I couldn't breathe, neck craned round to stare back at the park. The bus dawdled along and stopped at the traffic lights by Barkers. Running easily through the crowd came

Jerome from Singapore, smiling like a shark, head moving to and fro to see if he could spot me. He stepped on to the bus platform and watched me till I got off in the Earl's Court Road. Another Olympic dash took me to the flat but not before he'd seen me go in.

The point of all this is that my own terror frightened me, running away made me even more afraid, panicking made me panic. If I hadn't run, he wouldn't have chased me; as it was, all he did was ring the bell for a few days, and get bored. Why didn't I say: no thank you, goodbye, sorry, I don't want to? Because I was afraid of hurting his feelings, afraid he'd think that if I didn't want to see his etchings it must be because he was Chinese. For days afterwards Ælene would lean out of the window and say, 'Oh here comes Jerome.' Nina would say, 'Jerome on the telephone for you,' or 'We've asked Jerome round for supper.' Poor Jerome; but there was not a picture in sight in that second's glimpse I had into his eyrie in Bayswater.

Showing photographers your book was a pretty grim affair. The fashionable attitude towards models was that we were ugly old bags and feelingless idiots. 'You look like a pig but I suppose we can use you,' said one. 'Go away until you're not so ugly,' said another. This was, once you learnt it, only banter – but there was a bullying streak in many of the snappers. Hairdressers and photographers; crimpers and snappers. The first two photographers to use me were Crispian Woodgate, of the *Daily Mail*, and Roy Round. I owe much gratitude to them. They used me often and even if Crispian said, 'You look as if you've got out of a zoo,' I don't think he really meant it.

Dinx had joined the London Festival Ballet, Nina worked in an art gallery, Ælene did temporary secretarial work, and I was racing about with a model bag and curlers. The Beatles played at the Hammersmith Odeon and we went, swooned and came away deaf. We went to watch the Boat Race and hitched a lift back from a coachload of police drafted in from Essex. Dinx invited them all up for tea in the flat: they stood and sat and leaned everywhere and drank tea from tooth-mugs and jam jars. People came round in shoals: writers, painters, photographers, medical students, ballet dancers, architects, models – we took our jeans in, played 'All You Need is Love' on top volume at the open window, bought junk in the Portobello Road and ate at Nick's Diner.

Nick Clarke was an enormous Old Etonian with great humour, appetite and style. His small restaurant in Ifield Road in Fulham was on the lorry driver's route through London. The food was excellent, the conditions cramped, the clientele studded with Kray Twins, royalty, politicians and the glitterati of the day. Late, after most people had gone, Nick would get down rare bottles of wine and his favoured guests would talk and drink and smoke till three o'clock, all chairs on the tables, last waiter gone, doors locked to the night. Nick Clarke was a natural host – visiting every table, occasionally settling down, like Mr Jackson, all over a chair, honouring you with his presence for a whole course. The food was excellent but what made people go again was Nick's welcome and concern. 'Everything O K, lovey? Nigel, bring another bottle of the house red please – and a chair.' And at once you felt re-membered and cosseted, important. It's the secret of any really good restaurant, where food is not all – for that matter, of any grocery shop or garage or hairdresser – to be made welcome.

Hairdressers, led by Vidal Sassoon, were prominent members of the modelling world. Crimpers had groovy cars, Minis with blacked-out windows, and jeeps: you could have your hair done free if you were willing to put your head in the hands of apprentices in evening sessions. They would snip and bleach and tint, fingering your hair with resignation and disgust, talking to each other, often leaving you armless in your gown, half-cut strands over one eye or lobster red under an oven-hot drier. Blow-drying hair was the in thing. My hair, which had always been

wild, was now frankly unacceptable. I dyed it dark plum red and
flattened it with water and hairgrips, grew it long and made it
brown, bleached it, streaked it, hennaed it but it was never really
a great success. Ironically, now, when it really couldn't matter
less, as most parts I do demand a wig, it has come into its own,
curly, springy, thick, unflattenable, grease-able, buoyant, hopeless and completely fashionable.

The obsessive attitude I had to hair was reflected in the zeal
of the crimpers who changed their rules daily: don't perm, do
perm, don't use hair spray, backcomb it to the skies; only use
your fingers/towel/ray gun/oven to dry it, don't dry it, wax it,
wash it twice a day/twice a month, razor cut/scissor cut, rip it
off with your teeth – brush it, rinse it in hot/cold water, tea,
beer – don't ever brush it, cut it off, it must be long, on and on
and on – two months away from your favourite crimper and
the staff have changed, the look has changed and the disdainful
fingering starts again. You need a hot oil treatment, they say
sternly, and proceed to roll it round scalding tongs, spraying,
scratching and combing till it is a brillo pad. I love and fear
hairdressers. The good ones make you look as though you
were meant to look like that, the bad ones leave you weeping,
alone and nearly bald, in a washroom.

Chapter Five

There is always one moment, one day in your career which later you can point at and say, 'Then is when it started to go forward.' Mine in modelling was being booked for *Queen* magazine by the terrifyingly chic Lady Rendlesham. I went to David Montgomery's studio in Edith Grove, nearly fainting with terror. How strange to look back from now to then! Montgomery, a tranquil genius from Brooklyn, Clare Rendlesham, witty, generous, *Queen* magazine, zazzy, groovy, absolutely the best, all combined to make me want to saw my own legs off at the knee. Montgomery's studio was painted black and was reached by side steps to a basement, garden flat. Inside, I think it was black too: Bob Dylan's music, coffee machine, huge black and white photographs, a model room with bright mirrors, already occupied by two blonde skeletons applying the eighth layer of mascara to the third pair of eyelashes. Clothes grander than any you could afford hung on rails – shoes were huge (most models are tall) or tiny (brand new shoes are made in size $3\frac{1}{2}$ as samples). Boxes of jewellery and accessories and a stylist ironing things which will never be looked at, a feeling of occasion, seven pages to fill with a look, a feeling, a sort of air of knowing, nonchalant we're-here-already-where-are-*you*? Ben Carruthers, a sixties London hero, whom I never properly met, walked about in tall leather boots and a hat, exuding danger and *weltschmerz*. David Puttnam, Montgomery's agent, skimmed in and out again, smart, bright, kind, going places. He looked about thirteen and later grew a beard to stop being thrown out of pubs and began to run the film industry.

There was a restlessness, studied langour, nervous knots in case you suddenly blurted out something un-cool and fubsy; the essence was to appear as though this particular day was of no importance, was nearly a bore but was quite FUN. My face was round although I was fairly thin; my hair was cut short. But Clare Rendlesham put her own watch on my wrist and Montgomery used me more than the skeletons who had grudgingly made space for me ('Are you a model? Good Lord') amongst their Carmen rollers, diaries and nail varnish. By the next day I could afford to be so casual I was nearly horizontal: 'Oh yuh, I was working with Montgomery yesterday ... yuh, *Queen* actually, ... yuh, Benny Carruthers was there ... oh, it was OK, I suppose.'

People dropped into studios in those days. I was being photographed by Terence Donovan in his studio in Yeoman's Row, stretched out in the most ghastly contortion in a bathing dress, glycerine on my lips, wig obscuring most of my face, when Terence Stamp came in. Stamp was *It*: East End lad, immaculate Cockney whisper, movie star, dazzling face. He and Donovan repaired to another part of the studio to chat and laugh while I lay unmoving on the paper ('Don't move, you,') for half an hour till Donovan returned. At the end of the session I took my long blonde straight wig off and there was my brown short hair. I can hear that odd silence now. The photograph which I never saw was made into a poster and won an award.

None of this matters now, we all know each other – Donovan, Stamp, Montgomery, Bailey, Puttnam – we all view each other over the tops of houses, still floating, affection and respect increasing as time hauls us onwards. Like an endurance game, people slip off and fall behind; like musical chairs, we're all still playing but every now and then the music stops and someone else has to go to the side of the room. Those that remain, through luck and tenacity and talent, glance round at each other smiling, not smugly, not grimly, with what ... relief?

Some, of course, get up and leave because they want to –
Jean Shrimpton, the Shrimp, the Face, absolutely top of the
top models, packed it all in and left it far behind, along with
the indelible impression she made on the look of the time.
There were marvellous-looking girls around: Celia Hammond,
Paulene Stone, Tania Mallet, Sue 'Murraymint' Murray and
the zany Peggy Moffatt, Donyale Luna whose arms and legs
were a yard long, Nicole de la Margé, Grace 'The Cod'
Coddington, who cut all her hair off, right off (but Grace
went on to run *Vogue*); however no one caught the imagination
like the Shrimp and Bailey, bad wicked David Bailey grinning
like a pick-pocket, black gypsy eyes and bad manners and Jean
like a colt with legs right up to her armpits and eyes and
mouth two sizes too large. Just as she was turning her back on
the business there was a tremendous scuffle, a shiver and
shriek of excitement, craning of necks and gasps of glee as
Twiggy arrived: Twigs, who was being booked before people
knew what she looked like (tiny, vast-eyed, prep-school haircut, painted freckles, thin as a gnat), whose face launched a
thousand covers and eclipsed the second team, the *deuxième
équipe*, who soldiered on with the catalogue shots, crimplene
suits and knitting patterns, comforting themselves with comradeship and good-humoured professionalism.

In truth, photographic trips which were not scaldingly high-
powered were enormous fun. We had all heard the story of
Norman Parkinson who, photographing some girls for American *Vogue*, decided they were too fat and starved them among
the sand-dunes of Morocco. At our level, *Women's Own* or
Flair, or mail-order catalogues, we had no qualms about eating
everything in sight, borrowing shoes and hairpieces, laughing
ourselves sick and dancing all night at the local night-club.

We went to Torremolinos and Albufeira, Munich and Inns-
bruck, Tunis, Palermo, Bandol . . . charming resorts where
the weather was more reliable than in Britain. The location

could offer enough local colour in the shape of picturesque markets (in which we could be seen smiling at fruit), churches (wistful gazing on a step), sea (frolicking), rocks (peeking round), tropical vegetation (for striding through), to enable the photographer to get a wide range of backgrounds with the minimum of travel. The favourite snappers were those who didn't take it all too seriously, who would manage to finish our work for the day by lunchtime so we could disappear on to the beach ('Don't get too brown, girls' – ignored).

Sometimes the weather let us down. One trip to the Northern Italian lakes in midsummer was a fortnight of sodden shivering misery. Our location was a grand villa whose garden was re-landscaped every two years the better to display the Giacomettis. We, the models, were not allowed to enter the house in case we stole, broke or corrupted the treasures inside. Instead we were directed to a stone summer-house in a grotto, where the rain beat dismally at the windows and long-legged beasties bedaddered around damp deckchairs. The clothes (garments) hung on anything which offered a hook for the hanger, the suitcase of accessories lay open on the stone floor; plastic belts, nylon gloves, chiffon scarves, imitation leather bags. We had managed to borrow from one of the local Romeos, a charming and courteous boy called Ferrari, a portable record-player and two records. For two weeks we crouched shivering in heavy make-up, listening to the Rolling Stones singing 'Paint it Black' and the Beach Boys' bouncy 'Wouldn't It Be Nice'. I know every note of each by heart forever.

'Strange how potent cheap music is,' wrote Noël Coward. Strange in every way: how mundane little songs, sha-na-na, shoo-bi-doo, managed to creep in between your brain and skull and symbolize everything that was *then*, the feeling of a promised land, a possibility, a real change, a feeling that life did not depend on banks and arms deals but on a notion, admittedly fairly half-baked, that peace and freedom and love were all. It just managed to stagger to its feet, at the time

when London was called swinging and gear was fab; for a
short time anything seemed possible, probable – then there
were tears before bedtime, someone (everyone) spoilt the
party, and death, boredom and cynicism tore the tinsel
down.

The photographer's day starts very early, particularly on a
trip where lighting is not controllable, as it is in a studio.
Breakfast would be served in the hotel ballroom, or a partially
cleared dining-room, at five o'clock: black coffee, grapefruit
juice and the first cigarette, much moaning, hair in rollers.
Outside, in the Mediterranean villages, cocks crew, oranges
ripened on terraces, early gardeners watered the potted plants
and the sun slowly gathered heat. We would cram ourselves
and our model bags into a minibus and drive off to the
location, bare legs in sawn-off jeans, brown arms in fishermen's
vests or old cotton camisoles dyed lilac. A tiny hilltop village,
dusty streets, doorways being swept, a wandering dog, us
perched on walls with hand mirrors finishing our make-up
while black-garbed women stood in disapproving clusters. It
made me uneasy that we would encroach on their territory and
sense of propriety; but if you managed to speak to them in
broken French or Italian, it appeared that they didn't really
mind a jot and would like a closer look at your fake pearls.
Sometimes there was more open hostility. In Palermo, three of
us strolling in the market, decently clad with covered legs and
arms (but tall and blonde), were stoned and jostled and jeered
at but, remembering Jerome (walk, don't run), we got back to
the hotel safely, although one of us was in tears.

I noticed that models at home as well as abroad were treated
rather degradingly. Either we were leered at by waiters and
policemen ('Be a good girl and say sorry'), spat at in Paris
streets by honourable matrons who were shocked by our
miniskirts, or jostled by porters in Covent Garden: 'Allo,
darlin', I couldn't arf give you some.' Never mind: rather like
Quentin Crisp we merely went on looking marvellous, al-

though privately I was appalled at the amount of malice that floated around the business.

I took to wearing gold stockings, kohl-painted eyes, black-spotted veils, wearing nightdresses to night-clubs, carrying Czech newspapers and generally posing for the world. I bought a black Suzie Wong wig and green tinted half glasses, which you wore on the end of your nose as a face decoration, like Michael Rainey. Many times, leaving parties in the early hours of the morning, I would take off my high heels and sprint barefooted through the silent London streets, safe, swift, alone, happy as a lark, quite often trailed by a bored police car.

I bought the *Stage* and found an address advertising private drama coaching. I made an appointment and caught the underground to Sloane Square, walked a bit and came to the basement door, 'Ring and Knock'. It was opened by a tank of a woman, voice an octave lower than Paul Robeson's, cigarette in hand. We sat in front of her popping gas fire and read from Oscar Wilde. She furnished me, unasked, with a huge gin and tonic and said, 'What do you want to concentrate on?'

'To modify my voice, make it more – erm – normal.' I had taken quite a lot of stick about the accent I never knew I had: I wanted an actor's anonymous voice. And projection! And breath control! And everything to do with studying drama.

She eyed me through the smoke and smiled, poured another huge gin, moved closer. 'Your voice is perfectly all right,' she growled and patted my hand.

I paid my three guineas for a course of lessons, but when I reeled out into the winter night behind Peter Jones, into the tall wet streets (run! run!), I knew I'd never go back.

I went to Moscow with Roy Round to photograph fake furs for *Flair*. Inflamed by all things Russian, it was unbearably exciting to stand in Red Square, to see the Kremlin's red star shining in the freezing night, to visit a dacha. 'This is where the astronauts live,' said our guide Juliet, 'and here the musicians reside: Rostropovich, Shostakovich, Oistrakh . . .'

'All in there! What a fluke!' I carolled. Only when we were entertained by Maya Plisetskaya, Prima Ballerina, and her husband, a composer, did I realize that artists were housed together in Moscow. Plisetskaya's flat was tiny, reached by a goods' lift. Although we had been asked to dine, although Roy and his wife Georgina Parkinson were friends of theirs, we stayed only for a quick drink. They were nervous about it all, it was tense, we left in half an hour.

'What would you most like from the West, Juliet?' I asked.

'A flickering electric fire with pretend coal,' she answered promptly. I wrote to her but she never replied (never got the letter).

There were crystal chandeliers in the underground where the Trans-Siberian Express started its huge journey, old grannies sweeping streets with hand brushes, wild-eyed students in underpasses trying to exchange money or buy jeans, queues everywhere, black bread on the tables, a two-hour wait for each meal and an interview every day at the Intourist Office.

'I have no bathplug.'

'It is not necessary.'

'May we photograph these fine old buildings?'

'There are no old buildings in Moscow, only new.'

'May we photograph the Kremlin guards?'

'Their uniforms are all at the cleaners, in any case there are no guards at the Kremlin.'

I had been told that chocolate was in short supply so I took ten sixpenny bars of Cadbury's Milk Chocolate. I gave one to the maid who cleaned my hotel room (four beds, seven wardrobes, fifteen chairs) and she wept. I gave another to the maid who ironed a skirt for me and she knelt down, kissed my hand and took away all the rest of my clothes to iron. I know it's changed now, and I can't wait to go back, and to see more of the

USSR, Leningrad and Georgia, the vast Steppes. But then I only longed to leave: and we cheered silently as the plane took off, toasting each other in plastic cups of champagne.

The relationship we all experienced most frequently – friendship – is the one we can least accept to be true about other people. Gossips can't believe that men and women can actually just be friends and go on trips alone, like Roy Round and I did, and work professionally without falling into each other's arms.

By the time Patrick Lichfield got married the newspapers were billing me as an old flame, but the truth is rather different. Lichfield's studio used to be where the golden Berkeley Hotel now stands in Knightsbridge, just Harrods-ward of Hyde Park Corner. I took my modelling book round to show him, was fairly shocked to hear such an OK voice using such colourful phrases, and was booked for a session of bathing dresses, or what the trade calls swimwear. He worked at breakneck speed, told extremely funny stories ('Beans cold, butler tarted') about his relations, Europe's royal families, gamekeepers and butlers in a way which made everyone feel that they would be at home in, be accepted by, even enjoy, such elevated society. It must have been for him that the phrase 'living in the fast lane' was coined.

We were about to move flats: our new landlord demanded a social reference (to see if we were house-trained) and I wrote, 'Dear Patrick, you are the only Lord I know, will you give me a social reference?' He was still unknown outside the world of photography and he wrote back at once on House of Lords paper, in an ancient crusty style: '. . . have known this young person for many years . . . decent pedigree . . . good school . . . dependable' and signed with a flourish, 'Lichfield'. We moved into our new flat without a murmur, and Lichfield became a real friend. He has photographed me more than anyone else has, from bikinis in the Serpentine ('Look warmer! You've gone blue!'), to diamonds for Cartier, Jean Muir for *Vogue* and, much later, publicity pictures for *The New Avengers*. He has that magic quality, enthusiasm: no matter when or where, or how whacked and worn out, how ghastly the clothes were, he would leap up with a story, an idea, a bubble of energy and attack (and quite often another job booked simultaneously).

Improbably, David Bailey was a close friend of his. Their chalk and cheese characters and backgrounds attracted them to each other. I never really worked with Bailey then: only once or twice, almost as if I were invisible, by mistake, apologetic: he was screened by secretaries and assistants and mystique.

Most photographers are called by their surnames. Duffy, Brian Duffy, worked from King Henry's Road; he had a passion for military memorabilia and red-heads. When Molly Parkin presided over the orange and purple shoot for *Nova* (which Bailey said were the best pictures of the year), I wore a red wig for Duffy. Molly was inspiringly outrageous, even then. We were photographed sprawling amongst make-up, cleaning teeth, with bath towels, lighting cigarettes. Was it for Duffy we said, 'Monday, Tuesday, Wednesday, THURSDAY,' which made your mouth a pretty pout in a photograph? It was Duffy who said, 'When are you gonna do sunfink abaht yore bleeding accent?' ('When you do something about yours, Duff'.)

The 31 bus ran right the way back from Swiss Cottage outside Duffy's studio to the end of Trebovir Road, stopping by Earl's Court where Billy Graham came to spread the word so loudly that we could hear it all from inside our flat with the windows closed. We went, nevertheless: and shared a hymn sheet and saw people queuing up to be saved or merely blessed. We also went to Happenings at the Marquee. 'Hey, are you going to the Happening at the Marquee? Sunday morning, The Who will be there.' The Who weren't there, but several hundred of us loomed around looking deep, smoking cigarettes and wearing weird headbands and heavy make-up, all looking as though we did this Every Day, Man. Someone did something creative with a wheelbarrow, some of us played a sort of twelve-bar blues (for about three-quarters of an hour, I'm afraid), people danced in that mad, interpretive arm-waving zeeb-like way but, to be honest, nothing Happened.

The old Ad Lib Club having burnt down (where the chef appeared at midnight and danced in his tall white hat, high above Leicester Square, reached by a lift), new clubs opened, of which easily the newest was Sibylla's. At the first night there were several Beatles and many Stones, some Kinks I think, and wall to wall beautiful people, moving in a porridge of glittering humanity, between the newest sound system in the world, which sent beams of noise like steel hawsers across the tiny dance floor, where later the Four Tops sang 'I'll Be There' and they *were* there, snapping their fingers in electric blue suits, hands outstretched in unison, cool as American ice-cream.

Dolly birds! That's what we were called. I hated it, and for that reason could hardly bring myself to go to Dolly's, the night-club. Dolly girls skipped, swinging their shoulder bags, wobbled their heads when they did the Mashed Potato, wore white lipstick and knee-socks and were the invention of men. I was booked to appear on a television show. This was it! I was breaking into show business! There were twelve of us: we were to walk down a catwalk (sounds unpromising) to the tune 'A Pretty Girl is like a Melody' (bother). But the best thing about it all was meeting three men who have never changed and who never forgot me: Bruce Forsyth, Roy Castle and Lionel Blair. Brucie sang the song, Roy embellished on the trumpet, they both danced and joked (they can both do anything), and Li made us walk in predestined positions with as little embarrassment as possible. From this brief exposure I was unable to transmit my desire to play Portia but it was a beginning.

*

Ælene and I travelled to Stratford to see David Warner in *Hamlet*. He was the student prince with a scarf: when he died he was hoisted high by the soldiers and carried off feet first upstage. His head fell back towards the audience, pale straight hair flopping as they carried his corpse away. The strangest thing happened: the stage was real life and the audience bustling about collecting umbrellas ('Wasn't it marvellous') were fiction. We sat stunned with grief, still staring forwards for many minutes. Not much I have seen in the theatre since then has come anywhere near his performance. I went to shows in London, craning out of the gods to watch Jill Bennett in *A Lily in Little India*, Olivier in *The Masterbuilder*. Our favourite cinema was the Paris Pullman, where we smoked Gauloises and wore trenchcoats and saw every foreign film that played.

Paris was so near yet, for paupers, so far. My cousin Reay was at the Sorbonne sending lunatic postcards. The *Daily Mail*'s fashion editor, Judy Innes, booked me to 'do the Paris Collections'. The unbearable thrill of it! I stayed at the Hotel Castiglione in the Faubourg St Honoré nearly opposite the Elysée Palace. Doing the collections for a paper meant being photographed in a selection of clothes worn by the catwalk models. As their day ended, ours began. We would arrive at the studio in the evening and work through the night so the pictures could be raced back for the late editions. At three or four o'clock in the morning, a sprint to Le Drugstore at the Arc de Triomphe for le sandwich, and a taxi ('I sink you look a leetle like Bardot, non? Won't you sit 'ere in ze front seat?') back to the unruffled night porter. The night-clubs were Castels and New Jimmy's, the records by Jacques du Tronc et Les Playboys and Aline by Christophe. Sitting at the Deux Magots I heard the Beatles' 'Michelle' drifting out over the cold streets: the glass was fuzzed up, I was faint with hunger, the afternoon was dark, coffee and cigarettes lay on the tiny round table; a student sloped past, gesticulating, with a scarlet handkerchief round his unshaven throat. I travelled by Metro, buying tickets in tens (*'un carnet de dix, s'il vous plaît'*), to photographers' studios to show my book – which was, in France, odd; too English, rather safe. I wanted to be French. I bought antique buttons at the Marché des Puces, drank Pernod, went to big cinemas in the Champs Elysées and small ones in Boulevard St Michel, tipping the usherette as I took my seat, dreaming of an atelier where I could starve in Saganesque pallor. When Reay was twenty-one, several of us ate at Marius et Jeannette, in the Avenue George V – formidably good fish and boiled potatoes. Reay wore, as ever, an enormous old overcoat bulging with newspapers, magazines, Communist tracts, books in Greek.

For some reason our modelling fees took six months to be paid – we had no union, and nothing could induce the magazines and photographers to settle up at the end of each month. Consequently the money, when it did come in, fell silently into the overdraft, blotting it out for a few days before the spending started again. Apart from the most fashion-conscious magazines, who provided their own stylists, most clients expected the models to bring their own standard basic accessories, which we carried from job to job, in a vast model bag.

The basics were: black, brown and white shoes, boots and high heels, headscarves, junk jewellery, belts, gloves – short and long, polo-neck jerseys in white and black, tights in all colours, several bags (shoulder, clutch, evening), maybe different coloured berets, at least one wig and some hairpieces, body stocking, make-up, and Carmen rollers if you had them, hairclips, hair spray, false eyelashes and false fingernails. You were expected in one three-hour session to be able to metamorphose from a sleek lady executive in an office suit to a hair-swept-up-long-evening-dress-vamp to young mum crawling about with a rented toddler.

Models were the masters of the quick change, often in public places – I changed from a polo-neck jersey, tweed suit and boots into a ball dress with long tight sleeves on the pavement in the Mall in front of a crowd of sightseers, and I don't think they saw more than a wrist and a bare foot. I changed dresses in the back of a cab in the rush hour, stockings and hair too, and never missed a sentence of my conversation with the driver.

We became masters of tricks: to show a belt properly it should be buckled to the middle hole – usually we were thinner than that, so we would push a shoe into the small of the back between belt and person. Creases were abhorred, and we learned how to smooth several small wrinkles into one large fold at the elbow; or, worst of all, nylon threads were attached to trouser buttons or skirt hems and unseen assistants would drag on their lines while we, Gulliver-like, smiled and gasped and gazed for the camera. Bulldog clips clasped in extra material between our shoulder blades, and tweaked in skirts round our hips. Paper hankies were stuffed into toes of shoes which were too big, so your heel fitted into the heel; clothes which didn't hang properly were slit open and Sellotaped to the skin. Back-combed hair was propped up over concealed cardboard, tissue paper was inserted in sleeves, wind machines blew strands of hairpieces over lip-glossed, outlined mouths.

Il faut souffrir pour être belle: 'you must suffer to be beautiful'. How beautiful? What is beauty? We all thought it was the bravest thing imaginable when top French model Nicole de la Margé was photographed *sans maquillage* (bare-faced) in a magazine with a circulation of thousands. There was a sequence of pictures: after the shock of the first naked full-frontal face, Nicole showed how she applied her looks from tubes and jars, showed how she altered her slightly lop-sided oval into a latter-day Helen of Troy. The eyes were all important: they had to be huge, dark and haunted and just as our mothers reached for their lipsticks when the doorbell rang, we almost slept in our false eyelashes for fear of being found bald and piggish in the cruel dawn. Mouths were blotted out and our bodies were the forerunners of the ghastly thread-like apparition that emerged from the spacecraft in *Close Encounters*: emaciated, pale and bottle-shouldered. In photographs we turned our toes in to look knock-kneed and flattened our bosoms. Hip bones like coat-hooks were much admired. The look was waif – wistful and helpless. Most girls were still only secretaries and waitresses, not executives and company directors, so in photographs we skipped and propped ourselves on chairs like discarded puppets.

We were as far removed from luscious pearly Marilyn Monroe as we were from furious box-haired Grace Jones. Is there such a thing as durable beauty? I can remember looking with disappointment at postcards of Victorian lovelies with their tiny teeth and plump arms, and puzzling over the 'It' of Clara Bow. What would Rubens have made of Farrah Fawcett? Will the singer Madonna's face be remembered for half as long as Lady Diana Cooper's? The real Madonna has been painted more often than any figure in history: each artist has given her the most beautiful face he could imagine, and yet there is no feature in common between an icon and the Virgin on a Christmas card.

Symmetry and youth, I suspect, are the only prerequisites of beauty. After that, noses can be long or short, tip-tilted or Negroid, lips can be full or thin, eyes deep set or prominent, cheeks rounded or chiselled. Beauty is indefinable: the power of beauty, however, is indisputable. To begin with, it is very rare indeed. The word is over-used. Beauty queens turn out to be merely pretty girls; beauty sleep sees us all looking much the same the day after. All actresses and models are automatically titled 'beautiful': those who see them off celluloid know that they are attractive, striking, charming, but seldom if ever beautiful. Beauty is the stuff of fables, almost a dream quality, to make men mad, to inspire the painter and the poet, to plant in our gullible hopeful hearts the notion that it can be bought. '*Il faut mentir pour vendre.*'

It was a world of brazen artificiality, summer dresses photographed in January, thick coats in the midday Spanish sun. We wore fur coats then – two decades later none of us would touch them with a bargepole. Celia Hammond, even then a passionate defender of animals, organized an appeal for retired greyhounds. We would assemble at White City with collecting tins, and all the kind men who'd made a bob or two betting on the dogs would, we thought, drop coins with gratitude into our outstretched hands. We hadn't bargained for all the men who'd lost their shirts over the years and now couldn't care tuppence if the retired dogs became cat's meat or the Count of Monte Cristo. Sports crowds were usually rather difficult to motivate in a charitable fashion. Over the years I have made appeals to cricket crowds, football fans and racegoers with resounding failure. Wrong time, wrong place, and wrong emotion. Celia never gave up though, and went from feeding starving Roman cats from her own plate to founding her animal trust, CHAT.

The only short cut to an Equity card was through doing commercials. If you did five, you were given a card. My first was for Nimble bread. We filmed for two days on the River Cam in October. I was to pluck the hat from my bookish boyfriend's head, scamper, bikini-clad, to the river and dive in; emerge, laughing like Esther Williams, waving the hat to show how fit and lively I was. The river ran swiftly and was deep and reedy. An underwater swimmer was submerged downstream in case I got into trouble. The arc lamps made it brilliant day, but in fact the wind came soughing over the fens and the sky was slate grey. After each run and plunge I was dried off, re-made-up, fed half a mug of brandy and sent back. After the fourth dive, when I had missed my footing on the bank and slithered drunkenly into the river, they agreed they'd got that bit.

The next shot was of me waist-high out of the water like a

porpoise, grinning and waving. 'Tread water underwater till you hear "Action",' the director said: but the current was so swift that I was dragged away, the bottom so deep that I had nothing off which to spring; and to make it worse, when I was underneath I couldn't hear 'Action'. But, in the way of these things, the film was somehow made and I was paid £36.

Another commercial had me as a clean-toothed air hostess at Gatwick airport, but by then I heard that Equity had changed its rules – you could now only get a card after forty-two weeks of repertory theatre, or if you were cast in a film part. Jacqueline Bisset, fresh from her egg commercial as a young mum being pampered with breakfast in bed, had already moved to America. Jean Shrimpton had starred in *Privilege*, Tania Mallet in *From Russia with Love*. How could I even be considered for a film part? Bursting with enthusiasm and optimism, nothing seemed impossible. When I met the actor Richard Johnson at a Kensington party and said, 'I want to be in films,' it seemed part of fate that he merely said, 'I'm in a film at the moment, you can have a part in that.' He arranged through Betty Box and Ralph Thomas, who produced and directed the film *Some Girls Do*, that I was given an Equity card, introduced me to his agent, Terence Plunket-Greene, and saw to it that I had a speaking part (one line, 'Yes, Mr Robinson'). It mattered not a jot that I was blown up before the credits: I was In Films.

In that strange way that several exciting things happen at once – that three longed-for letters arrive simultaneously, that two excellent parts are offered in the same week – my début into the film world, indeed my life so far, was quite eclipsed by the birth of my son. Despite gloomy prognoses in my teens ('You're sterile, my dear, but you could always adopt when you're happily married'), despite negative tests, slimming injections, water-retention pills, much prodding of the lump ('You must be stricter with your diet'), an exercise bicycle and unspoken fears about a growth, James was born in the Kent and Canterbury Hospital at ten-fifteen p.m. on 16 October 1967. The gynaecologist missed the birth (he thought the baby would be delivered in February) but collected his fifty-guinea fee. I was put in a private room ('So you won't distress the other mothers') and they kindly allowed me to have visitors all day. James was put into an incubator: at just over four pounds he looked quite unbearably touching and fragile: he was fed through a tube and although I wasn't allowed to hold him for a week, I would sit beside his little perspex cot (Snow White's glass coffin) and watch his tiny heart hammering away in his baby-bird chest. I was sent home after six days – Jamie had to stay there for a month and a half until his weight reached five and a half pounds.

Nothing at all had prepared me for the new rush of emotions that arrived with motherhood, the greatest of which were incredulity and an overpowering devotion to the tiny chipolata figure in a nappy as big as a tarpaulin. I had dreamed about this years before: a dream in which I lay in a bed by the window in Salem, the dormitory which looked over the terrace towards the sea, and the other girls tiptoed down to breakfast, leaving me with my tiny sleeping son in the pale morning sunlight.

To marry or not to marry? Although Jamie's father and I had been together for two years, we had never discussed marriage: it seemed to me then (and still does) that marriage should not be entered into just to stop gossip, or for propriety's sake. There are as many opinions about this as there are stars in the sky, each supported by its own set of circumstances. Our decision was to remain unmarried, but to stay in close touch with each other and each other's families. I begged to be allowed to shoulder most of the financial burden as I was to reap most of the rewards. In this manner we have had an immensely happy, unorthodox relationship, no squabbling over money, no sulking over access, a shared pride in a son and a grandson and no end of affection all round. Half anticipating the strenuous curiosities of the press, I decided that I would protect Jamie and his father's family by anonymity. That plan backfired slightly, however, and the journalists and I continued our strange paper-chase which at the end of twenty years has produced no winner: the name remains a secret. I am the hare, becoming breathless but always half a field ahead of them, and they (the hounds) have given me a brisk run but the paper fragments are now difficult to see and have led them to many wrong turnings. It's like one of Aesop's Fables with an impenetrable moral.

There is a notion that actors plan their careers ('Some Shakespeare and maybe Congreve, lovey, then a sit-com for Yorkshire, a tour with a musical and a movie for Spielberg'), when in fact everyone I know grabs at a chance to do anything good and, quite as often, at anything at all. There are thousands of actors and only hundreds of parts: over eighty per cent of the profession is out of work at any given time and the smirking inquiry, 'Resting, are you?' stings more when you have been to seventeen auditions that month and the final rates demand has arrived. No one would dream of asking a redundant steel-worker if he was resting. I suppose actors themselves are to blame: it is their pride and dignity that sometimes makes them adopt the ridiculous pose of relaxing till the next blockbuster comes their way.

I realized at once that the burden of choice had been taken from my shoulders right at the beginning of my acting career: I had to work for Jamie and me to live, so I really had to consider seriously anything at all that was offered. If it turned out to be too awful, I could always escape the blame by murmuring, 'New shoes – gas bill,' which was at once true and self-defeating. Perhaps if I had gone to Paris to join Peter Brook's experimental theatre, or tried to get into drama school again and been a waitress in the evenings, things might be different now. (How different? And for whom?) It's always tempting to go back and say, 'What if . . .' What if I had followed my first true love and gone to art school like Anthea? I had, after all, taken Art O level at thirteen and been awarded the highest marks in the south of England. What if I'd studied languages seriously and gone to the Sorbonne like Reay? What if all the drugs and needles the doctors filled me with when I was pregnant had killed the baby? What if our dear family doctor Colin Turner hadn't been the only one to find out at six months that the lump was a child, not a cancerous growth? Everything would have been different for ever.

But all was well: it was 1968, I had a beautiful baby, a doting family, an empty purse and a new career in movies: and, as so far movies had only occupied two days of my life, I had my old job of photographic modelling to fall back on. Everyone greeted me and the news of Jamie with delight: even Duffy melted ('Good for a girl to have a hob-goblin to look after') and I think people made a special effort to use me to help fill the gaping coffers. Why hadn't I saved any money before, when modelling had been so plentiful and well paid? Because I spent it on clothes and shoes, on travel, on eating out, on giving away, on buying junk, on anything – I thought it would roll in for ever, and my middle name was Improvidence.

'You should go to 3 South Audley Square at two-thirty,' said Terence Plunket-Greene, 'to meet Harry Saltzman for a part in a new Bond film.' Yeek! On with the best of the best, the blusher, the lashes, arrive at number 3 as Mr Saltzman's great Rolls-Royce deposited its owner on the doorstep. Mr Salzman's hair was crew-cut over black eyebrows and a sturdy body held up a square head. The lift had broken: his office was on the third floor. We climbed the stairs. He crossed the carpet, sat behind a huge desk, almost speechless from the long journey up. Finally, after staring at me keenly till his breath returned, he said, 'You have the part,' and I skipped off down the street with a bubble in my chest like a helium balloon.

Like a great circus coming to town, the film unit rumbled majestically into Switzerland and up the narrow valley south of Interlaken to Mürren, where it settled for a few months in the autumn of 1968. Mürren is an astonishing little village perched high on a wide gorge in the Bernese Oberland. We arrived by train from Interlaken and took the funicular, grinding up nearly sheer mountain walls past the thin veils of the Lauterbrunnen Waterfalls. As we rose out of the valley, it became apparent that we were face to face with the Eiger, Mönch and Jungfrau, so close we could almost lean out and touch them in the cold September afternoon. We changed trains and went sideways, along a perilous track through the thick pine forests, with the valley darkening far below, though the sun was still bright on the high hills. The first and last view of Mürren was the Palace Hotel, a gaunt grey monster right on the edge of the cliff with no sign of life or gaiety. There were no cars in Mürren, except Bond's Aston Martin, which made its own fantastic journey there by crane and train and air. The village had somehow been roped off from the outside world. The film company treated it like an extended sound stage at Pinewood, and paid it handsomely.

But if Mürren seemed remote it was nothing to Piz Gloria, the restaurant at the peak of the Schilthorn that was being used as Blofeld's centre of operations. Only accessible, it seemed, by cable car, it was controlled by tight security: visitors were not allowed, and everything had to be taken up in the cable car or by the unit's helicopters. Blofeld's hideaway was opulently furnished and thickly carpeted. At 10,000 feet we had to walk slowly at first in case we fainted in the thin air. The Piz Gloria was ringed by range after range of mountains, the view was unparalleled, perfect: too perfect – it looked like a painted backcloth. A props man was given the task of enticing birds to fly around to show it was real, to give it location value: just before the cry of 'Action' came another less familiar call: 'Feed the crows!'

The Bond girls' part of the story was confined to the wicked Blofeld's mountain lair, where he was indoctrinating us with the secrets of germ warfare. Our names were: Ingrid Back, Mona Chong, Julie Ege, Jenny Hanley, Anouska Hempel, Sylvana Henriques, Joanna Lumley, Helena Ronée, Catherine von Schell, Angela Scoular, Dani Sheridan and Zara. Most of us looked vaguely Western, even vaguely similar. Helena Ronée, battling for Israel, looked as though she could have been the American girl, who was, as any fool knows, played by Dani Sheridan. Anouska was the Australian girl, Zara represented the great Indian sub-continent in a sari, Ingrid was sort of Central Europe, Sylvana was the black nations in general, and Mona Chong was the Far East. Jenny Hanley and I were Ireland and England. Angela Scoular was England too, but Scoular had a real part: more than one close-up, several lines, bed with Bond, the lot. Catherine had a real part too, but the leading lady of our film was Diana Rigg (who became Mrs Bond but was shot dead at the end of our film to make room for a new heroine in the next film). Blofeld was Telly Savalas with his earlobes Sellotaped back, and Bond was George Lazenby, an Australian model plucked from a chocolate commercial who was teaching himself to play 'Hey Jude' on the guitar.

Apart from eating and reading, there was not much you could do silently on the film set except write or sew. Someone showed me how to crochet and I bought wool at the Wollstübli Gertsch in the village to make a blanket for Jamie, who was staying with my parents in Kent. Soon the little blanket grew. Wollstübli would crack its knuckles as it saw me coming (*'Gruetsi, miteinand!' 'Salut!'*) and by the time the film was over, the blanket could cover a double bed and had to have a suitcase of its own.

Friday was our day off. Sometimes we would take the cable car to Stechelberg to reach the valley. It has the most hair-raising drop from top to bottom, almost sheer, one thin cable, an apocalyptic vision of the earth rushing to meet you. Interlaken, as October gave way to November, glimmered with fuggy coffee houses and shops selling chocolate hearts, wooden angels and fine gold bracelets. I bought a fat wooden bear for Jamie, and small toys for the five Armitage children. I had stayed with Tony and Celia Armitage for two months during the strangely short time that I knew I was expecting Jamie. The children, Caroline, St Clair, William, John and Lucy became very dear to me: their ages ranged from fourteen to four, and they wrote letters to me which I've kept to this day. The four elder children were at boarding schools – St Clair, the second was just about to start at The King's School, Canterbury (and thereby change the second half of my future life. But slow! All in good time).

I was homesick for Jamie. We saved our allowance money to make weekly telephone calls. Letters from home were lifelines, read and re-read. While I was away, Jamie stood on his baby legs and took his first steps. It was sometimes hard to pretend that what we were doing in the film justified being away from home for a day, let alone two months. I realized very early on that we were only set-dressing, like a vase or bright cushions ('Drape yourself somewhere there, Dani, that looks lovely'). Sometimes I replaced the Spanish comb in my hair with pencils or knitting needles, or twisted hairgrips over my teeth like braces and grinned out of focus in the background; but we were so unimportant that I was never even noticed, let alone reproved.

My bedroom overlooked the mountains. I collected armfuls of whatever could pass for flowers – bracken, daisies, twigs – and filled my gaunt room and clanging bathroom with rustling leaves and an army of insects. One night, leaving the bathroom and switching off the light, I saw a young climber sitting on my bed, undoing his nailed boots. He turned to look at me and vanished. Macabre stories were passed round of bodies still unretrieved, swinging forever on ropes across the north face of the Eiger, the time on their watches still accurate to observers using powerful telescopes. Some found the mountains oppressive and dismal. Once, travelling down from Piz Gloria to Birg over deep rocky valleys and chamois, the mountains blood red in the sunset, the village already shrouded in purple, I heard an electrician muttering, 'Effing view! What I wouldn't give for a decent pint of bitter.'

The stuntmen and Olympic skiers arrived, the former summoning champagne by helicopter, eating two steaks and four eggs for a snack and raising Cain at night, the latter, led by Jeremy Palmer-Tompkinson, walking like gods with muscle-bound legs, and faces sunburnt from the glaciers where the second unit was filming.

Every Wednesday was film night: one of the Palace Hotel's vast faded ballrooms was filled with chairs, a screen was erected and we would shuffle in like prisoners (like school, like the ship) to be entertained. Outside in the corridor stood the glass cabinet holding the trophies for the Kandahar Ski Club, founded by Arnold Lunn, whose father bought the hotel in 1910 and, by starting the first downhill race in the world, made Mürren the hottest ski-spot in Europe. The first snows came before we left, projecting a pale unearthly light on to the great ceilings and cornices of the reading and drawing rooms. We left in a flurry of suitcases and snowflakes one dark December morning.

One line in *Some Girls Do*; one line in Bond ('I know what he's allergic to'); and now my first television play, *The Mark 2 Wife*, in which my one line which came right at the end of the show I have since forgotten. I do remember my silver crochet mini-dress, Philip Madoc with a strand of hair between his teeth ripped from the head of a dancing partner, Faith Brook, pale and beautiful, and the great Gwen Ffrangcon-Davies, frail and myopic. I was paralyzed with fear: in television the videotapes start rolling, quite large scenes are played without a break and unlike filming, where several takes are to be expected, television frowns on mistakes, as the unwieldy apparatus takes so long and costs so much to re-set. You are performing in front of several cameras and your positioning is even more crucial than for a film camera, which can usually accommodate a lean or a step aside. The lighting is harsher, less satisfactory and comes from above: in films, each tiny fragment is re-lit, making it far more pleasing and effective.

I was playing a glamorous younger woman, the object of desire and jealousy, and it was then that started my horror of pretty parts. As they were to become the bulk of my work (pretty girlfriends in *Steptoe and Son, The Persuaders, On the Buses, The Cuckoo Waltz*), I had to grit my teeth and think how lucky I was to get any work at all. Playing a mindless lovely is depressing when you don't (in your opinion) look lovely at all. When you know so many real-life pretty girls with immense humour, bad language, courage and brains, to see women reduced to a session of 'gorgeous pouting' blondes (copyright *Private Eye*) is humiliating and a bore. The more dishy secretaries I played the further and faster I removed myself from any possibility of being asked to audition for a real part. It would be ridiculous to say that I felt bitter about this: it was part of my lot, having been a model, to have directors doubt that I could ever learn more than one line ('Which drama school? Oh, I see'). I met charming people, learnt how to say unsayable lines and lived alongside mediocrity and staggering banality with resignation and sometimes affection. (What made me think I deserved better than this? Everything. Everything I had been brought up with, learnt at school, read, seen, imagined: everything in literature and drama and poetry was better than 'Sally walks seductively over to the filing cabinet, her clinging skirt revealing her shapely figure and long legs. She pauses, lips slightly parted, a sensuous smile playing over her mouth . . .')

In some cases directors were sensitive enough to furnish their minor roles with thoughtful characterizations. Such a director was Roddy McDowell. Roddy was, of course, an actor, which explained his attitude. *Tam Lin*, which he directed in 1969, was taken from a Scottish ballad, the story updated to suit the late sixties. Glamorous older woman, a sort of latterday witch, lives with her coven of heathenish acolytes in London and Scotland. She falls for a younger man, who is rescued from her clutches by the daughter of a local minister. Work in those days got you work, and I almost took it for granted that I would be auditioned ('Oh yuh, I'm doing a movie – yuh, on location *again* but only for two weeks – yuh I'm on all the way through – eight weeks, not bad huh').

I was sent to be costumed by the splendid Bea 'Bumble' Dawson: thick black-rimmed glasses and a basement flat full of cats. We were terribly spoilt. 'I want all Jean Muir clothes,' I said (and got them) and Rupert Lycett-Green of Blades made me an ankle-length shocking pink shaved velvet overcoat that was on screen for twenty-three seconds. There were twelve of us in the Scottish coven, twelve others in the London lot. We travelled to Scotland on the train, each out-actoring the other, with dark glasses, guitars, feigned sleep, Russian phrase-books, and checked into the Hydro at Peebles.

Poor Peebles Hydro: it was not prepared for a film company, who refused to take supper at six-fifteen and seven-thirty (second sitting), who demanded that the bars were kept open till after midnight, didn't want clock golf and rose at five a.m. On our first evening I walked up the hill behind the hotel and picked a huge armful of briar roses from the hedges for my tiny room. Then, on second thoughts, I knocked at the door of our leading lady, Ava Gardner, and gave them to her maid Louise. 'Tell her they're from Georgia,' I said: my name in the film was Georgia.

None of us had yet seen or met Ava Gardner. She had arrived before us and been installed with Louise, Reggie her manservant and Cara her dog, in the Grand Suite above the Great Hall. Behind Louise, I could see the tall double doors ajar leading to the drawing-room. 'Thank you, I'll tell her,' said Louise and the door shut in my face. I went upstairs and went to bed. Three minutes later my telephone rang. 'Georgia, honey, this is Ava. Please come down and have a drink and bring your swimsuit.' Moving like a conger eel I was dressed and downstairs in cartoon time.

Ava ('Call me Big A') was sitting on a sofa in an old cotton shirt and trousers, her bare feet in a pair of tennis shoes. She wore no make-up and her hair was pushed back and untidy. She greeted me with great warmth, Reggie fetched me a drink and I sat in an armchair. 'I'd like you and Reggie to read through this scene for tomorrow,' she said, so I read her part and Reggie read Ian McShane's. When we had finished Ava clapped her hands. 'Let's go for a swim!' The hotel manager was summoned to open the pool in the basement. Reggie and Louise stood by with two towels. Big A dived in like a dolphin and swam expertly up and down, her neat legs and ankles hardly raising a splash. 'Come on, Cara baby!' she cried and Cara the dog leapt in with much yapping and spluttering. The three of us swam about for a while; when we got out the second towel was used to wrap Cara.

'Ain't you got a towel, honey?' asked Ava with concern.

'No, I'll just shake it off,' I said, pulling on jersey and skirt.

We went upstairs for another drink: the first day's filming in a few hours' time weighed on everyone's mind.

First days are always awkward. No one is quite at their ease, the pattern hasn't yet emerged, in-jokes and nicknames not yet invented. Some actors become conspicuous by their humility ('Good Lord, a chair, how marvellous! I was quite happy to squat by this lovely ladder till you needed me'). Others are impatient to show their pedigrees and connections ('So there I was, half-way across the river, Burton on my left, Guinness on the far bank . . .'). Because there is no rehearsal time as such, you are plunged straight into a performance without being able to gauge the voltage of your fellow actors' contribution. For this reason it is imperative that you learn as soon as possible to identify the lens they are using and to watch the camera operator as he rehearses his movements. No point in a quizzically raised eyebrow if you are the size of an ant, no reason to bury your head in your hands if the camera has already panned away from you. Similarly if your face is the size of a tablecloth the less you do the better. Once you get over the horror of close-ups (lined brow, open pores, blood-shot eyes) they are the most rewarding on film, although it invariably means your eyeline will be fixed to small camera tape crosses on the camera hood, or on the end of an assistant's finger ('Is that OK for the getaway car? It explodes here . . . I'll jiggle it about . . . and then here it is going over the cliff').

We were using Traquair House as Big A's Scottish base. The long drive to the Bear Gate (still locked until a Stuart king is restored to the throne) led up to the beautiful nearly French-looking house, with small irregular windows in its dove-grey walls. Cables and lamps and butty wagons (where you get your bacon rolls and currant buns) sprawled all over the grounds. The designer had added an extra porch to the back; miraculously, plaster, paper and wood had turned into centuries-old stone. Big A, dressed to kill, a million dollars, a cheer from us all, stepped out to say her first line, 'Scum!' and shooting had started. Two days later the Americans landed on the moon. I can't think why it was such a happy film for me. Some – such as Stephanie Beacham, playing the Minister's daughter – were unhappy; Kiffer Weisselberg, one of the coven, found the whole thing so unsettling that he decided to give up acting. We split easily into the grown-ups (Roddy, the producer Alan Ladd, Big A, Ian 'McMouth' McShane) and the children, with Maddy Smith and Sinead Cusack, Pamela Far-brother, Hayward Morse and Michael Billyard-Leake, among others. We went riding on local ponies, motored into Edin-burgh to see a film, sat up all night and dreamed through the hot afternoons, as our parts demanded: a group of decadent pleasure-seeking satellites.

When we returned to London I gave a party and everyone came, from the second assistant David Wimbush, crazed from lack of sleep, black shadows like mighty Agrippa's inky finger-prints under his eyes, to Big A herself who arrived last of all. As I opened the door I could smell the wonderful scent of tuberoses and up, as slim and lightfooted as a seventeen year old, came Ava, dressed in Spanish finery, eyes gleaming green, Reggie following with an enormous basket full of every kind of bottle imaginable. 'A big jug, honey,' called Ava. 'Some of Momma's Mixture!' And all the bottles were tipped in and everyone stayed till dawn. I have only hazy recollections of the night: Big A leaning tenderly over Jamie's cot, stroking him and whispering, 'Little baby'; of four people standing on the foot-wide parapet outside the window, of people up to the ceiling, down the corridors, glasses on every flat surface, dancing till the sky grew pale above the tall trees in Addison Road.

The flat was number 7 on the top floor of a solid Victorian house. After Patrick Lichfield's lordly commendation, Dinx, Ælene and I moved in. Nina stayed behind in Earl's Court, moving into a dampish basement which did her bronchitis no good, where she painted her exquisite miniatures, married Hamish Colyear Walker and produced her first daughter after a year. Dinx moved to Islington; Ælene married a brilliant teacher and inventor called Martin Frey and moved to Putney. Into the vacuum came Jamie and an au pair girl, Delise. For Jamie and me, 86 Addison Road was to be home for the next eighteen years, although if I had realized it then I should have slumped to the ground with despair. Facing east, the sun had gone by ten-thirty each day. On long summer evenings, some-times rays of the sun would glance off the windows of the houses opposite, creating a false, welcome sunset in the drawing-room. Then someone would open or shut their window, and the sunlight would snap off like a light in a cellar.

In the flat downstairs lived a strange collection of bohemian people. They had no problems with locks or windows: it seemed they could shin up anything, click any door open. There were young and old, several men, some girls, mostly good-looking with tously dark hair. One afternoon, when Aunt Joan Mary was having tea with me, a knock came at the door. Would I like to buy a Rolls Royce? 'Of course,' I cried. It was down the drive: we peered out. 'How lovely! How much?' £550. The car looked delectable; black and maroon, with runningboards and huge Lucas headlamps. My overdraft would only permit me another £200. 'I'll lend you the rest!' said Joan Mary, digging at once into her bag for her cheque book. It runs in the family: the more grotesquely unnecessary and expensive something is, the fewer reasons we can think of for doing without it. We had the rent to find and my dear Delise to pay, Joan Mary was scarcely flush either: still, we handed over the cheque, were given the key and the deal was done. It seemed there were no papers, no dreary formalities – there it was in the drive – mine!

She was a Silver Wraith, 1949, with a Mulliner Park Ward aluminium body, a $4\frac{1}{4}$ litre engine, a kneeling sprite, walnut fascia and tables, curtains, footrests, a right-hand gate gear lever and no brakes at all. Getting into first gear demanded a special skill, although she started in third. She had an old-fashioned wireless, piano-lid bonnet and windscreen wipers which you had to start manually. Her hugely heavy doors opened forwards: if they weren't shut absolutely tight the air would get in and wrench them open, smacking cyclists to the ground. The rear window was the size of a courgette, the indicators were tiny orange flippers which flicked invisibly into feeble salutes, and when cancelled dropped like broken wings. Somehow I got her to Jack Barclay's garage in Wandsworth, slithering along, crashing into reverse and driving entirely on the gears. No one ever, then or since, remonstrated with me during these operations. Her charm was so immense that when she suddenly stalled one day, during the rush hour outside Earl's Court underground station, seventeen men abandoned their own cars and swarmed around, rolling up their sleeves, crawling under and over her like mechanics at Le Mans. When I parked her near other newer Rolls Royces, their drivers would offer to 'look her over' and I would leave her in their loving hands. Having her to worry about took all the worrying away from how to cope at home. She managed about nine miles to the gallon. Her number was inappropriate: 288 TUC.

I may not get back to her in this book so I should tell you her story quickly: one miserable winter, when I didn't understand about draining the engine, the block cracked, and I think her heart weakened. She spent months in a garage, but I was advised to keep her under cover in London. How? There was no question of renting a garage. Like someone whose child outgrows its pony, I began to realize that, after two years, I may have to sell her. I advertised her as subtly as possible in *The Times*; some young executives from a Knightsbridge advertising agency leered and jeered at us both ('Come round for a drink when you've chucked that thing away') and then her battery stopped holding a charge. The garage had to bring jump leads and start her for every customer. One Thursday morning, the telephone rang and the Prime Minister of St Kitts and Anguilla's Aide rang to say that the PM was interested in viewing my car, would two o'clock suit me? After the garage had jump lead-ed her into life (at £20 a shot they considered me the perfect woman driver) I kept her engine running and waited for my VIP in the drive. He arrived in a black limousine: I was too afraid to take my foot off the accelerator so I shook hands humbly through the window and waited while he eased himself into the passenger seat. Into the back seat climbed an enormous woman in a uniform, with a gun jammed into her already bursting jacket. We set off towards Shepherd's Bush, never quite coming to a standstill in case she packed up, anticipating lights like a clairvoyant and crawling or racing to get through them. We chuntered round Shepherd's Bush Green: in my rear mirror I could see the scowling face of our armed guard, grunting disapprovingly to herself. When we got back to 86, the Prime Minister hopped out and was gone into his limousine in a trice. The guard was slower but never looked at me once. They drove away.

Friends urged me that the car was only fit for scrap. I had her painted cream like the car in *Borsalino*, but 'Oh!' said the purists, 'Oh of course now she really isn't worth ANY-THING,' and I drove her to a dealer in Acton who gave me £700 in cash. Two weeks later I heard she had been sold to a German for £3,500. However, the injuries caused by money fade away: the memories of that car have quite subdued my enthusiasm for her more modern successors.

Auditions were being held for a Brian Rix farce, a new play by Michael Pertwee called, *Don't Just Lie There, Say Something*. Backstage, we were offered pages to read from the four girls' parts. I chose the shortest piece: at first glance they all seemed the same. Half-way through my reading on the dusty empty stage, a disembodied voice called out from the stalls: 'Why are you reading that part?'

'Because it's the shortest,' I replied.

'She's supposed to have a huge bosom,' came the answer, and I slunk off. I was recalled, however, two days later and was given the part of Miss Parkyn, a severe secretary who lets her hair down and becomes embroiled with an MP.

It was a hilarious play, and most of my scenes were with Alfred Marks, who was dangerously funny to act with, even when you were well prepared. After touring outside London for a month, we came in to the Garrick Theatre. I shared a dressing-room with Deborah Grant, and we set up an innocent routine of opening a bottle of white wine at the half (the half hour before the play starts) and slowly drinking it throughout the show, whenever we came off-stage. It is unthinkable now: many actors today won't touch a drop of alcohol at any time during the day of a performance, but our glass of cheap white then never seemed to impair or improve our performances (which were fairly undemanding) and we treated the whole engagement as a pleasant cocktail party, before going out to dinner. This is the Robert Morley School of Acting: the idea being that it's great fun to do, as much a pleasure for you as you hope it is for the audience. A long run can become like a boring office job, each performance blending in with the next, until you exercise real concentration to find out whether the scene you're about to do has in fact been done, or whether that was at the matinée five hours before.

Although the show was a great success, there were many Wednesday matinées when the Raffia Hat Brigade would come in out of the rain and doze through the whole play, bolstered by rows of empty plush seats and yawning usherettes. On such a day, in the second act, when the entire cast was gathered around a double bed in which Rix and Marks were discovered in a mistaken clinch, I glanced across at Donna Reading (who had got the part with the big bosom). Donna was trying out some new contact lenses, tinted blue: as she looked back at me with her sweet pretty face, I could see that the lenses had drifted slightly giving her eyes four pupils. I dropped my head and my shoulders began to heave. Debbie, standing beside me, whose line it was next, became mute, fighting back hysteria. At the lack of a line, Brian and Alfred and Peter Bland the Policeman looked up; Nina Thomas was shaking, and in a few seconds everyone on stage was completely speechless, sobbing silently, quite unable to speak. Some of the audience woke up during this lull, and laughed hugely: for three extraordinary minutes we clutched each other on stage, yowling with mirth and the tiny audience roared and guffawed. It is, of course, like laughing in church; utterly forbidden and fuelled by terror.

During the run of the show, amidst deadly secrecy, Alfred's *This Is Your Life* was being planned. At the end of the play, as we took our bows, Eammon Andrews stepped out of a cupboard holding the big red book. Alfred's amazement was genuine, and the audience was delighted at the surprise. After the programme had been made, Alfred told me that they had left out the only thing he was truly proud of, singing at La Scala in Milan. I have since been on *This Is Your Life* five more times as a guest, and each time the most impressive thing was Eammon's undimmed enthusiasm and nervous energy.

At home, Delise, my dear au pair girl, had left and been replaced by Marcella who had stayed a year. Both girls became like younger sisters and were completely absorbed as family (hard not to be, with our cramped conditions and only one bathroom). The flat was arranged round a horseshoe-shaped corridor, fanning outwards. At the left heel was the kitchen, with a pine dresser stripped by my father, bought for £3 10s. The sink was a deep white china square, an Ascot heater grasped the wall and coughed its fumes backwards through a tube to the outside air. There was a gas stove, old but serviceable, a fridge which we paid off on the gas bills and a large store cupboard where an army of busy little black beetles lived. I've always liked insects and used to find it touching that beetles only came out to clear up the floor in the middle of the dark night. If you suddenly switched on the light they would run apologetically for cover. Spiders jigged in their webs on the ceilings, which were unusually high for a second floor. The bathroom, next door, was a tall dark shoebox set on its side with an enormously long Victorian bath, surrounded by tiles which clung unevenly to the walls. If removed, bits of wall came away too, so they were heavily grouted and pushed back into place. The top of the window opened inwards if you stood on the lavatory and pulled strongly. It could never be cleaned from the outside and its flowery opacity was dimmed further by London grime.

Next door to it was the drawing-room, on the left-hand side of the horseshoe curve; a lovely square room with an open fireplace. In this room I managed to cram almost all the junk I had collected over the years; an old sofa, which gradually sucked you away into its broken springs till only your head and feet stuck out, walls of books, pictures, statues, rugs, plants, sets of scales, old gramophones, chests of drawers, corner cupboards and chairs, a gate-leg table . . . there was just room to sidle round the furniture and sit down. The paintings went up to the ceiling. Many were torn from magazines and framed, many I bought. The huge looking-glass above the fireplace came from the Portobello Road market for £4. The curtains had already seen action in Trebovir Road, and even as I write are still going strong in Fulham. Behind the door was the telephone, beside it a blue canvas director's chair, sagging from the hours of conversation it had supported.

At the apex of the horseshoe was another sheer slim room which went from bedroom to dining-room to study and was too small for them all. Estate agents reckon that if you can drag a bed into a room and can stand beside it, it is a bedroom. We had by this reckoning four bedrooms. Mine, half right from the front door, was filled with cupboards installed by the previous tenant, a Norwegian with a propensity for pink. The top cupboards needed ladders to open them, and a netball-trained arm to toss plastic bin liners of decaying but well-loved clothes into the space. There was a constant leak just above the foot of my bed. The landlord couldn't fix it, so for many years I put a small bay tree there, to catch the drips. The tree flourished until I had my tonsils out when, thinking I had had my throat cut, it died that day in sympathy. My carved wooden bed came from a warehouse in Hastings and cost 70s, the original horsehair mattress 30s. My room contained everything that didn't fit anywhere else, and my dressing-table was my Aunt Toona's writing desk. I set about tiling the floor as my footsteps were too loud on the bare boards for the downstairs flat. Nailing down the hard-board was easy enough but I ran out of steam when it came to cutting tiles to fit round the fireplace and they stood in piles under the bed along with suitcases jammed with winter clothes and the tin of tile adhesive.

Jamie's room was next to mine, same abundance of cup-boards with handles near the ceiling, a small window facing south above a radiator of immense proportions which would come on in the middle of heatwaves. Beside Jamie's room and at the right-hand end of the horseshoe was the au pair's room. Dear girls! After English Delise and Marcella, came Berit from Sweden, and Kari from Norway, Mehri from Tehran, Lotte from Austria and Dörthe from Germany. They all stayed in that tiny bedroom which just held a narrow bed, a chest of drawers and a whitewood cupboard. They never complained about its size, although Lotte woke me apologetically on her first night to show me the appalling evidence on her back of bed bugs (Kensington and Chelsea Health Department, ex-terminators, sprays and drenches, burnt mattresses and so forth). The interesting aspect was the bug itself. Shield shaped and reddish-brown, it lived for six months in a plastic bag without food or air (I had forgetfully put it in the hall drawer) and, upon being released, it strolled out as fit as ... well, a flea. The meek and weeny will inherit the earth.

When we moved in we paid £14 a week rent, which gradu-ally rose to £25, remarkably good value. It was depressing, however, that journalists would always refer to a spacious (once 'palatial') Kensington apartment. Certain areas attract certain adjectives: Kensington and Chelsea are 'luxury' areas, but no journalist would dream of writing about a 'cramped' Belgravia flat or a 'luxurious' Acton penthouse. These abodes are turned easily into 'love-nests' inhabited by people who 'vow', 'storm', and 'spell it out'. The tabloid press despairs of the humdrum normality it observes and seeks to bring urgency and colour into the most ordinary situations. If the reader also experiences envy, well and good. 'Whirlwind romance' is another favourite title, and my marriage to Jeremy Lloyd was just that.

I met him when we were both at Berman and Nathans, the theatrical costumiers, trying on clothes for a film. He was wearing satin high heels, size eleven, for a grand ball scene in which he would be dressed as a woman. (The film, *Two Girls*, was a comedy and also starred the splendid Richard Wattis.) We were married three weeks later at the Chelsea Register Office: I wore the silk Jean Muir dress and jacket I had worn at Jamie's christening and a black hat I had bought for a funeral. There was no honeymoon as we were still working on the film, which had now changed its name and run out of money several times. How quickly good can go to the bad! Jeremy, Dickie Wattis and I, along with Nan Munro and Diane Hart, had read a funny script and agreed to do a comedy film: it gradually became less professional, more makeshift, more seamy. We filmed against backdrops from other films, and once refused to work as none of us had seen any money for three weeks. One of my happiest recollections was of a cupboard from which Dickie and I were to emerge; Dickie would sing bits of Noël Coward songs, 'Someday I'll find you, moonlight behind you ...' My favourite was 'A Talent to Amuse'. 'Heigh ho,' sang Dickie *sotto voce* in the cupboard, 'if love were all.'

Everything I've learned about acting tricks I've learned from actors: how to breathe, and do voice exercises, how to 'pong' words, how to 'shine lamps' on people which means drawing the audience's attention to another actor on stage; where the prompt corner is (on your left, if you're facing the audience), how to get a close-up (make sure your face can't be seen at all in the two-shot), how not to sneeze (press your fingernails into the ball of your thumb), how to say an impossible line (very loudly and clearly). What emerged was: it is easier to play a big part than a small one; to act well is tremendously difficult, although most people can perform in some way (hence the hundreds of amateur dramatic stories I've been told); and you can never be better than your script: if it stinks, so, I'm afraid, will you. Dickie Wattis was destined to play civil servants and malevolent butlers because of the way he looked. I wonder how he would have handled a heroic part: probably marvellously. That's the swinish thing: no matter what we feel like, we *look* like something completely different. I look like a glamorous secretary and that's that. How often I've prayed for a longer nose, less height. Gloom about my looks would surface every year or so and I would dye my hair dark brown and cut if off and wear no make-up (and cut my fingernails off, too) to promote that no-nonsense, caring, sawn-off, distracted talented look. It never worked.

Jeremy (JL) and I went to the South of France for a few months after the film was finished. JL was writing with Jack Davies and we took a house called Le Cercle, a disused restaurant on Les Hauts de St Paul. Jamie and Delise came with us, and the cicada-filled days and starry nights were a happy change from the London flat. There was a swimming pool, sunk among tall grasses, filled with frogs and dragon-flies; wide dusty verandas, oleanders and pine trees. Quite a large number of English people lived around Vence and St Paul: there would be dinners on terraces, high above the twinkling lights of the distant coast, elegant people in beautiful clothes. During one dinner party, Jeremy told the true story in which, heavily sedated, he was forcibly prevented by a nun from leaving a hospital where he was due for an operation. I saw one man put a napkin to his mouth, his body bent forward in a spasm of mirth, while another fell slowly backwards off his chair to lie like an upturned beetle, tears rushing down his face. There was, it seemed, five minutes of silence, broken only by dull quacking sounds and people feebly beating the table; the elegant women's faces had come off black and red into their hands, their previously sober lustrous eyes now red-rimmed and miniscule, their chests heaving and wheezing. He was dreadfully funny: a kind of Englishness crossed with Los Angeles, where he had spent time writing the Rowan and Martin *Laugh-In*. I was then twenty-four, he was sixteen years older than me. When we parted, we stayed close friends.

Jilly Cooper was already well known as a humorous columnist when she wrote her first comedy series for the BBC, *It's Awfully Bad for Your Eyes, Darling*. It was about four girls sharing a flat and was destined to become muddled in people's minds with *Take Three Girls*. I was cast as Samantha, the *femme fatale* of the foursome. There was a dotty one, a morose one and a plump person called Pudding. Pudding was played by Jane Carr.

We started rehearsals in a room in a pub near the Chiswick flyover. Jane arrived in the smallest car the Italians ever made. She was late, having driven all the way from Loughton in Essex. She was very much shorter than most people and had a rounded figure and huge eyes. Perhaps she would like to stay with me in Addison Road during rehearsals? It was arranged at once. She came for six weeks and stayed nine years. We have never quarrelled about anything, not even had a cross word. She could tap dance: her Granny taught her when she was tiny, whipping her ankles when she went wrong. She had been to stage school, toured with a play when she was fourteen and made her name as the stammering Mary McGregor in *The Prime of Miss Jean Brodie*. As Pudding, she played a doleful frump, always left behind, teased by the others, gloomily scoffing leftovers in the kitchen. In real life she was the absolute opposite, much in demand, a demon dresser with a passion for shoes and an enviable career with Real Parts (like Shakespeare and Brecht). We were paid £50 a week: I seem to remember I managed to get £5 more than the others. I only put in these figures rather plonkingly because I think a myth has grown up about how much actors earn. All we read is 'on the dole' or 'six million a movie'. Most actors are living on the breadline, and are thrilled to do commercials to boost their incomes. Many actors can't face the strain of not knowing when they'll next be able to pay a bill, and leave to find a 'proper job'. The Equity minimum, which most performers are paid, is very near the bottom of the table: certainly no self-respecting transport worker would consider those fees. ('Ah! But actors don't do vital work. Entertainment isn't really necessary.')

Jamie moved into the dining-room study, opposite the front door. By now I had left the farce at the Garrick with what I think was a sort of nervous collapse. It started slowly, like a drip of water running down a wall, and steadily increased in intensity till all I could do was sit on my bedroom floor and cry. I had started to hallucinate every night on stage. I would see the dull gleam of a gun barrel as it nosed up on the velvet plush of one of the boxes, and levelled its sights at my chest as I moved downstage to sit on the end of the bed. I could hear the crunch of splintered bones, and had to stop myself from throwing my body across Alfred Marks to protect him from the gunfire. In retrospect, I was anxious about a great deal: my cousin Maybe was near to death in St Stephen's, fading away daily (she didn't die, thank God); an interim nanny had bolted back to Scotland; I was recovering from an operation which had already taken me out of the show for a month; and I was finding it very hard to make ends meet on £50 a week. The machine gun was the final straw, far worse than the flasher in the front row (who the management refused to move because he bought a ticket every night). For a long time after I left the play, I found difficulty in the easiest things, like shopping or even crossing a road (if too many cars came along, the tears started to fall). How fragile is the balance of a mind! And once the scales tumble over, how laborious the process of setting it back to its former position! It seems to take a long time, but improvements begin to show in a very few days if you're lucky, and I was.

My parents and the Freys, my brother-in-law's family, had joined forces with Ælene and Martin and booked the annexe of a small hotel in Zeneggen in Switzerland for a holiday. As soon as they heard I was out of the show, Jamie and I were included in their plans, and eleven of us converged on the tiny village by air, road and rail. The Alps were full of flowers and clonking cowbells, the hills around ideal for walking. Jamie and Kate (Ælene's daughter) made houses in the fir-tree roots for their toys and model animals – when we walked too far they would be hoisted on to shoulders and passed around like rucksacks. In the evening we would cook spaghetti or rösti, and read or play cards. When I came back I cut off my long dyed yellow hair and made it brown, to signify a Serious Actress.

Although the flat was rather cramped with four of us in it (Jane, Jamie, the au pair girl and me), there was, in summer, one huge extra room: the roof. Outside on the landing a white-painted ladder led to a skylight; push that open, creep along a narrow ledge, double-over and you were out on the top of the house, which was the tallest in the street and was therefore overlooked by no one. What a view! The pitched roof of the house hid the east and the road, but facing west was a huge flat roof, covered with gravel and tar which stuck to bare feet. From here you could see all the gardens of Addison Road and Holland Villas Road lying back to back: some very grand, with swimming pools and conservatories, some rather threadbare like ours at 86, which was laid to a dismal municipal plan, with two small lawns and a kind of birdbath, a black summer-house facing due east, and gravel paths which grew wider each year as lazy gardeners chopped off earthen edges to make them look smart. We could see the back of the Kensington Hilton which, being on the Shepherd's Bush Roundabout, we called the Shepherd's Bush Hilton; the Cardinal Vaughan School, where occasionally our gaze would be returned by beady eyes trained to a telescope from the laboratory; and, nearer by, every kind of ancient trembling chimney pot and sloping slate, and clusters of tangled aerials. On hot summer days we would proceed to the roof, with cushions, rugs and hats, dark glasses, books, scripts, bottles of ginger beer, a wireless, cigarettes and sun-tan oil. By leaving the skylight wide open and the flat door ajar, you could hear the vital ringing of the telephone.

We invited people up for tea and for the sun: it was absolutely splendid, silent, isolated and baking hot. (The land-lords at once put a lock on the skylight, which we picked off: then a padlock, which we detached. The thought of enjoying something rent-free appalled them, although they claimed our safety was their only concern.) Many years later, when I bought my flat, I tried to buy the roof-space: the attic side of it would have turned into a forty-foot drawing-room leading out to the huge balustrated west-facing terrace: one of the best aspects in London. At once a thousand obstacles and objections were raised, although there were roof conversions all down the street. It would upset the neighbours (no one could see that high, even on tip-toes with binoculars), it would spoil the back of the house (a fantastically dreary hotch-potch of odd windows and additions) and, worst of all, from my terrace I would be able to see into other people's gardens (comfortably visible already from every window in the house). I have long since left and the roof remains untapped. Somewhere a dog in its manger is rubbing its paws together.

As often as was possible, we went down to Kent. Sparkes-wood was our bolthole, the place where Jamie stayed if I was away working, the place to go for sanity, sleep, food – in fact, home. When I did two lines in *Not Now Darling* at the Marlowe Theatre in Canterbury, I commuted from Sparkeswood. My lines came right at the beginning and end of the play ('May I take my coffee break now?' and 'I'm back from my coffee break, sir'). We were a merry little company: I shared a dressing-room with Georgina Simpson and Jane Seymour, who both had proper parts. I found it very difficult to learn much from doing such a teeny part. Harrison Ford once said that he was so successful at playing bell-hops that he was in danger of never graduating to larger roles. If you play a maid, I think you ought to see what she has to do, what part she contributes to the play. If she's there to bring in the telegram or tea-tray, that's all she should do: you shouldn't notice her. Here is a dilemma: do you become a theatrical device ('Dinner is served m'lady') or do you mug like mad and make people notice you, and let the play go hang? I think prizes should be given to extremely successful small-part players, top marks going to extras who manage not to wear ridiculous hats or walk strangely and servants who melt into the background. Don't ever think you can start as an extra and end up as Barbra Streisand. Don't put on your best clothes and hang around films being shot on location in the hopes that they may spot you and use you in a scene ('Say! Who's that pretty girl! Maybe she could walk past camera as Redford posts his letter!'). This never happens. No one would notice if Sophia Loren was standing watching in the crowd, let alone allow her to appear in front of their lens. In the theatre, small-part players often understudy the leads: the show must go on. In movies, if the star falls ill, there are different priorities, as the audience is not sitting expectantly in the darkness waiting to be entertained at that exact moment – insurance means time to re-cast or re-shoot or re-schedule.

The drive to and from Canterbury took me through Godmersham where the Armitages lived: often I would drop in to see them, to hear how all the children were doing at school. They had a bright tall-windowed kitchen snowed under with children's chaos, heated by a coal-fed Aga. They said that St Clair was happy at The King's School and had made friends with a very talented musician. The boys were apparently as different as could be: St Clair, fair-haired and easy going, his friend black-haired and slightly truculent. They were due to come out one Sunday for lunch, to which I had been invited. When St

Clair arrived alone, I was disappointed (and puzzled to be disappointed – it was only a fourteen-year-old school-friend I had missed meeting). Caroline was at Wycombe Abbey, writing letters, 'screeds and reams', long and funny and clever. The small boys, Will and John, wrote letters too, full of match results. Lucy, the littlest, was still at home. If you're lucky (and I am) you can develop several families in a lifetime: you can sprout more sisters, grow brothers you never had, inherit children and great aunts. None replaces the original ones, but unlike acquaintances or the friends who spin like weathervanes, people who become neo-family never let you down and are always glad to see you. Later on in life the process reversed, and I found, after *The Avengers*, that I had developed a brother at Eton, at least five extra flat-mates, two schools and no end of country properties.

The film *Tam Lin* was not released. It ran into money problems soon after principal photography ended and was shelved. The film I did after that, my first big part, my starring role, name above the title, the big one, *The Breaking of Bumbo*, was not released either; at least not until it was completely out of date. Then it was put on television on a Sunday afternoon, five years too late. The important thing about work is not only doing it but being seen doing it. So my working life during the making of these two films had been operating in a vacuum for six months, as it were. Then M G M asked to see my photographs and that night they folded up or were swallowed up or dissolved: my pictures (my life so far!) disappeared with them. This shouldn't have mattered half as much as it did. Every photograph was, I thought, the best ever taken of me: they made me look like other people, almost normal, nearly beautiful. Now, without them to prove what a swell I was, and with no track record, what was I? They were only pictures but they were me. I tear up bad pictures of myself (and bad pictures of people I really love). There is a lasting quality about really bad photographs. Once I was shown a colour snapshot of a body decomposing in the water: it turned out that body was not decomposing but on holiday in Antibes. It should have been destroyed on sight. At school, Anthea, Sarah, Penny and I would cut out photographs of film-stars and snip round their faces, giving them Dr Spock ears and neanderthal foreheads. We had to put our heads right inside the desks to stifle the sobs of mirth. Some newspapers nowadays make a point of using bad pictures and adding captions or comments. They can make anyone look ridiculous or demented (that's their attitude: we put you there, we knock you down). If you can't stand the heat, try to keep out of the *Sun*. If you *can* stand the heat and do go into the kitchen, be prepared for napalm in the frying pan.

It came as a great relief and excitement to be asked by Richard Stilgoe to join his revue for the Nottingham Festival. We rehearsed above a pub in the Harrow Road; Russell Davies, Frank Abbott, Dickey and I. The show was composed of about seventy songs, sketches and gags which lasted sixty minutes. Frank was working on the slowest double-take in history. Usually depicted in cartoons with speed lines whizzing as the head swivels back seconds later, Frank's version allowed many months, even years, to elapse before the final realization. The head-turn by this time was so extreme that it would yank the whole body into a back flip. Russell played the trumpet and we called him Dai. We all wore candy-striped costumes, mine a bikini, the chaps in pyjamas. To make the point more strongly of how male chauvinist piggy the whole thing was, it was called *Poking Fun!* Sometimes, people not getting the irony of the piece sidled up to me after the performance and said they thought I was being exploited. I thought it was very funny.

Like all festivals, Nottingham was full of events of different sizes in unlikely places. We performed twice nightly in a hotel ballroom, at ten and eleven-thirty p.m. Dickey, forever fiddling about with words and anagrams, came up with 'Julia Trevelyan

Oman – I avert Joanna Lumley.' The director of the festival, Richard Gregson Williams, became Dr Igor Swelling-Charisma. Christopher Langham and David Rappaport were there from Bristol University, shocking people with the dwarf sketches (Rappaport is a dwarf): their anarchic looniness jostled happily beside Kyung Wha Chung and traditional jazz.

There is always some new fad to drink or eat or smoke. At Nottingham it was Guinness with a double port thrown in. Years before, it had been trying to smoke banana skins dried in the oven. (Clue: Donavan singing 'Mellow Yellow'. 'E-l-e-trick-er bananner'), completely ineffective and repellant and impossible. On *Tam Lin* it had been dipping the end of your unlit cigarette into Sailor's snuff, taking a swig of Nirolex and lighting up. (Result: nothing, but no more bad coughs. Sailor, the props man, used to melt away when he saw us coming.) At school it had been Coca Cola with aspirin in to make you faint before exams (never yet known to work).

Then there were the diets, the pills, the exercises . . . the meditation, the medication, the mastication, the motivation. Always, just ahead of you, was T H E marvellous one, the one which allowed you to eat whole chickens smothered in dumplings (like Roald Dahl's disgusting farmer in *The Fantastic Mr Fox*) as long as you drank two pints of water forty-five minutes before you ate the meal before last. Your exercises, if you did any, could be anything from yoga to a four-hour run, anything from three lengths in the pool to half a day attached to a series of milking machines which gave you electric shocks. Face care could be anything from Royal Jelly to soap and water.

Eventually you tire of the whole lot: you don't have the time or the interest to go on and on fighting. The same effects you are seeking to achieve through dieting and exercising can be had by buying larger clothes and being nicer to people. Whenever I'm too fat I eat less. I think we should try to look like healthy zebras on the wild African plains: sleek, shiny, healthy, not thin or fat, just person shaped. Most people stay fat because they eat meat. Humans used to be frugivores, fruit eaters. When in doubt, eat fruit. I live off bread, cheese, fruit and vegetables when I'm alone (and when I'm not). I eat most things raw out of laziness. I would much rather spend money on good olive oil, pesto sauce and brazil nuts than on poor old blood-stained meat.

But it was Guinness and port in Nottingham as Frank sang, 'I'm in love with the girl who models the corsets in the ads on the Underground stairs . . .' and I walked past trying to look like a Little X by Silhouette advertisement in a corset bought from Weiss (pronounced 'Vice') in Shaftesbury Avenue.

Coronation Street! But how? I would be Elaine, the daughter of the headmaster of the school where Ken Barlow taught, who had gone away to university and come back posh (so no stab at the accent, and no scenes in the Rovers). To show I was brainy, I unpicked wireless sets and explained circuitry to Ken Barlow, who was smitten. To show I was, well, not street material, I drank and offered sherry. Ken Barlow asked Elaine to marry him but she had set her sights higher, and turned him down flat, left for richer pastures. I took rooms in Manchester while I was working on the *Street*, a furnished flat in a building with dubious tenants half glimpsed in negligées behind swiftly closed doors. The neat, unchanging pattern of work was long established for the *Coronation Street* cast who were Granada's greatest stars. They had two Green rooms, one as quiet as a tomb for the bridge players, the other with its own coffee and soup machine and an unspoken pecking order for comfortable chairs. Violet Carson, the great Ena Sharples, worked her way quickly through *The Times* crossword before leaving early for her train to Morecombe, I think it was. Lunch on Fridays was provided by Granada, real salads and pies, not a canteen sandwich. (While I was there, an Australian party arrived: they were on a round-the-world tour, visiting the Grand Canyon, Taj Mahal and the Pyramids. The high spot of the holiday was a trip to meet the cast of *Coronation Street*. Television creates the strangest cravings.) I was made so welcome by the cast, and afterwards, when, as always happens, people said, 'Yes, but what were they REALLY like,' I could answer truthfully that they were collectively charming, hard-working, professional and entirely friendly. This, I thought, is it. It will be Ken Loach and theatre workshops, Stratford East, improvisation . . . I've cracked it! I hadn't. I left the show after a month and my next part was Jessica van Helsing in a Dracula film.

In the best Dracula films there must be Peter Cushing and Christopher Lee: anything else is counterfeit. Our film started life as *Dracula is Dead and Well and Living in London* but became *The Satanic Rites of Dracula*. Why couldn't I be in single-word productions like *Klute*, *Oliver*, *The Entertainer*, *Hamlet*? (What about *Tam Lin*? It wasn't shown, so doesn't appear on my curriculum vitae.) Hair: red. Role: Peter Cushing's granddaughter who is chosen by Dracula to be his Bride for eternity but is saved just before the Bite by an exploding ceiling. We filmed in frosty weather: outside running through bracken till your throat hurt from the cold air, and snooping along through dark squeaking undergrowth to the forbidden mist-strewn cellar door. There were tremendous special effects – buildings which like the Burning Bush burned but were not consumed, mouldering bodies and flying cloaks and Christopher Lee's three sets of eyes: prepare to bite (a few veins), ready to bite (riddled with red squiggles), and bite (blood red). His cloak was enormously heavy, weighted at the hem so it swirled round him as he walked. It was tailored from the stuff from which policemen's coats are made. He is very tall: his lighting stand-in, once he had his wig on with its widow's peak, was eerily like him. From his dressing-room next door I could hear Christopher Lee singing snatches of Italian opera in a pleasing baritone ('How lovely, Chris! Do sing some more.' 'Goodness, can you hear me?'). He always carried Bram Stoker's original Dracula with him, and protected the reputation of the evil Count by refusing to sensationalize or update him. (I had seen Christopher Lee in *The Mummy* at the Hastings Roxy: all his villains are somehow victims at the same time, and his victims as noble as kings.)

If he is the eagle then Peter Cushing is the dove. Gaunt, mekon-looking, with haunted eyes, Peter Cushing is one of the gentlest and most generous men you could meet. A firm which makes the best board games used to test their prototypes on Peter Cushing. He smoked a great deal, wearing a white cotton glove on the hand that held the cigarette, to prevent the fingers from becoming nicotine-stained. Immaculately elegant, he would join us as we sat at the edge of the set on our chairs with names on them, with kindness and courtesy positively whizzing out of him. All people are equal to him, every electrician and runner and carpenter was greeted, every make up girl made to feel like a duchess. It was an agreeable and amusing cast: William Franklyn, wicked and making us snort with laughter just as 'Action' was called; Richard Vernon, who although he is not a duke ought to be, his pencil poised over a crossword puzzle. He taught me how to do crosswords: when I was with him they seemed easy and inevitable as he led me, link by link, to the solution; but when he was gone, chaos was come again. I never do a crossword now without thinking of Vernon.

From where we sat in our dark little ring of chairs grouped over cables and weights, surrounded by polystyrene cups of coffee, we could watch the set growing or being dismantled around us. In another incarnation I shall become a set designer or work in the paintshops – something about the majestic artificiality, the fairy-tale falseness of movie-making, enthralls me. In *Tam Lin* I watched the chippies assembling, from wood, a colossal baronial stone staircase, cold, echoey, trodden by medieval feet, granite grey. When you were almost upon it you could perceive the plywood and paint, and the here-today-gone-tomorrowness of the whole thing. Outside windows you could see the rooftops of London, or the cupolas of St Basil's Cathedral in the Red Square: behind the flat (canvas or wood wall) you might find a painter half-way up a ladder painting with absolute surety and unnerving perspective, enormous vistas and mountains or a doorway in Marseilles. In the plaster shops, they prepare marble pillars, dead mammoths, wooden Adam fireplaces, all made from hard white plaster. After filming they all get thrown into the graveyard, gryphons and coats of arms, statues of Rameses III, sides of volcanos, garden urns. They lie there looking false as water and you wonder how they fooled anyone.

The camera, however, is a liar, and the lighting cameraman its accomplice. On film, there is nothing good or bad but lighting makes it so. Cheap things don't look so tawdry, expensive things lose their glamour. People don't look very ugly or pretty until the lighting cameraman starts in on them. Cameras are a great leveller, cruel and flattering at once, like Uriah Heep with a chainsaw. Technicolour, for all its marvellous qualities, has robbed the cinema of the drama of black and white. Monochrome demands much straiter disciplines than colour and, I think, offers much greater visual rewards. (Not for nature photography, or snooker, or for that matter, sport or children's game shows: but drama and politicians and horror and, quite often, humour work best in black and white.)

I have never understood the cavalier way in which television sit-coms treat lighting. All is flat and bright and comes from overhead. Of course it's cheaper and easier, but what is the point? Everyone looks tired and ugly and you have to work extra hard if the audiences' eyes are not charmed. In theatres they seem to have done away with that most important rack of lights which used to be set in the front balcony or dress circle at ten o'clock from the performers' faces. Now they slice in from the side or bash down from the top and are impossibly hard to work in and trying to watch. Lighting is more important than costumes or sets but less important than content, script or music. (They take precedence: but all are interdependent.) Lighting should draw its inspiration from great painters, who can be as diverse as Jan Steen, Rembrandt, Gauguin, Turner, Picasso, Hockney and Goya. It doesn't mean everything should look like an old master, but it should look good. Lighting cameramen are sometimes called Lucifer, bringer of light, a beautiful name. When you think that Lucifer the Devil was once a Senior Angel, it rather turns the theory of original sin upside down. I think we are born angels and unless we're careful we turn into de Debble. Religions are there to advise us how to regain our state of grace. I think when we fall down dead we probably become angels again, as no God worth worshipping would want a host of ne'er-do-wells milling around in the hereafter.

On the set they built the interior of the house where Dracula kept a cellar full of coffins each containing a dormant vampire girl. Disobeying orders I (Jessica) broke in through a side door, strung with cobwebs, to rescue a poor secretary who was chained to the wall, apparently waiting to be bitten by the Count. As I fumbled with the padlocks to free her she turned and smiled showing ghastly fangs. All the coffins creaked open and taloned fingers appeared as the vampires awoke, smelling lunch. At that second help arrived in the form of a detective who, wrenching apart a coffin lid, drove a jagged plank deep into the secretary's heart. Valerie van Ost, the secretary, had been rigged up with an ingenious device. A metal brace encircled her chest, with an indentation in the front in which was inserted one end of the stake. The stake was telescopic like a stage dagger; as it drove in a blood bag filled with Kensington Gore burst and she howled like a wolf. A visitor to the set had to be helped away, it looked so realistic. In another part of the studio they had laid out a room prepared for a black mass, with stars and points and an altar surrounded by self-igniting black candles (for my sacrificial wedding to Dracula). Coffins and black mass always cast great gloom on the company and although it was only a film and we were all only acting, it was a relief when those scenes were over. Everyone got headaches and tempers were frayed. Black magic is not much fun.

I went up for the Steve McQueen film *Grand Prix*. Mr McQueen was installed at the Royal Garden Hotel in Kensington; he and the director talked to me politely about the film ('Miss Lumley, are you vulnerable? This girl is very vulnerable'). When the director said, 'Would you stand up alongside Steve there so we can see how the both of you look together?' I towered over him. This was a disappointment to me. He was not a small man but he couldn't beat five foot eight and high heels. Also I fudged the vulnerable question. It's rather like answering questions on modesty or a sense of humour. No one who hasn't got a sense of humour admits it; in fact they are usually the first to boast of it as their most endearing quality. I've also noticed that people are quick to claim bad temper ('Wow! You should see me when I get going!').

Each time work has melted away like snow in the sun, something exciting has turned up. One sunny day my agent telephoned: would I like to work with Richard Lester? He was shooting some commercials for Italian television, and would I call him to discuss it.

Me: 'Is that Richard Lester?'

Lester: 'Would you like to come to the Sahara Desert?'

Me: 'How wonderful.'

Lester: 'See you there!'

After I put down the telephone I felt his information had been a bit sketchy. I rang him back.

Lester: 'Fly to Tunis. There will be a hired car and some other actors. Do you drive? Travel south for about 500 miles and turn right at Gabes. Drive to the end of the road and I'll meet you there. It should take you a day.'

At London Airport I saw Ben Aris, Ronnie Brodie and John Bluthal, and they saw me: but their information was as vague as mine and only when we were all standing in front of the hired car did we realize that we were the cast of the Lester commercials. We each drove for about 150 miles, due south as instructed – Sousse, Sfax and on to Gabes. The tarmac was only just wide enough for one car so when any oncoming traffic threatened us we drove off steeply into the sand avoiding the camels. We stopped to fill up with petrol and drank some wicked white arak which would have stripped the paint off the Forth Bridge in a trice; arak and warm Coca Cola. 'Kebili?' we asked, and they all nodded and waved towards the desert. 'Gabes – then right – Kebili.'

All over Africa the skies are twice the size of European skies and in the desert the heavens seem half as high again. As evening came we saw the sign to the right in Gabes and sped off straight towards the sandy bare bosom of the Sahara. An hour later in the darkness we saw a 'Parking' sign with a camel drawn on it, and in the middle of the road, grinning like a guru in a white robe, waving a benediction, stood Richard Lester. 'Wonderful!' he cried. 'Have a wash! Have a drink! We'll talk about what we're going to do!'

The hotel was a low bungalow, built round a square, with a swimming pool in the middle. Outside the square were a few palm trees, some bicycles, camels and, rolling away for ever, sand dune upon sand dune. Our rooms were spotlessly clean: the sand cleans everything all the time, and I didn't wash my hair for a week. There was no hot water and erratic electricity. Food was bricques, delicious egg and potato in a crisp greasy envelope of pastry, dates and warm Coca Cola. Sometimes we had hard-boiled bantam eggs and grey bread: always we had warm Coca Cola.

There are many many places in the world that I would recommend people to visit but none more strongly than the really vast desert. Mirages like Lake Coniston appeared and reflected camel trains and jeeps. The soft sand, like baby powder, assumed wrinkles and ridges which changed perpetually with the wind, which in turn whipped up a sandstorm against which the only defence was a cloth tied round the whole head. The sun sets fast, leaving the huge navy blue bowl of night upturned from horizon to horizon, blazing with stars. Distances cannot be perceived accurately, the sun is hot and the moonlight cold: charming oases, where palms curve and bow over picture-book water holes, are sour and brackish. You can lose your way simply by turning round.

Richard Lester, whose film *Help!* had marked him out as an innovator, was not a man for sticking to scripts. In this case he didn't have any. We were to shoot five commercials; and as he drew us all together round a table at night, his eyes were gleaming at the prospect of making things up as we went along. The product was an Italian peppermint: the notion being that if you became hot and bothered in some awkward or unpleasant predicament, you would pop a peppermint into your mouth; and in a flash you would find yourself cool, calm and refreshed (and transported – the second half of each commercial was to be shot in the snow on the slopes of the Matterhorn). We carted the cameras and tripods and props by hand from the jeep, our feet sinking into the baking sand. 'Close your mouth, Joanna!' cried Lester. 'I'm getting a flare off your teeth!' And we filmed away; pretending to sunbathe, driving around in circles with only a schoolroom globe to guide us, crashing into the only palm tree for seventy miles. We had to remember exactly the position we were in when we consumed the peppermint, for that was how we would be found in the cold April snow in Cervinia.

From Tunis we flew to Rome, from Rome to Milan. We nearly didn't make the connection as there was a baggage handlers' strike at Rome Airport. In a frenzy, we rushed off to find a huge vehicle-drawn cart (with no vehicle), raced with it, puffing and panting to the aircraft, bribed the ground crew to open the hold and leapt in, hurling out all the suitcases, all our cameras and baggages. The passengers on the Tunis flight stood round pointing and shouting, 'That-sa my suitcase! Get me thees *baggagio*! Find *il rosso* trunk, queeck!' Swearing and sweating, we sifted all our stuff from theirs and trundled, rat-like (Mr and Mrs Samuel Whiskers), to our distant plane half a mile away across the runway. By the time we took off several bottles of duty-free arak had been opened and consumed.

But all this was only ten days' work. I did a brief stint in *General Hospital* as a beastly woman with a broken leg who makes a play for the nation's favourite doctor. Having turned down the nation's favourite bachelor in *Coronation Street*, I consolidated my position as a Bad Person. Kind Jeremy Lloyd cast me as a German customer in *Are You Being Served?* but I was very short of money and despairing of being anything more than camera fodder. Why didn't I draw the dole? Because, having been a model, I was categorized as self-employed. I tried very hard to make the DHSS understand that I simply couldn't employ myself and all I wanted was to draw the dole like my fellow actors. 'But you're employed!' said one official. 'We've seen you on *Coronation Street*!' The same thing happened when I applied for child benefit. 'We'll have to come and look at your flat,' said another battery-hen official, 'and we'll need to see your bank balance.' For child benefit? I tore my frightful card up into tiny bits and pushed it through the bars where the woman had gone quite pink. No sick benefit – no dole – no child benefit. But I still humbly went on paying my stamp. What a weird form of insurance! From that day onwards I decided never to consider depending on the State.

There's always a great rumpus about private medicine. To be perfectly selfish (and most actors are perfectly selfish), if you are due to have your tonsils out, or your hernia trussed or your wisdom teeth removed, it must be scheduled to fit in with your few-and-far-between bouts of work. Imagine losing your only job because the hospital can fit you in that week (and no sick pay, remember). Jamie was snoring like a tramp, ashen-faced, mouth ajar. Every three months he was back on penicillin for his septic tonsils. If he hadn't had a private operation, we couldn't have managed. As it was, I stayed in hospital with him for the two nights and was presented with his tonsils and adenoids in a jar. Bits of my baby's head in a jar! All my admiration for Alan Fuller's skill was eclipsed by a longing not to see these bad-news things in formaldehyde. The boy ate toast, slept like a dormouse and three days later, started to grow, gaining colour and weight. He was at the Fox School in Notting Hill Gate, a first-class primary school: people moved into the district to be in its catchment area. Later, when *The New Avengers* changed my life by its constant claims on my time for filming, Jamie went to a private school, a boarding prep school. Roy Hattersley took me to task at a *Punch* lunch, years later, over this:

'You shouldn't send your son to a private school.'

'There are no State boarding schools, Roy. It has to be a boarding school.'

'Why don't you stay at home?'

'Because I have to work, and I have to go wherever I'm sent.'

'Why don't you get a job at a local supermarket? You could work at the check-out till.'

I often wonder if I have done everything wrong. Should I have got married, for decency's sake (and maybe divorced later)? Many would find that more acceptable. Should I have given up acting and found a more secure, less potentially rewarding job near home and not sent James away to school? Should I have taken John Counsell's advice when he told me at the Theatre Royal Windsor that my name was a drawback, ridiculous, and I should change it? Maybe I should have turned down all those bit parts in sit-coms. Maybe I tried to. I sat on the roof and wrote fifty-three letters to every repertory company and provincial theatre in the land. I wrote down what I'd done and offered my services for anything: acting, assistant stage manager, tea-maker. Only two companies replied, both were full up, thank you for inquiring.

I accepted an invitation to be a guest on *Seven To One*, a television interview show in which seven students grill a victim of their choice. They were charming to me mostly, but suddenly I was under attack:

'How can you justify living in your vast luxurious Kensington flat?'

'What do you ever do for other people?'

'Don't you feel guilty lording it when some people can't get work?'

I felt guilty for everything: guilty that I wasn't on the dole, did have hope, would not depend on the State, couldn't talk about my charity work. I was guilty of a happy home life, recklessly advantaged education (books), and good health. I felt ashamed of being so lucky. I felt abjectly depressed that life hadn't dealt me a meaner blow, and that I had a posh voice and didn't have to wear glasses. When I had grovelled my way into a sewer of self-pity, the telephone rang: Max Stafford-Clark asking me to be in a John Osborne play at Greenwich. John Osborne! My empty cup was brim full again, and, par for the course, the play had a long title and I had one line.

Chapter Six

It turned out to be eleven lines – John Osborne took pity on me and added the other ten. Still, my costume punctured my serious brown-haired approach to the play: black leather shorts and boots, stockings and suspenders. It wasn't really a small part, as we were all on stage for Act One and Act Three, although Act Three only lasted for about seven minutes and we all talked together like a Greek chorus. Counting lines is ridiculous anyway. In *Mistral's Daughter*, a purple-faced actor rushed up to me on the set in Paris. 'Imagine!' he puffed, 'I had twenty-seven lines and I've just been given another five! That's thirty-two! My agent will be thrilled.'

Max Stafford-Clark had the most generous and creative attitude to rehearsals. We were all encouraged to improvise and relate our backgrounds, until Rachel Roberts cried out, 'Oh Maaax! Let's get on with it!' She had an explosive character, swooping between gloom and hilarity: after the performance, when we would join the front-of-house bar for a drink, Rachel would entertain us, and any left-over theatre-goers, with tales of drama and fame. It was a huge cast, and a happy play. Jill Bennett had a teddy bear who was propped in the wings every night, and before we went on stage we were obliged to mutter, 'Good evening, Mr Teddy.' I never dared forget. Five of us shared a dressing-room: as one's name rides up the billing you get dressing-rooms on your own. I prefer to share with someone; being on my own is boring and frightening, an uneasy mix.

Driving to rehearsals in Lupus Street from Kent took about two hours. Usually I stayed in London but after delivering

Wearing Jean Muir, black tights and ballet dancer's make-up.

Celia and I in the middle of friends and greyhounds. Grace Coddington
on extreme right. I am brown from a photographic trip to Spain.

Pretending to mend the *beloved* Roller in the drive at Addison Road.
You can just see the *rare* kneeling sprite. The Lucas headlamps
were like searchlights.

In a Moscow underground station in
a fake fur.

Thyra Letitia Alexandra Weir –
better than Mrs Patrick Campbell.

Michael Billyard Leake watches me being a groovy
acolyte in 'Tam Lin'.

The Armitage children, 1968: William, John, Lucy and
Caroline, with Jamie. St Clair was away at the King's School.

Janie in the flat.

Jamie in the garden at Addison Road.

Jeremy and I by the Thames. He was yet to write *Captain Beaky*, *Are You Being Served?* and *'Allo 'Allo*.

When I said 'no' to Ken Barlow. Note the sherry: Bill Roache has got hold of the decanter.

Rachel Roberts and I at the
photocall of *The End of Me Old
Cigar*.

The hi-jacked stocking at the launch
of *The New Avengers*.

With Jamie on the set at Pinewood.

Jamie to my parents for a weekend, I drove back up through Goudhurst on the A21. Just where the heathland appears near Pratt's Bottom, a fox ran into the road and was knocked down by an oncoming car. We all stopped: the fox lay prostrate, a foot from the wheels, and the driver couldn't bring himself to drive over it. I leapt out and felt the fox's heart: still beating. I carried him to the side of the road, watched by a small queue of people waiting for a bus among the silver birches. The cars drove on and I sat rather helplessly with the un-conscious fox in my arms. I would be late for rehearsal! I wrapped him in my accident blanket, which only a week before had enclosed a woman knocked over on a zebra cross-ing, and put him in the back seat of my Mini. He was handsome, sleek and bushy-tailed, and he smelt very strongly of fox. I drove on, trying to think what to do. Twice he crept between the seats and put his head on my lap, twice I put him back and wrapped him up. The third time I settled him on my knees and drove rather erratically in the direction of Earl's Court. He had a broken tooth and a bleeding lip, and his poor tail drooped painfully.

When I carried him into the veterinary surgery in the Earl's Court Road, the vet sighed: 'A-aa-aaa!! A fox! We usually only have budgies and cats here!' They kept him for the night to operate on his broken tail and I rushed down to Lupus Street, smelling very foxy. The next day the surgery rang up: 'Your fox is ready for collection.'

A second floor flat in Central London is not really spot-on for looking after foxes. In the absence of an au pair girl he got the tiny bedroom, with a makeshift bed, and food and water on the floor. He must have been an urban fox, possibly tamed at some time. Whenever I went in to see him he greeted me, but he was listless and his recovery was slow. After three days of telephoning, I found a place to take him, the RSPCA in Putney. Oh Foxy! Off we went in the car, a friend driving and me holding him. They had made a cage available for him, tall enough to hold a giraffe. He lay on the ground looking lost and depressed. I visited him each day, until, on the fourth day:

'May I see my fox please?'

'He's not *your* fox.'

'Well, may I see the fox I brought in?'

'He's been re-homed.'

And he had. And that was that.

I hate the arguments we use to justify killing animals. Because of the unnatural way we keep hens, all cooped up with not enough perch room, when a fox breaks in and kills them all (and he will take and bury them all, given the chance, and eat them all when they are nicely rotted), we blame the fox. If the chickens could escape, they would: but we prevent them from doing so (because we're going to use them ourselves). How often are mink described as 'nasty, vicious little things' when they nip our fingers from their cages. 'Nasty' and 'vicious' are wholly inadequate words to express what we are, who plan to kill them for their soft coats. We bludgeon seals and slaughter dolphins, who deplete fish stocks. Deplete! Nothing can compare with the destruction humans have caused to the world, on a scale that beggars the imagination. At every level, from lost hedgerows and their wildlife sanctuaries to disappearing species of insects, butterflies, birds, animals of every size, trees and plants, prairies, seashores, lakes and rivers and their fish and mammals. All, all because men must eat. But wait! We were originally frugivores, fruit eaters. We don't need meat or flesh at all, ever, in any diet. Meat is a gruesome luxury, afforded mostly by the West, the sophisticated first-world West. If the land we used for fattening livestock were turned over to crop production, nearly all the killing would stop. (Not quite: there would still be people who think fur coats are glamorous, still rich fools who think rhino horn will improve their sexual prowess, still wicked traders who defend the use of ivory, almost indistinguishable from plastic: still people who shoot for pleasure, still scientists who insist against all contrary evidence that animals must be used for experiments.) How many more times do we have to be told that we will live longer and be healthier if we stick to fruit and vegetables, rice and corn? (And be better off: meat tends to be very expensive. When it isn't – such as chicken – the birds are produced in such horrifyingly cramped circumstances that disease spreads like the wind, killing them and those who eat them.) So: away with blood and bloodshed, and all the degradation and pain it entails. We are staring at the answers to the problems, but we are in danger of forgetting the questions.

Good old modelling. Good old Grattan Catalogue trip to Amalfi! After Greenwich came another yawning space of unemployment. Word was around that *The Avengers* were to be brought back to the screen: Patrick Macnee would still be playing John Steed, the compleat Englishman, but there would be a new woman. Hungry eyes all over Britain lit up: it would be a plum part, formerly filled by Honor Blackman, Diana Rigg and Linda Thorson. My name was put up but rejected at once. Only when I heard of fat women of fifty and sixteen-year-old weaklings auditioning did I have the courage to try again. By some jiggery-pokery I managed to get on to the list, and drove down to Pinewood where they were seeing people. We sat on chairs in a waiting room, shuffling up when the next candidate went in. The average interview took about eight minutes. In the inner sanctum were Albert Fennell, Brian Clemens and Laurie Johnson: three kind, courteous and reasonable men. They didn't want me. 'Please! Please at least test me!' I cried, slamming my back theatrically against the door. 'I've done nothing yet, I've got nothing to show you! You must test me!' The kind men sighed and rubbed their chins and agreed. I read from a script and was put on a short-list. Three weeks dragged by and I went off to Amalfi with Grattan.

The hotel was just outside the town, on the steep rocky

coast road that runs down south from Naples. We could see Amalfi, squashed against the stony cliff; a beautiful ancient Italian village, with the Mediterranean at its feet and Vespas zimming through its hot streets. Cool villas clung to the cliffs, reached by steep white steps; you could look down on their terraces of grapes and peaches and see into their vivid blue swimming pools. We drove in a coach to Paestum, and were photographed in nylon frocks leaning round Roman pillars and posturing on sunken Roman roads. A message came from England: I was needed for a screen test for *The Avengers*. May I go? Grattan said yes, and docked my fee.

I flew back one evening, spent the next day kicking stuntman Vic Armstrong about a studio with an actor called Gareth Hunt, late of the Royal Shakespeare Company, and flew back, exhausted, stiff and unhopeful, to Naples. (My luggage went to Budapest.) I trailed back to the hotel in an expensive Italian taxi, and tottered into the room I shared with Sandra Soames. The telephone rang. It was my agent, Dennis Selinger. 'Are you sitting down?' he said. 'You've got the part.'

It was rather like winning the football pools. Sandra raced down to the bar where everyone was gathering for a drink before supper. They cheered and called for champagne. 'To success!' 'Don't forget us!' 'Get in there, Lumley!' Their kindness and generosity of spirit warms me still all these years later: I can see them in front of me, glamorous girls, handsome male models, the photographer, assistants, stylists, all wreathed in smiles at my good fortune, holding up their glasses in the crowded bar: 'To *The New Avengers*!'

There was a lull before the storm of work began. We were all sworn to secrecy to keep up media interest. There were meetings and meetings, with dress designers, stunt arrangers, script writers, all building up to the Press Launch at the Dorchester Hotel one misty morning in London. Catherine Buckley designed some fragile gossamer clothes and much talk of suspenders went on. Anticipating stocking interest at the launch, I went in tights. The Dorchester was crammed with journalists and photographers, all anxious to get an eye-catching picture.

'Sorry,' I said demurely. 'I can't show my stocking tops – I'm wearing tights.' There was immediate pandemonium.

Albert Fennell took me aside behind a pillar. 'If you don't show stocking tops they're threatening to boycott the whole thing.'

'I can't, Albert, I haven't got any.'

A minion was sent scurrying off; he returned two minutes later beaming, 'We've got some!' and I was hustled into the ladies' lavatory. There I found an anxious middle-aged woman being stripped of her nether garments. She was wearing stockings, which, alas, weren't a pair. We seized her suspender belt too and left her half-clothed (with a fistful of money, I hope). Outside in the street, I was photographed in Patrick's bowler hat with a gun tucked into the top of a stolen stocking, which, coming from a shorter woman, didn't reach far above my knee. Stockings and suspenders; stockings and suspenders. What if the press had remained under the spell of another kind of clothing – flared trousers, or cloche hats, for example – or even Dr Scholl sandals?

I decided that the character should have short hair. The producers looked glum: 'You can't be a heroine with short hair.' I agreed to wear a wig if it was a disaster, and went off to Leonard's, the grand hairdressing salon in Mount Street, to search out John Frieda, who had cut Sandra Soames's hair so beautifully. Mine was cut, and streaked blonde, and straightened: 'It'll fall out.' It didn't. The character's name had changed, too: originally it was Charlie. Brian Clemens allowed me to offer an alternative: the name of the finest English gun (and, in secret, a tribute to the modelling world I'd left behind; with its passion for surnames, one of the current top models, called Sue Purdie, was Purdie for short. It seemed, all in all, a tough good name).

Gareth and I went on an Olympic crash course for three weeks, chiefly to build up stamina and suppleness. Every morning, so early that only blackbirds were around, we drove to Pinewood and the Bandroom, where big orchestras rehearsed and recorded, and were put through our paces (and the paces of several other animals) by a woman called Cyd Child. She was the heavy-weight Judo champion of Europe, later of the world – gentle-voiced, placid-looking and lethal. 'Cyd, I can't!' 'Cyd, stop!' but she drove us on and on. The worst was the shuttle run. The session was divided into ten minutes. At the beginning of each minute we had to sprint to the end of the hall and back three times, then spend the rest of the minute catching our breath. Then at the start of minute two, off we went, flat out, to and fro, then puff pant and wait for the third. It was almost all right for the first four minutes but by then we were slowing up on the sprints, and therefore recovering time was shorter. 'Cyd, I'm coughing blood! Cyd, I'm dying!' We never got off the hook. Gareth, far stronger and quicker than me, suffered less but had a grimmer time on 'loosening up', when Cyd would crouch peacefully beside you, pulling your ankle past your ear.

Gradually our heartbeats slowed down: the Olympic goal is forty-five beats a minute. I got down to fifty-one. After an hour each morning with Cyd, Gareth did weight-lifting and I did an hour of ballet – Purdey was an ex-ballerina and her method of fighting was to include balletic spins and high kicks. Ray Austin, stunt director *extraordinaire*, watched over us with proprietorial interest. 'Kick my hand,' he said, holding it above his head. 'See that, Albert! She couldn't do that two weeks ago.'

The rest of those preparatory mornings were spent doing press interviews. *The Avengers* had built up enormous worldwide audiences, and they were all interested to see how the new format would work, with Steed very much the lead and Gambit and Purdey his rather recalcitrant sidekicks. Gareth's

(Gambit's) background was to be of flinty toughness in a high-tech package, Purdey's of decent international upbringing with a bishop as a stepfather. Purdey's own father had been shot as a spy. In no time I was reading articles in which Purdey and I became one, and my own father was reported as extinct and people asked me how life had been when I studied at the Sorbonne. Our first episode, shot in Scotland, predicted the future fantasies, with its scenario of Nazis disguised as monks and Hitler's body in suspended animation. The first bunch of flowers in my dressing-room was from Peter Cushing.

Each episode, all shot on film, lasted fifty-three minutes, and took two and a half weeks to shoot. Very few were actually completed in that time, but every two weeks we started another story. Sometimes we were filming three – and once five – episodes simultaneously; out of sequence, as all films are, with different costumes, different plots, different directors and actors, second units and a host of street doubles. There are degrees of doubles. A lighting stand-in takes the actor's place during the slow and laborious lighting of the set. A street double is someone who is dressed as the actor and looks as similar as possible. They do things like getting out of cars in a long shot, driving past in shots where the camera hardly sees them, lurking in woods so you can see the right coloured jacket or dress. Stunt doubles dress as the artiste (artiste! the word is used on the call-sheet) and undertake all the difficult and dangerous work, from fights and falling down stairs to leaping out of windows, crashing cars and galloping on horses. I couldn't ride a motorbike. To be fair, they gave me part of a lunch hour to learn, but I only ever managed to do the slowest, most gormless things. A stuntman did many of my bike stunts, and Wendy Cooper did the ones which really had to show it was a girl. All the other stunts I did myself, not out of bravado but because I had been trained, and there is nothing duller than having to sit and watch some terrific scrap or dare-devilry without being able to join in. I learned how to throw a 'haymaker' right hook, which had to miss the stuntman's jaw by an inch; he would snap his head back and fly across the room, making my power look immense. I punched them in the stomach, but at the last second you pull the punch: they double over and crash head first through sugar-glass windows. I kicked Jim Dowdall under the chin on the top of a train and he hurled himself backwards in a huge somersault. Gareth smote Rocky Taylor, who was dressed as a mechanical Cybernaut, and Rocky 'Raccoon' clattered and clanged head over heels down two flights of stairs.

I enjoyed the stunt days more than any other – but not all stuntwork was fighting. Once I had to run along the ridge of a disused hospital roof, about four stories high with no safety nets. A chronic sufferer from vertigo, I found that steep slopes didn't alarm me a bit. I never attempted anything I couldn't do. Twice I was very afraid: once, jumping from a window on to a pile of stunt boxes covered with a mattress: 'Don't land on your feet or your knees will come up and knock your teeth through your skull,' I was advised; as I waited to jump, my expression cool and devil-may-care, I could feel my teeth preparing to drive into my brain.

Another story took us to an army assault course, full of ghastly tests, webby rope walls to climb, then wires to manoeuvre along through high trees, gappy slippery poles to step up, with no hand holds. There was a platform, which seemed as high as St Paul's dome, from which we had to swing on a rope, in a wide arc, before letting go at the far end and flying into a mesh of bony knobby ropes. Of course, I had on high heels through these tortures; standing on the platform with Jeremy Child, who was playing a grim-jawed officer, I muttered: 'I can't do this.' Just then, a sergeant's beefy head appeared at the top of the steps: 'A word of caution: when you swing on the rope, pull yourself up on your arms like this –' (he demonstrated, elbows tucked in, hands clenched at chest-level), '– or you will swing too low and you'll smash your kneecaps off. Good luck.' 'Action!' yelled a distant voice and Child and I, serene-browed as blancmange, exchanged our lines:

'Was he here, Major?'

'I'm afraid I can't help you at this stage,' and off we went, flying from the heights, terror filling my arms with the strength of ten sumo wrestlers, so my knees cleared the ground by six feet.

The rush of adrenalin prompted by the cry 'Action' also enabled me in subsequent episodes to scale high wire fences, sprint down disused railway tracks in ballet shoes and dangle from hovering helicopters. I learned how to skid a car with the handbrake, how to fend off arrows flying towards me with my bare hands, how to strip down and reassemble a Beretta and how to run over rocks in high heels. I was given twenty-five minutes one lunch hour to learn how to tap dance ('Come on, Jo: anyone can do it') but, as that was not an immediate success, a charming thin dancer appeared, was put into my clothes with a Purdey wig slapped on to her head and off she went, tickety-tack, on the empty stage of the Wimbledon Theatre where some showdown was taking place. Because of all the rapid changes, I kept the same small gold earrings and mushroom hairstyle, so even if I forgot which door (and which story) I had just burst through, the audience would be fooled by my identical appearance.

Crazed with tiredness one evening, I drove three times round a roundabout unable to remember which exit to take, or which town I was approaching. After that, the production company kindly provided me with a car and a driver. Each morning I was on first call: make-up at Pinewood Studios at seven-thirty, which meant leaving three-quarters of an hour earlier. On winter mornings it was exciting to drive through slicing rain or sleet, the yellow of the street lamps illuminating cold, bundled paper boys and hurrying milkmen. On summer days the pale gold dawn had come two hours before we set off, driving through avenues of blossom and birdsong. Sometimes we would encounter a mounted regiment, men in green tunics, leading one, riding one; black gleaming horses in headcollars and snaffles, clinking and clip-clopping through St John's Wood. Always we travelled the opposite direction to the commuter traffic, and usually we were too early for them anyway. The world was ours as we drove past curtained windows and closed garages: only newsagents' lights gleamed, and mighty London seemed as benign as Ambridge.

At the studios Andy Armstrong, second assistant, waited to herd us into make-up. The second assistant has to be responsible for many things, chief of which is assembling and dismissing the workers. If the star has fallen down, dead drunk, in a gambling den, it's the second's job to haul him out and have him sober on set. If a leading lady storms off in a fit of pique, it's the second's fault if she can't be persuaded to return, unblotched and docile, to finish the scene. It is his duty to make sure everyone has a call-sheet for the next day, and knows what time they must arrive, which often means that the second assistant is still on the telephone well after midnight. To be a successful second, you need the tact of a saint, the power of a sergeant major and the staying power of a limpet.

Apart from my recently acquired stamina and the ability to drive a car, the only other skill I could offer was riding. In the weird way the industry has of transmuting abilities, Gareth was given riding scenes although he had never been on a horse, and I ended up with the motorbikes and tap shoes. I was also consulted about the colour of Purdey's flat: was there any particular colour I wasn't keen on, couldn't abide? Yes, I answered clearly: I'd rather not have mauve. At once Purdey's apartment was painted lilac, with touches of purple. The bedroom was partitioned off by dangling mauve bead curtains: 'Like a tart's boudoir,' muttered Patrick Macnee. It looked very pretty but it was distinctly mauve.

Many of the crew members had worked on earlier *Avengers* episodes and I quickly got used to being called Diana. That wore off after a few months, but I never felt offended. Because we didn't own a television set when the first two series came out, I had only seen one episode with Diana Rigg.

I could easily understand the fascination of the so-called 'rivalry' between Patrick's co-stars, but it never existed. We all praised each other to the skies in the interviews, whether we had seen each other's work or not. I left it up to the taxi-drivers to say,

'That Diana Rigg (or Honor Blackman) – now she was my favourite.'

'Mine too,' I would chime in.

No one ever mentioned Linda Thorson, but I owe to her my part in the show. The French had gone overboard for 'Leenda – vairy sexy leddy' and had come up with a large sum of money to make a fourth series, assuming Linda would take the lead. When I was put in her place, there was quite a lot of French unease about my lack of allure. 'Joanna's not sexy enough!' honked the tabloids, and indeed, I had taken pains to present Purdey as a keen, no-nonsense head girl of a secret agent, with easy-to-keep hair and no real boyfriends. I wanted her to be tough and reliable, competent in scrapes but in bed alone by eleven. No matter what you think of the character you're playing, however, you must say the lines that are written and act out the story. 'Have you researched the part?' asked keen reporters and I always answered yes. The truth about research, a much respected word, is that if you have to jump feet first through a plate-glass window, it doesn't matter if your character reads Kafka and had a soft-boiled egg for breakfast: nothing you can do can show off this knowledge, so you might as well save your breath to cool your porridge. Of course, it's vital when you play a real person (I never have), but with cartoon characters, as Patrick called them, and fast-moving stories, it is essential not to become too wedded to your character's character.

Small quirks were allowed. Patrick hated guns and violence, so Steed never carried firearms, preferring to prod villains with his umbrella. I didn't want Purdey to show disgust and terror at a monster rat, as I love rats and think they've had a very bad press. Gareth just didn't want Gambit to appear a complete duffer in comparison with Steed but otherwise Gareth didn't mind much about anything. We laughed inordinately, all three of us, all the time. Gareth had a character he assumed when things were boring, a pub-singer who thought he was Tom Jones and sang into anything that could pass as a microphone: a vase, a shoe or an electrician's bald head. We were as thick as thieves, endlessly conferring, consulting, complaining, applauding. Patrick had a nickname, 'Bits', derived from his habit of snipping bits out of newspapers that he found interesting, or thought we should read. Medical journals, travel magazines, history, politics, money pages: it would be marked out and pushed under the dressing-room door, 'Darling, I thought you'd like to see this.' Our lives centred round Pinewood Studios: our dressing-rooms and chairs bore our names. Restaurant tables were reserved on a long-term basis, faces became familiar friends as we outstayed successive productions on the other stages.

After a few months, the series began to be shown on television and nothing was the same again. Up till then I was unknown. People had said, 'Weren't you in . . .' or 'We saw you in *Coronation Street*,' but now all at once it seemed that one walked in a perpetual spotlight with trumpets playing. No matter how scruffy and un-made-up I was, a watching eye would recognize me across a supermarket or half-way down a street. It would be naïve to say I hadn't expected it, but I was naïve about fame and have since discovered that you never get used to it. The first few times I was recognized, it was fairly thrilling, it meant people actually watched the show we had taken so long to make. Then a slow panic started as I realized that soon, like Katy the Oxo Lady, I would remain remembered long after the series had finished. Instead of being an observer, I was the observed. People behaved differently in my presence, and were prompted to say and do things that they would never say or do to their next-door neighbour.

How can you enter the world of showbusiness and want to remain anonymous? I don't know: but I do know that when you become well known, you lose a most precious part of your life, possibly for ever. Fame brings all kinds of extra treats: unexpected kindness and praise, respect (often un-deserved), flattery (mainly extravagant), riches sometimes, but by no means always: opportunities, presents, platforms from which to utter the least important and ill-informed of opinions. Your advice may be sought on cooking, slimming, child care, current events and fashion, home decoration, car maintenance, holiday tips and investments. You will be criticized for lack of brains, untidy hair, bad manners, louche living, choice of coat at the Cenotaph, choice of wife, children's names, girth, back-ground, football team and very occasionally performance. Your house and car will be scrutinized: the former will now, of course, be called 'luxury' but the latter often fails to please. ('Gaw! Is this your car, Joanne? Why don't you get sunnink decent?') You will be pitied for lack of work and criticized for over-exposure. Terry Wogan, for ten successive years the most popular television personality (male), only has to put his nose round the door before the baying starts: 'Wogan again! He's everywhere, that man! Three times a week is three times too often,' and so forth. Undeterred, the greatest living Irishman, appearing to be asleep as he speaks, dozes onwards to the top of the next popularity poll. He is quite unmoved by it all (as most clever people are); he leaned over to me, just as we were about to go on air in front of millions and yawned, 'It's only television, for heaven's sake.'

Only one thing brings you to this strange goldfish-bowl existence: television. You can tour the country in a play, sing at the Royal Opera House, be a brilliant juggler, a prima ballerina and still walk unnoticed through crowds. But appear on television – as a newsreader, in a thirty-second commercial, or as a presenter of a games show – and you will become a Celebrity. Television has no regard for the absence or presence of talent: it merely makes you 'famous'. Even the cinema cannot now match television for the stars it produces. Noël Coward said, 'Television is not for watching: it's for *being* on.'

After filming the first thirteen episodes, we took a break for several weeks. There were Purdey stockings and sheets, Purdey look-a-like competitions, even an ill-conceived scent called Purdey, which was brewed up and sold without permission and sank without trace. I was invited over to Holland, which had taken to the show with fervour, to appear on a live variety show. 'No problem: we all speak English here,' said the organizer as we sped away from Schiphol Airport. 'You will first fight with our judo expert, then you may give a karate demonstration.' Sweating freely, I tried to make them understand that Purdey did these things on film only: I, as a puny actress, could barely slice bread, let alone karate-chop blocks of wood. Gloomily, they sent the judo expert away, but I had to chop the planks. 'Really it will spoil the show if you don't,' they said, eyeing me with contempt. They kindly agreed to saw the planks three-quarters of the way through: I walked on in my Jean Muir dress, answered some questions in English, and crashed my hand through the wood with as loud a yell as I could muster. As I drove back to the airport nursing my bruise, I saw that eight out of every ten heads had a mushroom cut.

Holland loved the show; Sweden, Denmark and Norway decided it was too violent and refused to buy it. It was the *Infallible Tre* in Italy, *Schirm, Charme und Melone* in Germany, *Chapeau Melon et Bottes de Cuir* in France, and *Los Vengatores* in Spain. We were dubbed into Greek and Japanese, made into cartoon strips, sent to New York and South Africa and presented to the Queen Mother. (I was wrongly introduced as

Carol Lombard, whom we both knew was dead. Her Majesty looked at me with compassion and interest but I was unable to start on the muddling process of re-identifying myself, particularly as I had just overheard Princess Margaret saying to Gareth, 'I'm afraid we don't watch that.' How exciting these big moments can be! And when they go wrong, how dismaying.)

Must we go into money again? Yes, we must, for by now people were saying, 'Where do you keep your yacht, tee hee.' Gareth and I were paid £600 an episode for the first thirteen episodes, and £800 for the second thirteen. There were no repeat fees: for some tiresome reason, everyone ran out of money, and the French finance failed and sold us on to the Canadians, who went into a package deal with an English independent company who, presumably, have collected all the funds owing to the producers, writers, composer and actors. But what the programme did for us in the way of publicity and exposure cannot be measured in terms of money; and maybe whoever got our share of the loot gave it all away to charity.

You can be sure that when people stop quoting exact sums, they've become richer than they want to admit. We all like a good hard-luck story: we imagine the sympathy flooding towards us ('Poor beggars, and yet they always kept cheerful'); but sympathy zips away like a Ferrari when you announce that you have just earned £40,000 for appearing with a yoghurt pot in a commercial. I'm very interested in what money does to people. When there's not much around, people give it most generously: they can see the bottom of their purse and know to the nearest pound how much they've saved, and yet those are the ones who almost invariably give the most, spend the most. As you get richer, you get more seized up with the stuff. It becomes important in its own right, has to be treated differently, behaves independently, goes up and down, and prevents the owner from admitting that he is rolling in it. Very, very rich people look careworn and haggard ('Constipated with money,' said Joan Mary, 'you must get rid of it; then more will come along'). At the upper end of the curve, they must imprison themselves, appoint their own guards, starve their bodies, work long hours, worry for twenty-four hours a day, have electric fences and blackened bullet-proof windows. They live in perpetual dread of kidnappers and blackmailers: their jewels must be returned to safes after supper, not left in an ashtray or soapdish. These are wild generalizations, wild but true. Exceptions prove the rule. When I was nineteen, being photographed for a knitting pattern in Shepherd's Market, we saw a very shiny taxi parked by the kerb. It had carriage lamps and, inside, lovely leather seats and thick carpets. We posed delicately round it, leaning an elbow here, a finger placed there. When we had finished, a figure in black, black Homburg, black coat with a huge black persian-lamb collar, sprang out from a doorway where he had been watching. 'How wonderful! Will you send me a photograph? I'm so proud you used my car! Such beautiful women! Such wonderful jerseys!' It was Nulbar Gulbenkian; and this was the taxicab of which he said: 'I hear it can turn on a sixpence, whatever that may be.'

Surely I am not hauling out the artist in the garret, running that old one up the flag-pole to see who salutes it? Well, well. I don't think Peter Sellers was ever happier than when he was doing the *Goon Show* on the wireless and that maybe goes for the incomparable Spike Milligan. Rod Stewart is not the only rock star who looks back with affection and nostalgia to the days of the transit van, the gigs in clubs and shared clothes. After he had bought Lord Bethell's beautiful Georgian house near Windsor, Rod showed me round: huge rose gardens, gravel drives, tennis courts, sweeping staircase and a spacious room lined with cupboards holding a seething mass of glossy clothes. 'Oh! How splendid,' I cried. 'I liked it better when I slept on a mattress and hung all me clothes round the walls,' said Rod.

Quite soon, money turns into possessions: houses, cars, furnishings, gadgets and paintings. All these things cost even more money: the maintenance and insurance and replacements make you feel more pressed and hounded than ever before. Everything becomes more complicated. You must first buy the jewels, then insure them, after having made a burglar-proof place in which to lock them. On the other hand, moving over to plastic bin-liners from folded newspapers, or using a washing-machine instead of treading on sheets in the bath, makes a daily difference and has given me a lasting sense of well-being. I knew I was rich when it didn't matter in which shop I bought a jar of coffee. Not counting out the change to see if you can buy brie instead of cheddar – that, for me, was the threshold between luxury and scrimping. Shame washes over me as I write the word 'scrimping'. Only when I had travelled back to India and Pakistan, and seen villages in Kenya and houses in Soweto, did I realize properly how huge is the divide between us and them, let alone between our rich and their starving.

Chapter Seven

To Paris: after six episodes of the new series, our producers were preparing the show that would absorb them for the immediate future, *The Professionals*. We, like gypsies, packed up and departed to France, where there were funds to film three more episodes. It was unexpected and unsettling: James was now at a prep school, and seven weeks away from home cut across his holidays. We left our entire crew behind, all our friends and colleagues, and started again, in a foreign land in a foreign tongue. Patrick could speak French but only did so under duress; Gareth didn't know a word. The French had a different and most agreeable way of running the day. The first thing the electricians did every morning was to light a brazier and start cooking *andouillettes*, sausages made out of unspeakable bits of animals. At lunchtime, a huge marquee was erected and a delicious three-course meal set out – fresh asparagus, *knèfles paysanne*; soft cheese and *tarte aux cerises*. Bottles of wine and baskets of bread studded the white tablecloths and, unlike Pinewood, where there was both a canteen and a grand restaurant, we all ate together. Every other day was a Saint's Day and whoever bore that Saint's name offered everyone a drink at the end of the day's work. In the Avenue George V at five-thirty, a trestle table would be set out with drinks spread upon it, and, '*A vous, Etienne!*' as we raised our glasses in our private cocktail party in the rush-hour street.

We were billeted in a hotel almost underneath the Eiffel Tower. It was midsummer, 1976. We would walk or drive to the Latin Quarter to eat in open-air restaurants and watch the world go by. My French got better and better, from translating between director and crew to the few English people with us. Gareth's grasp of the language remained rather slight. He had no difficulty in communicating, however: he just made French sounds and gesticulated. '*Bonjour maintenant Toulouse Lautrec* ee haw ee haw.' We sat at a table in St Germain des Prés; narrow cobbled streets led away in each direction, our chairs wobbled on the paving stones and the candle guttered in the hot evening air. 'This is the life,' we said: and ordered wine and food. A small boy stood on his hands, balancing his hat on his feet, then with a leap he was the right way up, hat on his head. 'Bravo!' we called, and Gareth handed him a few francs. 'Lovely kid,' he said. The lovely kid disappeared round a corner and came straight back with a tiny sister. She clambered up the boy, and balanced on his shoulders. 'Well done! Clever kids,' said Gareth, hunting out the rest of his loose change. The children disappeared, but before we could raise our forks to our mouths, the whole family appeared at the trot: mother, father, two uncles, three tall sons, two daughters and the clever kids. With cries of 'Hop-la' they assembled themselves into a human pyramid, grunting and straining a foot away from our table. 'Oh *matelot bonjour bouillabaisse encore*,' said Gareth, paling slightly and riffling out two large notes. The pyramid leapt apart and scuttled away. 'Great stuff,' said Gareth, 'marvellous family enterprise.' We started to eat quickly, keeping our heads down. A poet sprang into the roadway and declaimed one of his works, smacking his forehead and dropping to one knee. The other diners waved him away, but he was already on his way to our table, palm outstretched. 'Fellow performer,' said Gareth, 'good man,' and took another large note from his wallet. No sooner had the wallet been returned to the pocket, than a juggler came, ignoring everyone else, eyes only on Gareth, who might just as well have worn a lighted hat with 'Sucker' written on it. The juggler dropped one of his balls into a wineglass at our table, causing a spray of beaujolais to hit Gareth's chest. 'One of your balls is in my glass, old squire,' murmured Gareth, tears of mirth streaming down his cheeks. By the time the fire-eater had arrived we were paying the bill; but Gareth gave him his last twenty-franc note as the four-foot flame crisped the hair of a woman sitting behind us.

The chef who cooked our unit lunch each day had worked for most of his life at Maxim's, the legendary restaurant and night-club. One day, each grilled steak *au poivre* was encircled by a chain made of potato, and deep fried like a chip. If you picked up the chain at one end it dangled down, each link unbroken and hooked through the next. I went into the cooking tent to ask him to show me. 'It is a grand secret,' he said, sternly. 'But I'm not a chef! I only want to learn how to do it.' With a sigh, and trying not to look too delighted, he picked up a raw potato. 'It must be waxy, not floury. You peel it so – and so – and then cut here and like thees and in thees way and so and in here and cut and – *voila*!' It was about eight links long and as beautiful as a mayoral chain. Going slowly, he showed me again. My chain only had three links, 'But you will improve,' he shrugged. I kept his chain in a bottle of water but it has long since gone and with it my memory of how to cut the potato. I can't remember these tricks for long – can't remember how to get solitaire out, have to be told the rules of backgammon every time. I can still do the sign-language alphabet but it's been superseded by more advanced methods. I can't remember the order of the hand movements in the handjive and to make pastry I have to read the recipe book each time. I have a silver ring which is made up of thin intricately shaped rings which assembled correctly look solid. I learned once how to do it but have since forgotten and it lies tangled and unwearable in my jewellery box.

Seven weeks went by. Most of our actors were French, struggling manfully with their English: 'Zair ees ollways one rotten eppel in ze berrel, Steed.' We had one shot full of old French extras, dressed as soldiers from the last war, lying dead and wrinkled on the lawns surrounding a château. On 'Action', the Major, actor Pierre Vernier, was to stride between them gazing at their corpses in dismay. But on 'Action' all the old actors struggled upright. It was explained again and again that 'Action' was for Pierre Vernier, they must lie still. '*Ah, oui!*' they said: but on 'Action' they all cranked their old limbs into a sitting position. By this stage of filming we used to laugh like drains at anything. Pierre was a wonderful companion and a fine actor. Immaculately courteous, he dressed like an English country gentleman, had a passion for racehorses and solemnly translated the French nursery rhymes and songs, that I learnt, parrot fashion, as a child.

> *Il etait un petit navire, il etait un petit navire,*
> *Qui n'avait ja-ja-jamais navigué, o-he, o-he.*

Lousic Loftus Jackson used to sing it in Middle Lights at Miekledene. Now we were on location at a French morgue, where an actor dressed as a villain pretended to lie dead in a drawer, with greyish make-up and a painted bullet hole. In real life, only twenty yards away, stood the grieving parents of a teenage girl, whose body lay in the morgue awaiting identification. Although we were promised that our use of the morgue would not coincide with any visits, corners were always cut, maybe palms greased. (In South Africa, Patrick, Gareth and I had only agreed to be sent there if they would guarantee mixed audiences everywhere. There were thousands in the crowds, but hardly any black faces. 'Where are they?' we asked. A *Rand Daily Mail* reporter, who was accompanying us, said with bitterness: 'You don't understand anything about this country. How can they watch television if they don't even have electricity?')

As our trip to France came to an end, we learned that we would be going straight on to Canada. I returned to London, collected Jamie, whose summer holidays had just started, and set off for Toronto. The film editor flew out with us, to cut the films in the Canadian studios. 'Joanna flies off on holiday with mystery man,' burbled the papers as we left Heathrow.

The Harbour Castle Hotel towers over Lake Ontario, with a revolving restaurant on the roof and an enormous heated swimming pool. The views were magnificent but none of the windows opened, confining us in chilly air-conditioned sun-dimmed glass. Gareth's son, Gareth, exactly Jamie's age, had arrived and Gareth Snr and I hired an au pair girl to take care of them while we were filming. To make ends meet, we moved into two double bedrooms, divided by a drawing-room: the two Gareths in one, Jamie and I in the other, and, to save laundry bills, one bathroom full of boy's socks and T-shirts, which hung dripping over our supplies of fruit juice and cornflakes. Sometimes we would take food from the unit lunch and smuggle it up to the boys for supper: our per diems were a valuable source for phone calls and cinema visits, and I was saving every cent to put down in advance for Harrow School.

When the boys went, I moved to the Windsor Arms near Bloor and Bay, a low built, old-fashioned hotel covered with virginia creeper, with scruffily friendly rooms and windows which opened. It was favoured by actors; the management showed me an impressive list of visitors; and one cold morning, as I left for work, I was obliged to duck under a lanky arm flung across the front door. 'Well hello,' drawled Donald Sutherland, forget-me-not eyes half closed with charm and fatigue. I had been lent a car, on condition that I drove myself to whichever location was listed, far easier than it sounds as Canada has very straight roads. The hot summer turned suddenly to fall, and I saw for the first time the colours that people are forever trying to explain. Knowing they wouldn't last, I filled a box with fallen leaves, scarlet and fire, blazing orange and blood red, brilliant yellow and Indian pink, to bring back to England.

Our storylines were getting rather wild: a building with a

mind of its own, an island in Lake Ontario which was (of course) a Russian submarine. Nevertheless we enjoyed meeting Canadian actors and, after a dour beginning, made friends with the Canadian crew. Money was running out again. On location, we had one Winnebago which served as make-up, wardrobe, shelter and lavatory for the entire unit. One rainy morning, we arrived to find that the chemical thunderbox, which hadn't been emptied, had spewed its grim sewage all over the floor and the roof had started to leak, soaking all our costumes. 'A scout smiles and whistles under all difficulties,' said Gareth, retrieving a shirt from the sodden floor. We filmed an episode which centred around an old jalopy called Emily. A villain's handprint on the roof was the vital clue to the owner's identification. At one point, Purdey, seeing the car about to enter a car wash, flung herself on to the roof and thereby protected the handprint whilst getting drenched in the process. To make it look good on film, I was smothered with detergent, a whole packet of washing powder stirred in a bucket with a little water, and smeared all over my hair and clothes so that I would foam spectacularly when the jets of water hit me. It was two degrees below freezing on the day: I went through the car wash twice, each time the detergent being re-applied. 'Cut,' called the director and the stuntman, Val Musetti, pulled me off the roof, as by now I was blinded and had a mouthful of soap. Too cold to speak myself, I heard Val saying, 'Where does she wash this off? Where's the bath?' There was a murmured consultation: there was no bath and no hot water for several miles. 'Clear the car wash!' I heard, and after hauling off my jersey, skirt and boots, I stood in my underclothes as they turned on the icy jets of water. There was so much soap powder in my hair that I foamed and bubbled for a full five minutes, clawing at my head with mauve unmoving fingers. 'Break for lunch!' I heard; but lunch for me was spent in a bewildered woman's bath, in a bungalow seven miles away, lying full length underwater as the suds continued to pour off me. No food: full make-up re-applied, hair dried (and by now looking like the whizzing brushes in the car wash), and back to work.

It all ended, not with a bang but with a whimper. Patrick flew to Palm Springs, Gareth stayed on in Canada for a week or more. The series was to be discontinued, not to be resuscitated. The Americans, flushed with a new anti-violence wave, had not shown us coast-to-coast on network television as they had done in Diana Rigg's days: and when we did appear, it was at about two o'clock in the morning on selected stations. We had taken such care not to be offensive, to adhere to the early cowboy films' rules; 'Aieee-ee!' as you fell off your horse, 'Tell . . . Bates . . . I didn't mean . . . eurgh!' as you died, no blood, no guns to the head, no smoking, no nooses, that I was bitterly disappointed, more at being branded too violent than not getting a network release (which wouldn't have paid us anyhow). We had each signed a five-year contract – now after two years it was all over. When I arrived at Heathrow, a laconic taxi driver stacked my suitcases in beside me.

'Don't I know your face?'

'Maybe. I'm in *The New Avengers*.'

'Cuh! Hope you don't mind me sayin' but I can't stand that show.'

The show was over, but the repercussions go on until this day. Advertising opportunities reared up: careful selection was like tiptoeing through a minefield. Coffee yes; cough mixture no. Newspapers, cars yes; corn plasters no. Jeans yes. By this time I had grown the mushroom-cut out and my hair was like bindweed again. Disappointed clients, expecting a sleek bob, were pleased when I pulled on a Purdey wig that I found on sale in Selfridges. My image was of a cool self-reliant woman, equally at home in a palace or a garage. I was photographed overwhelming assailants: wrestlers, mafia men and a punk rocker. The punk was full of safety-pins, through his ears, lips and nostrils. He had a husky voice and looked rather like a young Laurence Olivier. During the coffee break, he carefully took the pin from his nose: the sharp end was covered with sellotape so it didn't pierce the skin. 'Worst thing about gigs is people gobbing at you,' he said. He played in a rock band called The Police, was married with a child and was worried that if they called their first album 'Police Aggravation', it might cause offence.

'Good luck with it,' I said. 'What's your name?'

'Sting,' he replied.

When the sessions ended, I took off my wig and he removed all his safety pins. He melted away into the afternoon of Covent Garden, all in black, looking like Hamlet in search of a skull.

Whenever possible, I used public transport, mingled with crowds in shops, walked in the streets. The best way to overcome stares was to smile back or, if a panicky feeling arose, to start a conversation. Out of sheer laziness I always wore old clothes so it was not surprising that in a bread queue the woman serving behind the counter said, 'Know who you remind me of? Wossname in *The Avengers*!' The queue, who had recognized me, winked and nudged each other and smiled secretly at me. 'Purdey, that's it!' said the woman. 'Dead ringer. I bet you wish you had her money.'

It struck me that I would be saddled with Purdey for a long time. 'Does that worry you, being typecast?' queried reporters. The answer splits into two. No one wants to be typecast because most people act to show off their skill in portraying many different people. On the other hand, it is very gratifying to be remembered for a role: better, in any case, than being overlooked or forgotten. To a certain extent, we are typecast by our appearance, height, weight, colouring and the pitch of our voices. Miracles can be done with wigs, contact lenses, skin dyes and make-up, false noses and wrinkly skin: some actors thin down to skeletons to play prisoners of war, some put on stones to look like out-of-work overweight boxers, but on the whole Mogul princesses are better played by Asians and not by a blue-eyed girl with brown stain on her arms and face. Having said that; a thousand examples proving just the opposite spring to mind. Alec Guinness and Laurence Olivier playing an Indian and a Moor, Ingrid Bergman as Golda Meir, grown-up women playing Peter Pan, and Harriet Walter as a boy in *The Ragged Trouser'd Philanthropist*. Casting always provokes debate. Should Macbeth, historical figure and Scottish king, be played by a black man? Should Othello, Moor of Venice, be played by a white man? Should the black man paint himself white, as the white puts on black make-up?

Type-casting doesn't just mean racial stereotypes: it means getting so used to Raymond Burr playing Perry Mason that people wouldn't accept him playing Stalin. Les Dawson, he of the weary Playdoh face and voice like a sack of rubble being dragged around a cellar, would like to play King Lear, and I for one would dearly love to see him do it. I suspect he has a snowball's chance in hell of being offered the part. After *The New Avengers*, I knew I would have to be very lucky to have the chance of playing someone who was not a secret agent or policewoman. When *Sapphire and Steel* came along, I snapped up the part of Sapphire with gratitude.

Chapter Eight

P. J. Hammond had thought up a rather different kind of mystery series. Sapphire and Steel were aliens, sent from outer space to Earth to combat a shifting sort of evil which tampered with time, changed history and stole children. It was given an early evening slot with two episodes a week; and although it was fairly frightening, it built up a healthy following among children and people who had the time to think and the willingness to suspend disbelief. David McCallum was Steel; his appearance hadn't changed since he broke hearts as Illya Kuryakin in *The Man from U.N.C.L.E.* We filmed at ATV in Elstree; by filmed I mean recorded, because it was all done on videotape. Before we started the first of the thirty-four episodes, there were make-up tests and consultations about special effects. One of Sapphire's skills was being able to manipulate time herself – we had to discover a device that the viewers could see, so that they'd know that Sapphire was exerting her influence. The first idea was a throbbing vein in the temple. Apart from looking funny, I feared what the vein might be required to do under pressure, spread across the whole face, say, or grow huge and burst. I would have had to manipulate its pulsations by squeezing a rubber bulb in my hand, like a buttonhole flower that squirts water, a rubber tube running up through my hair. Contact lenses which flashed a vivid sapphire blue seemed a safer alternative and I went to have my pupils measured for clear soft lenses that would easily absorb ink-like eye-drops. On the shelf were Christopher Lee's prepare-to-bite eyes; I was in good company.

McCallum and our director Sean O'Riordan used to work

very hard to make sure that each story, lasting four to eight episodes, had its feet as firmly based in possibility as science fiction can be. Should there be a shadow from that wall, if the wall ceased to exist in the mind of a ghost? Should the children see the attic room stretching as long as a football pitch, or from their point of view was it normal until Evil set the music box working? McCallum had the sort of brain that thrived on these problems. He studied astronomy and was in the process of building his own house near New York where he lived with his wife and children. Fearfully fit, he would walk and run for miles each day and was keen on a healthy diet.

'What did you have for breakfast today, Jo?'

'Coffee, bread with the fur cut off. And you?'

'Two walnuts, half a satsuma, an ounce of melon seeds.'

This was probably how he kept his ridiculously young looks. He hated smoking, and if someone lit up in the cold rehearsal room, he would fling the windows open like a schoolmaster. His enormous experience of working in films gave the show an extra sheen of professionalism.

So much of the series depended on special effects that during the shooting there were periods of *longueur* for the actors. In the studio next to us was *The Muppet Show*, and we would sneak through to watch them at work. The Muppets stayed in character even when the cameras weren't rolling, and Gonzo and Kermit would lounge around on their high sets chatting desultorily in Gonzo/Kermit voices. I watched Christopher Reeve singing to Miss Piggy as he played the piano. She swooned until he mentioned her weight. Hell hath no fury like a pig insulted. Down the corridor, Petula Clark was preparing a variety spectacular, and the canteen filled up with leggy dancers and backing groups.

Talking to a group of children at a Saturday morning cinema group, I asked how they thought my greeny-grey eyes were suddenly able to flash so blue. A small boy put up his hand and said, 'Double glazing.' It was in fact an ingenious run-of-the-mill effect, which goes roughly like this. Pick a primary colour (in my case blue), and key it out, which means remove all that is blue on the screen. I had to wear blue lenses to make my pupils blue enough to be keyed out. Into the space that's left from the absent colour is transmitted whatever another camera is seeing; flames, galloping animals, or, in our case, a make-up girl's overall, which just happened to be a good turquoise colour. So: one camera fills its screen with turquoise, and the other camera focuses on my face (not my blue dress) and as the blue is taken from my eyes the turquoise is inserted rather like a backcloth. Setting all this up involved minutes of non-blinking, non-moving. Contact lenses made it easier not to blink.

I became accustomed to wearing them quite easily, so easily that a story was written to show all my eyeballs going black as the Evil Thing tried to take over my brain. I had to have plastic lenses made to the size of my eyes, painted black and put in by our eye man. I simply wept and couldn't keep them in. Anaesthetic drops were inserted: at once my eyes lost their sensitivity and their ability to focus and for a short while I was completely blind. That day there was some rumpus about an electricians' strike, and we were plunged in darkness as the crew took an early lunch. I was left behind on the set: in the heat of the moment, everyone forgot that I couldn't see. I sat glumly in a chair, terrified to walk over the cables and weights, unable to take out the lenses as my eyelids had by now been anaesthetized as well. Blindness closed round my head like a blanket and got into my brain, whispering, 'Did you ever think of blindness? This is blind.' I was rescued: much fuss was made, lenses out, much soothing and apologizing. As my eyes slipped in and out of focus, I could see blindness standing in the shadows.

It's much easier to support a charitable cause if you have some first-hand experience of the problem. People who have lost relations through a disease set up funds and societies, and work with all their energy to raise funds for research. People who have witnessed floods and famine, cot deaths or anorexia are fired by painful memories and try to raise public awareness. It's much easier to help when your heart is involved. When a call went out on a London radio station to say there had been a fire at Erin Pizzey's refuge for battered wives, I put blankets and clothes in the back of the car and drove round to Chiswick, half curious and half concerned.

Nothing had prepared me for the scene. The fire was out, and the building was still standing. It was difficult to tell how much of the dereliction was caused by flames or simply by poverty. There were about twenty women of varying ages and twice as many children. The tall, once grand, house had cracked filthy windows, peeling paint, one lavatory and rooms like dormitories crammed with sodden mattresses and tottering wardrobes. Bare light bulbs hung from the crumbling ceilings. The kitchen had two tiny stoves and thickly greased walls. The women, some bruised, all weary-looking, gave me tea in an uncracked mug. Despite the squalor, they were safe, and for the time being that was the best they could hope for.

'Safe from the fire?' I said.

'From the men,' they answered.

It seems incredible nowadays when there are refuges up and down the country that once they were seen as unnecessary, luxurious even, an easy way out for idle, troublesome women. The complications which make up the backdrop to wife-battering are formidable: the police are unable to interfere in marital rows, women become too scared to leave home earlier, beaten wives often go back to be beaten again and, worst of all, all the children are infected with violence at an early age and grow up to be stimulated only by violence (the nor-adrenalin syndrome). The local council, bound to enforce rules on sanitation and habitation, threatened to close down Erin's refuge, but a reprieve was granted after royal intervention: we understood that the Queen had sent a message of approval and sympathy to Erin.

There was a slightly slap-happy disorganized approach to life in the refuge: its flexibility and small number of rules were part of its strength. There was immediate security for a woman and her children, food and many sympathetic shoulders to share the burden of being suddenly homeless. There was a nursery school for the smallest children, and the older ones went to the local school in Chiswick, not always the easiest of integrations. There was also petty theft, bedwetting, some cases of heavy drinking, and many of heavy smoking. Erin and her team, particularly Anne Ashby, counselled the women, heard their stories through and helped them make some plan out of their chaos. No one was turned away, there were no hours when the refuge was shut. Men were always on the staff so that it shouldn't become a viperish, anti-man organization, and so that the children shouldn't lose faith in men as fathers and friends.

I took to dropping in from time to time: books, blankets, shoes, clothes and make-up were all needed, and everything was received with enthusiasm. The population was always changing: contrary to accusations, people left as soon as they could find alternative accommodation, although many returned for counselling or simply for the feeling of comradeship, and curiosity about their fellow sufferers' fates. In their demoralized state, the women took little interest in cleaning the house and indeed there were almost no brushes, hoovers, dusters or bottles of bleach. Everything was so gloomy, cracked and grimy that it was an impossible mountainous task for one or two people to face. But eight or ten?

Assisted by friends and their daughters, some actors not working that day, some stepladders, buckets and scourers, I led a working party down to the refuge and we performed a one-day blitz on the interior. Windows, opaque and yellow with nicotine, suddenly sparkled: mouldings round the ceilings yielded up soft moustaches of black fluff – rotten mattresses were taken outside and burnt, as was a cockroach-infested cupboard. The children who weren't at school were all given tasks, and we must have looked like several Snow Whites and the animals cleaning the dwarves' cottage. The enthusiasm was contagious and soon after lunchtime several mothers rolled up their sleeves too. The kitchen was scrubbed, curling lino hammered down, the poor little lavatory polished and knifed clean. We washed down the walls and wallpaper, shook out the greasy rugs and vacuumed all the pokey whiskery corners. It was, apart from being very satisfying, extremely enjoyable.

There must be thousands of people like me who would rather help in some practical way than contribute to yet another sponsored run. And why always a run? I would like to see far more sponsored litter collections, or helping old people with gardens, sponsored white-washing or sponsored graffiti removal. Those of us who draw raffle tickets and sit on committees sometimes look with envy at the field workers, while at the same time realizing that our own skills are not specialist and therefore not very valuable. Actors are useful for being famous and attracting crowds by handing out autographs and handshakes. I wish I didn't feel so phoney when at the end of a brief visit to a children's home I am handed the flowers and thanked by staff when of course it should be absolutely the other way round. The people who do it – who nurse and care for the handicapped and chair-ridden, who run the homes in which autistic children blossom, who tirelessly put disabled ones through therapy, who care for dependent people at home, thereby losing half of their own life – to these people should bouquets and thanks and praise be given. And support: just one day off a fortnight can make the difference between an overworked mother and a child-beater.

Long ago it became apparent to me that it was worth taking matters into your own hands, and not waiting forever for the authorities or the experts to act. Take your neighbour's dog for a walk, feed the cat, collect their children, sit with their

My birthday at Pinewood Studios. Patrick and Gareth celebrate with me.

In the kitchen at the Chiswick Family Rescue with industrious helpers.

Eric and Ernie danced liked dreams. My stagefright seems to have vanished in this shot.

McCallum and I. My dresses were always blue and were meant to be of an indeterminate style denoting timelessness.

With Niven in the south of France.

Cutting Shimshali's hair.

Passing the Shimshal test. The Passu Cathedrals are in
the background.

Rajah Sahib outside his old house in Shishkat. The
low wooden throne-seat is on the verandah.

My seven companions for seven days. Asif wears a
white hat.

Hyder Ali, Gordon and Ray outside Shams. You
couldn't stand upright inside.

Hyder Ali led me across like a horse.

The path to Shimshal.

Hogarth waded across like St Christopher.

On the headman's yak in the valley of Shimshal. She
had been brought down from the high pastures.

Gordon, self and Oram-Sahib with our trusty staves.
Mine was a ski-stick. We had walked to Shimshal.

The Glyndebourne photograph taken by Jamie.

granny or baby, do their shopping, help paint their sitting-room. Give lifts in your car: for all the times that you will be coshed on the head, ten thousand times more you will be helping someone who will in turn help someone else. So suspicious and terrified have we become about 'getting involved' ('Don't have a go,' warn police chiefs), that we walk neatly round the victim assuring ourselves that the good Samaritan is just around the corner and that we probably couldn't have helped and what do we pay our rates for anyway? As well as Neighbourhood Watch, I should like to set up Neighbourhood Grab and very occasionally Neighbourhood Wallop: and the permanent vigilantes I would enlist would be the same tough young men who presently frighten old women into staying inside.

When did it change? When was it that the sight of a strong young man would make an old spinster's heart unfold with relief; he would carry her bag, walk her home, wave a big stick at an attacker. What an extraordinary volte-face that our protectors have become our molesters. Well-publicized terror doesn't help ('I daren't collect my pension,' confesses eighty-six-year-old woman), as fear is contagious and villains are flattered by the power they wield. Why haven't we taught our children how to behave?

If for just one budget I were given the Exchequer to distribute, I would make the most enormous settlement on Education. Nothing – not Defence, Hospitals, Homes, Pensions, Police – nothing is more important than Education. If you are educated, you go on through life learning more and more from experience; and books, for books contain everything that has ever been thought: how to be, do, and understand everything. To know all is to forgive all; resentment and envy would take their proper place at the bottom of the pile, as we understood more. Education is not for special people: it is for everyone. Recognizing that families have changed shape (divorced, two parents, both working, single parent or whatever), I should have weekly boarding schools up and down the land where for four nights a week the children would have the chance to do prep unhindered, follow particular sports or arts; learn practical skills, with driving, first aid, typing and cooking high on the list, followed hotly by decorating, child care and how to fill in forms. These schools would be mixed, and the teacher-pupil ratio would never be more than one to twelve. It would be compulsory to board for at least one term; with any luck, my schools would be so happy that people would beg to board all the time, with weekends at home. In this insidious way, the poorest children could be properly fed, the mutinous observed, the fanciful stimulated and the studious encouraged. And at last the teachers would be paid properly – they would be second only in society to the politicians, and would undergo the most stringent training justifying their salary.

The schools would be housed in magnificent buildings so that, just for once in a lifetime, there would be a feeling of being at home in splendour and beauty. All the fine buildings at present being snapped up for conference centres I should requisition for the schools. While I was about it, I would make tax-free all money going towards research, the arts and charities. Industry would avalanche funds in these directions with the right incentives, and the sweaty search for a pound here and there would vanish, enabling medical research to set up long-term programmes; the healing effects of theatre, music and art to become more widespread and accessible; and charities could be encouraged to group together, rather than form splinter groups.

I realize my ambitions may seem financially naïve. When I was twelve I wrote to the Chancellor of the Exchequer, Mr Selwyn Lloyd, suggesting that if he doubled the value of the pound overnight we should all become twice as rich. I received a courteous reply, saying he had read my recommendations with interest, and thanking me for my valuable advice: nowhere did he accuse me of sending him a recipe for galloping inflation; I suspect he could see, from the timbre of my letter, that economics were not my forte.

If I ruled the world . . . if I had a million pounds . . . and now, in *Sapphire and Steel*, we were able to change history, enter old photographs, take revenge for slaughtered animals, set ghosts free and bring back the dead. It was an absorbing and often terrifying show which I was sad to finish. To our dismay, the last episode had Sapphire and Steel banished in a time-lock, in a garage in the black distances of outer space. The Darkness appeared to have beaten them, but only temporarily, we were assured, we would be released in the next series. There never was another series, and our characters are still up there, waiting to break free and continue the fight. It's like a film of someone diving, inched forward frame by frame but never hitting the water. It interferes with your breathing.

Chapter Nine

Every year since 1972, with a soothing regularity, came *Call My Bluff*: Jeremy Lloyd had put my name forward as someone who might make an acceptable guest and it remains one of the great, if too brief, pleasures in my life. In the old days, the show was recorded in some sort of scout hut in Manchester that was one of the BBC's standby studios. We would travel together on the train, eat lunch, do the crossword puzzle. (I got 'Strathspey' as an anagram. Frank Muir was pleased with me, and, as I said the word, I could remember when I last uttered it ten years before; Scottish dancing in the gym with Miss Gregson.) We would record the two programmes and then dine together or travel back by train. Now it's all rushed through at the Television Centre, probably a blessing for the three regulars but for their guests there may be a tinge of disappointment that the clock has moved forward.

The ritual is splendid. A rehearsal: there is a trial game, to teach newcomers how to play, both less and more complicated than it looks; and what we call the Oxfam display: the Holding Up in front of you of the clothes you hope to wear that night. Then the Handing Out of the Envelopes to each team leader and the stealthy withdrawal to the leader's dressing-room where coffee and sandwiches are provided as you deliberate over the words your side will define.

We were customarily chastised for our appalling attempts at regional accents by the unchanging Robert Robinson, and the whole event was as comforting and uplifting as golden treacle on sponge pudding and re-runs of the *Navy Lark*. When they altered the arrangement of the signature tune I had to be revived with brandy. Some things should never change.

When Paddy, the great Patrick Campbell, was alive, I was once put on his team instead of Frank Muir's. Unfortunately I couldn't stop laughing at him all the way through, which is only allowed if you're on the opposing team, otherwise the cameras don't see you and all you can hear is stifled screeching and snuffling. Frank has been lumbered with me ever since and I have perfected a silent hysteria for when he speaks. I was allowed to guffaw openly at the unforgettable Arthur Marshall. When he died it seemed as though one of the last links with the past had been snapped; a past England, a gentler, happier place, the land of Betjeman and Saki, Richmal Crompton, Miss Read and Arthur himself.

Frank is a perfect example of the public and the private man. Managing to appear an amiable ass, never downhearted, a Wodehousian character in public, in secret he works away on scholarly books, one of which has been on the boil for many years, and drapes his marvellous brain with a cloak of humour. He and Denis Norden approach everything with a style and elegance that is inimitable. We don't seem to be breeding replacements with the same combination of humour, brains and kindness.

Any chance I had to go abroad, I seized. Everything you see and hear is different, from the shape of rooftops and the design of toothpaste packets to the language and the sound of birdsong. We all become slightly changed people abroad, I think; never more so than when we are travelling alone. How tragic to cross the world and find hotels that have prawn cocktails, good English spoken and a fax machine. I foresee an alteration in the great conga-chain of tourism. Soon, people will only want to go slowly, insisting on mosquito nets and bicycles; local food and lack of telephones will be added attractions. Even now the very grandest and most expensive holidays are returning to grass-roots exercises, riding, walking, camping, lugging heavy equipment, cooking for yourself. In the crumbling days of the French aristocracy, they pretended to be shepherds and milkmaids; now we pretend to be explorers, shipwrecked fishermen or anthropologists. As the top end of the graph curves down to even humbler, costlier holidays (working as a maid in a Belgian guest-house, operating a dumptruck in Istanbul), and the yachts are emptied of people pretending to be Onassis, the new wave will click into a different cog in the wheel; Torremolinos kiss-me-quicks queuing for Egyptian Tombs, sun-soaked Seychelles visitors awaiting their turn in the paddy fields. Soon the 'civilized' world will be full of people travelling enviously to unsophisticated lands, finding to their amazement that everywhere looks a bit like Croydon now, returning home with memories of the Disco Night in a Mombasa beach hotel and a jogging track in Jakarta, and wondering secretly what all the fuss is about, and whether they should have taken different things to wear.

The British insist on travelling in hot countries in ill-fitting underclothes, shorts and gaping T-shirts, regardless of the way the local people dress. Not only the British: I saw a German woman in Kenya walking through a Muslim street in the skimpiest bikini. We tend to view any place we visit as a holiday resort. Still, suntans are going out of fashion, and soon the oil wells will run out. Then there will be slow journeys, time to learn a bit of the language and the history, time to enjoy getting closer and closer, on a ship or a train or maybe a horse.

The most disappointing thing about going to the Seychelles is that everyone who has been to those tiny glorious islands has been to the same few restaurants, lain on the same beaches. ('No, we went just north of there, where that huge rock – remember? – sticks out just where you can see Silhouette Island . . .'). David Hemmings first told me of the Seychelles, arriving late at a dinner party, burnt dark brown, brimming over with the paradise he'd just visited. It had taken two or three days to get there, on a ship from the rim of Africa – two years later the airstrip was built, and a steady queue of 747s started to disgorge thousands of people a week, including me, and the islands changed forever.

On Mahé, the largest of the Seychelles islands, I met a man who came over to shake my hand. 'Thank you for bringing us here,' he said, indicating his wife and two daughters. 'I was an ordinary hairdresser, doing quite well, until the Purdey cut came in. Then – boom!' and he threw his hands in the air, laughing with delight, and the equatorial sun beat down on us all. It seemed absolutely right that, at the end of it all, my impossible hair had brought some wealth and happiness to the very breed of people it had so disappointed earlier in my career.

For me the best kind of travelling involves work or a 'project'. Twice I have been lucky enough to sit on the Drama Jury at the Monte Carlo Television Festival. For a week you lead the life of a character in a film, always dressed in your best clothes, staying in hotels creaking with chandeliers and gnarled with grand balconies overlooking the harbour; trotting down to the viewing-room with a briefcase bulging with information on forty-five programmes; cocktail parties at the Palace, helicopters to Nice Airport. The extra frisson was having to conduct your discussions in French and sometimes even German and Italian. There was a glittering award-winning dinner at the end of the week. One year, at our table, a man was arrested by police as we plunged into our *gâteau au chocolat*; two tables away, Leurs Altesses Sérènes graciously kept their royal heads turned towards the stage. For a week you pretend to be the sort of person who sleeps in a satin nightdress, changes for dinner at home, uses leather suitcases and fountain pens, and carries several air tickets tucked into a battered passport. When you get back, on go the rugger socks and holey jersey; out comes the tin tray with baked beans on toast in front of *Blind Date*.

*

Headaches. I became used to having headaches several times a week. It was obviously stress, I was told, and possibly referred pain from the back, but not eyes and certainly nothing more sinister like a brain tumour. The Old Harrovian Players invited me to be Rosalind in *As You Like It*. We would rehearse every Sunday for a month and perform it in front of the school and general public on the first weekend of the summer term. As Jamie was not yet at the school, I knew I wouldn't be embarrassing him by appearing and it was my second chance to do a Shakespeare play, the first having been *Othello* with the same O.H. Players five years before. Four days is not an ideal amount of time to rehearse a play, but we met in the evenings as well as during the week, in the cold semicircular Speech Room which Nehru, Churchill and Rattigan knew so well. The play would be performed without scenery and only the most basic props, with almost natural lighting and on a stage similar in almost all ways to the original Globe Theatre. There was no backstage to speak of: characters leaving stage-left could be seen sprinting round the parapets in full costume by passers-by to enter again stage-right. The costumes were lent, as always, by the Royal Shakespeare Company. I found myself in Dorothy Tutin's jerkin and knickerbockers, rather at half-mast as I am about six inches taller than she is. (I had made, for *Othello*, the handkerchief, roughly painted and embroidered, which Othello gives to Desdemona and which she loses, causing her to lose her life as well, poor Desdemona: this time I made flowered and ribboned coronets for Celia and Rosalind to wear for their weddings. Twiddley-fiddley, snip, snip, glue: never happier than when making something.) We would bring thermos flasks and blankets and put them on the seats: I remembered this large amphitheatre from long ago, when I came to stay with Anthea Warman during the Lent holidays. Harrow hadn't broken up, and we came to the Speech Room to hear Haydn's Creation, every face visible, parents this side, boys packed on that, beaks and choir on the stage, orchestra in the pit. There was a very quiet part of the singing when I was terrified that I would leap up and yell, 'Ble-aargh!' and I had to grip the seat with damp hands to stop myself. I envy short-sighted actors who can't see beyond the footlights.

Rosalind's part is long, the longest Shakespeare wrote for a woman. His blank verse is, however, not hard to learn: by that I mean not hard to 'quick studies'. I used to be a quick study. I used to be a photographic study, sometimes only reading something once before I knew it. Anything well written, no matter how long, is easier to learn than something that is badly written and poorly constructed. I took Rosalind home with me, and spoke her lines out loud in the car. But by now a band of metal, like a crown round my forehead, was being inched inwards by unseen hands, and the inside of my skull was filled with molten fudge and white-hot concrete. My eyes hurt to move; the fudge poured down through my spine, which became hotter and hotter. It was the week before Easter, and there was no rehearsal on Easter Sunday. Rehearsal period was half-way through – only two more days, at weekly intervals. If I could just lie down and sleep, I could learn the part easily afterwards. I went down to Kent to stay at Sparkeswood. On Good Friday, I couldn't get out of bed, and light was now unbearable to see, even water difficult to swallow. No kind of pills made the slightest impact on the pain, which seemed to have taken over my whole frame, round which I clung like a prawn's shell. It was viral meningitis.

As soon as it was diagnosed, and the drugs administered, the pain retreated and in a short time I could walk about fairly feebly. My brain, however, seemed to be operating strangely, with vast gaps where memories used to jostle, and an unnerving way of packing up completely when hunting for simple words like 'car', 'potato' and 'skirt'. Should I pull out of the play? As I learned the lines, they went into my head and straight out again, like pieces of a jigsaw puzzle swept off a table on to the floor. But no one else could stand in for me at such a late date and, beside everything else, I realized that if I didn't go on now, I might not be able to go on again. Sometimes I couldn't remember my address in London. Earlier that year, my cousin Michael Neale had had meningitis, and a few months before I'd visited Brian Alexander, a close friend, who was stricken down in London with the same disease: both men had had a far more virulent strain than the one I caught.

I began to pray to Shakespeare. I've always prayed, at any time of the day or night, usually to God; but this time it seemed that Shakespeare was the one who would have the time and the specialist knowledge. 'Let me not forget the lines, dear Shakespeare, and let me get some sort of Rosalind in good enough shape to show your play to its best advantage.' On the day of the performance I could see every line, written in my head with a light shining on it. A huge gale of energy blew into my panicky heart and all the lines came out perfectly and I didn't let down the cast, which was what I most dreaded. It was enormous fun, too, and exhilarating, but by the next day every one, every single one of the lines had left me and from that day to this I cannot recall one word of Rosalind's part.

This, as they say, gave me pause for thought. The stage, my goal, demands a retentive memory, or at least an ability to take a prompt when you dry. I feared that I would now forget not only my lines but also which play I was in, and possibly which country as well. Push the thought away: like Scarlett O'Hara, 'Tomorrow is another day.' (Take therefore no thought for the morrow: for the morrow shall take thought for the things of itself. Sufficient unto the day is the evil thereof.) Or, as Jeremy Child would say, 'Just get on.'

When I was at school I read *Cider with Rosie* by Laurie Lee, a book so deliciously visual that it scarcely needed illustration. The few provided, in my paperback version, were by John

Ward. They were in black ink on white paper, not wholly substantial in that you could see through a person's arm to the chair behind. They were sketches, illuminations, and they had the most profound effect on me. I met him and sat for him when I was expecting James and staying with the Armitages at Godmersham. John had been commissioned to draw the interiors of some pubs and needed bodies sitting in them. So I perched on bar stools and relaxed on sofas in his huge Elizabethan studio, and John twinkled and grinned and drew, with several pairs of glasses on different parts of his head like Professor Branestawm. It was always very quiet and rather cold, just the scratching of his pen and the clink of brush in the water jar. All around the walls were books, hats, shelves, busts, dried or dead flowers, canvases, twists of cloth, broken dolls, anything that charmed his eye. Above the studio door, at the other end of the room from the big open fireplace, was a striking painting of Alison, his wife, in lovely shiny satin evening gloves and a look of tremendously lofty kindness. Alison knew I was expecting James, John didn't notice. 'Oh are you? I say, how marvellous!' he cried; and drew me for the cover of a collection of Chekhov's short stories, wearing a King's School straw hat: his elder boys were at school there with St Clair. Behind me in the drawing was a distant scene of countryside in Russia and I sat in the foreground in a high-necked Indian cotton dress with the straw hat. All was terracotta, light and shade, and scratchy etched lines, and a terracotta shadow on my face. Alison came in with some tea and looked at his drawing over his shoulder. 'Put in her face, John. She must have a face,' she said, and John beamed. 'Marvellous! A lovely face!' and set to work to draw it in. When Jamie was born, he gave him a painting of trotting ponies and boys with bicycles, drawn in Italy. I became a dedicated collector of his works, and they fill the walls and our lives with pleasure and kindness. Like Ardizzone, John Ward seems unable to draw an unkind thing. That doesn't mean he flatters; he simply sees people as rather marvellous and sets to work. I've only seen one of his portraits which made me feel uneasy. Later, John said, 'Did you see the picture I did of so-and-so? Didn't like him,' and it showed.

There is a vogue in art (both in painting and 'Art' as a heading), that ugliness is somehow more real than beauty. Aggression and 'raw anger' are valued, while charm and courtesy, infinitely harder to achieve, are seen as 'flabby' and 'middle class' (which has, in turn, become a term of opprobrium, although it's always used only by middle-class people). Theatre groups ripple with tense contempt for the audiences who always want 'shaking up'. Mind-numbingly awful music is composed and played and critics praise it to the skies for fear of appearing unperceptive. In youth perhaps it is easier to admire death; but when you think how long it took to grow a tree, or a person, it seems incredible that anyone can applaud its destruction. Why America still hasn't changed its gun laws is one of the great mysteries of the twentieth century. How anybody can see anything awesome, attractive or admirable in someone who walks about with a gun taxes my brain sorely. People with guns simply look silly and rather cowardly.

There are very many films glorifying robbers, murderers, prostitutes, in fact all the occupations that are really easy to do. (Shoplifting is, I suspect, far easier than trying to catch the assistant's eye.) I may have become 'Disgusted, Tonbridge Wells'. But I do believe that most people are perfectly ordinary, they just like to biff along, caring for their families, feeling sympathy, indignation, love, roaring with laughter, getting bored. Most people don't need jolting or shaking up or scaring or bullying. Now and then something happens which sends them to their ballot boxes, or reaching for their wallet or marching in the street. But most of us, most of the time, just want life to be good, for us and those around us.

John Ward sees this innate goodness in everything, which is

why his paintings give such pleasure. While I was lying in my fever-darkened room at Sparkeswood, my parents drove over to John's studio to collect the finished drawing which they had asked him to do of Jamie. When they came back I was impatient to see it, and they propped it up by my bed and I squinched my eyes through the light and saw Jamie, twelve years old, shiny hair and sloping eyes, fine dark brows, one hand cupped to hold birdseed, the other pinching up some grains to feed some canaries in a huge old-fashioned cage. The cage is at the front left side of the drawing; the birds hop about with bright little eyes, millet sticks through the bars which curve up and away in a generous dome. Behind and to the right is Jamie, intently watching the birds so we can study his face. It is the most beautiful drawing of a boy and some birds, and just about the most exciting present I've ever been given. There is no doubt it helped me to recover more quickly.

Chapter Ten

When *Private Lives* came my way, I seized the part of Amanda with joy. James Villiers, who played Victor when I saw it first with Maggie Smith and Robert Stephens in the leading roles, was to play Elyot. It was to be a tour of the production which started life at Greenwich with Maria Aitken. Rehearsals were held in a room high above Her Majesty's Theatre, a room where the Prince Regent used to dine during the long intervals in plays a hundred years before. The floor was marked out with Sellotape, boxes and chairs were placed to mark the balconies. There is a huge world that divides a rehearsal room and the final set – only the measurements are the same. With a play as 'proppy' as *Private Lives*, it is important to rehearse with the real glasses, gramophone records, and breakfast things, or you will find yourself completely thrown by the difference. It is traditional for the stage manager to announce over the tannoy anything new that you may see on stage that night. ('Good evening, company. In tonight's performance Mr Leo Franklyn's slippers will be dark red, not dark blue. Thank you.') There is also an unwritten rule that you must not call 'Fire!' if your dressing-room curtains go up in a blaze. Each theatre has its own emergency code, usually something like, 'Mr Green has left the building.' This is so that there shall be no panic, but as the whole company knows the awful implications of Mr Green's announced outgoing, a stampede may well take place anyhow. The iron curtain is to protect the audience, the plush auditorium, the outside world from the flaming inferno backstage, where unreality rat-runs between painted backcloths and miles of lethal electric cables.

During rehearsals, a tight knot which never untied had formed like a turnip in the pit of my stomach; every time I thought of performing the play in front of an audience, a sheet of shock swept through my brain. My mouth could chatter away about parking places, where we would go for lunch, the lovely costumes by Peter Rice, but in my head all was brewing up blackness and terror. I could never get away from it: the first thought as I woke up was of the play, which had itself reached gargantuan proportions, as if I was a fly struggling in a saucepan of jam. Fear of letting my fear be seen became another burden: the whole of my life seemed to be a slow-motion nightmare. We travelled to Norwich to open the show and start the tour, eleven weeks in as many towns. I gave blithe, confident interviews, posed for photographs, even on the morning of the first night. Jilly Cooper telephoned me at the Norwich hotel, to tell me that in the Common Entrance exam several people had taken for a Sunday newspaper, I had come out on top. It was only a light-hearted affair which we'd all done with humour and some trepidation – my convent background gave me good marks in Divinity and French, and John Rae marking them unseen had said of my papers that he'd like to have this boy at his school.

'Jilly, we open tonight,' I whined.

'You poor old thing,' she said sympathetically. 'I just thought you'd be pleased to know. I'm so *thrilled* it was you.'

This generous gesture of hers calmed me for a few minutes, then the sheet metal flashed again. The evening was only hours away and in my head I jabbered the lines over and over, sweat lining my shaking hands.

No matter how I looked at it objectively, that it was only a play in a theatre in a town, that it would end one day, that it wouldn't really matter if I forgot my lines, fell over in a dead faint or missed a cue, no matter how I tried, I couldn't shake off that stage fright. What was worse, the fright became more intense during the show, not less. The more often I did the play, the more terrifying it became. John Caird, the director, a close friend of Jane Carr's, came with Janie to see the play at Cambridge. 'You should . . . *play* with it a bit more,' he said, 'have more *fun*.' But the truth was I only wanted to remain alive and still speaking; there was no energy left over for interpretation, or, for heaven's sake, for fun. We travelled on, packing up on Saturday nights and driving home on Sunday to get clean clothes, before driving on Monday to the new town, hunting down the theatre, walking on the empty stage, looking at those dear empty seats, knowing that by the evening a head would come round the dressing-room door. 'House sold out tonight, Joanna.' 'Please don't tell me.' In Lincoln, I nearly enjoyed it when we opened to only forty-three in the audience, but by the end of the week, due to our untiring, smiling publicity, the house was full again. Sometimes we stayed in hotels, sometimes in digs. Both were a gamble as the accommodation lists sent to us are not often checked, and it's best to go by word of mouth or your 'friendly family pub, cosy rooms, full breakfast' can mean damp beds, mice-infested walls, 40-watt bulbs and cigarette ash in your scrambled eggs.

We played the Alhambra, Bradford, the week before it closed down for an extensive face-lift. There were no posters outside to show the play was on, no publicity handbills up around the town. We opened to a pitifully small audience. The Alhambra is a large theatre. Even I was moved to concern. 'We'll have a competition,' we said. 'We'll fill this house by Saturday night.' Word got around that two lucky programme owners would win the star prize of being allowed to have dinner with Jimbo Villiers and me – a pretty measly lure, but it worked. Tuesday night's house was almost quarter full, Wednesday was half full. On Friday a small group of us drove over to see Haworth, the Brontë home on the bleak moors. It was extremely spooky, we all thought. 'Veddeh, veddeh gloom-eh,' said Jimbo, looking lugubriously at his half of shandy in the pub, frequented once by wild Branwell Brontë. 'Veddeh disagreeable.' That night there were only a hundred or so seats unsold and we swung into the show with gratitude at the Bradford response.

At the end of Act One, Amanda and Elyot, now remarried to different spouses, decide to elope together. As we exited stage-right, leaving our cocktail glasses on the balcony overlooking the Duke of Westminster's yacht, Jimbo staggered slightly. In the wings he hissed, 'Your little shoe, lovey, gave my leg an awful kick.' 'Didn't touch you, Jimbo, look, I'm miles behind.' In his dressing-room, with the doctor probing Jim's calf with anxious fingers, the cast standing around flapping, with our cups of tea and cigarettes, the truth was told. The tendon in his lower leg had somehow snapped clean in two; the doctor said the feeling would be exactly as if one had been kicked savagely with a pointed toe. Jim was absolutely incontrovertibly lame. Act Two, just Elyot and Amanda. We somehow managed, with him staggering from piano to sofa, although the end, the great cushion fight and record-smashed-over-head bit looked one-sided and cruel, as Jim couldn't do anything but be belaboured. By Act Three his white face and the huge distances between doors and chairs absorbed us all and the play clonked mechanically to a close (although Jim never lost a single laugh). By the end of the show the dear man was nearly weeping with pain, and the whole company went into a complete dither.

The cast of the play is small; Timothy Carlton, Amanda Parfitt, Susan James and I mere satellites around Jim's languid sun and although understudy rehearsals had gone on, of all parts to recast, Elyot's was the hardest. Chris Norman, the company manager, understudied Elyot, but he was the company manager and his hair was shoulder length and he was a foot shorter than Jim. Frantic telephone calls flew around. The message came back from London: on Saturday, the show must go on. We sat up late into the night refilling our glasses round Jim's bed. 'Another drop of Vera, lovey, this is the end of my life.' (Vera Lynn – gin). By Saturday, with the matinée cancelled to make way for rehearsal, an idea had formed in my head. I would buy the theatre out. I sat at my dressing-room make-up desk and wrote in my cheque book. 'Pay the Alhambra Theatre the sum of three thousand pounds'. There was a knock at the door. It was Chris Norman; his long hair cut very short and slicked back, a dinner jacket and bow tie beneath his anxious face. 'I'm game if you are,' he said. 'The house is sold out.' I tore the cheque into tiny pieces, feeling more ashamed than I'd ever felt before.

Well, we went on, and what is more Chris remembered every line and every move and there was a storm of applause for him at the end as I handed him a special bouquet. We took curtain call after curtain call: later Chris told me that he'd always longed to act, and that his favourite part of all time was Elyot Chase in *Private Lives*. Now he'd played Elyot to a crammed house and a standing ovation and his cup was full. I thought of my cheque and my craven course of action which would have made all our lives smaller. The motto of Mick-ledene School had been 'Courage'. What had happened to mine?

But a replacement had to be found as there were still four more weeks to play. On Monday we were to open at Newcastle, and the show was a sell-out in advance. I went back to London on Sunday to await developments. On Sunday even-ing, when despair was growing, a telephone call told me to catch the ten o'clock train to Newcastle with a first-class ticket. James Roose-Evans, our director, would rehearse me and the replacement actor on the journey. His name was Simon Cadell.

Somehow over the weekend, Simon had been persuaded to take over the part, which he had played before, despite the fact that he was filming in the south of England and would have to commute between Newcastle and London every night. We met on the platform, rehearsed madly in our first-class carriage, love scenes, fights, business with glasses and cigarettes, singing

'Some Day I'll Find You', to the disbelief of other travellers. There was no wardrobe for him so he brought his own dinner jacket and a light coloured suit. (I thought then, and know now, that he was a workaholic and a glutton for punishment, apart from more obviously being sent from heaven.)

The Theatre Royal, Newcastle, has a most grand and sophisticated audience. When, before the show started, we peeked through the curtains, the place was full of first-night jewels and hubbub and excitement. James Roose-Evans went out to speak to them before the play started. 'Ladies and Gentlemen,' he began, 'you are about to see a drama – a real-life drama,' and he went on to explain about Jim's accident and Simon's lightning study and there being no clothes for him; and the audience rustled and chuckled and spread its hands and waited and the curtain went up.

How we got through the night I can't remember. We were perfect strangers, embracing, bickering, dancing together; in the play as familiar as a pair of gloves, in life staring across the stage with eyes glittering with tension, as alert as rattlesnakes. I knew everything that ought to happen, Simon divined every move and pause, and at the end, quite rightly, the reception for him, and for us, was tumultuous. For the second night running, I handed my leading man a bouquet from the cast, a prize for living through the actor's nightmare.

Because Simon was in the popular television show *Hi-de-Hi*, and I'd been in *The New Avengers*, sometimes teenagers would come to watch the show to see television stars in real life. Often they had never been inside a theatre before, or seen a straight play. One of the most rewarding parts of the tour was meeting small groups of young people after the show at the stage door, all smitten by the play, the plight of the characters, and Coward's writing, and every thought of *Hi-de-Hi* and Purdey banished. We played Southsea, where the week before there had been an ice show on stage. When they removed the ice rink, water had seeped through on to the wooden stage, creating huge bubbles on the veneer floor. As we glided on in evening dress, the bubbles flattened underfoot only to bulge up somewhere else, and our progress was marked by quiet pops and clicks. It was Wimbledon fortnight while we were playing Southsea. On Saturday during the matinée, we devised a way of indicating the score of the men's finals to each other, Simon's expression getting blacker and blacker, as the boy McEnroe beat Bjørn Borg.

I stayed during that week with Prue and Jack Madden, dear friends of the family, whose house at Emsworth looked out over the sea where, as a child, I had sat fatly on the shallows on home leave. In Emsworth was Ramleh, the large house where my Great Uncle Pat and Great Aunt Minna had lived. The garden was full of roses, lavender and fruit trees and contained the summer-house, a sort of shed called the Delapidations, where on a wind-up gramophone we had played George Formby records. Uncle Pat was a naval man, windows were kept open at all times, washing up of glasses done in cold water in the butler's pantry. Strange sea shore: whiskery grass and mud flats, sailing boats and driftwood, dogs racing with sticks in their jaws and seagulls crying. Then clong! The theatre, and Amanda's evening dress and Coward's marvellous dreadful play, and freedom gone.

Only one week to go, and that at Richmond. During the Richmond week, I rehearsed for the Morecombe and Wise show, which ought to have been far happier and far more fun. I was so flattered to be asked and thought that the stage fright was just that: fright of the stage, not television. But it is fright of life. Eric Morecombe and Ernie Wise were a delight, effortlessly generous and charming and it was just my bad luck that although I said I couldn't sing or dance, they had arranged a Thoroughly Modern Millie routine to bring fresh terror to my self-obsessed torture.

And then, quite easily, it was all over. There were parties, farewells and expressions of regret. 'It's been such fun – I wish we were going on and on,' although my chief feeling was of betrayal to my character Amanda Prynne. I had betrayed her, not portrayed her, and somewhere in the ether Coward thought so too, as I could tell he was pretty disappointed with my lacklustre performance. One day I will, if I may, have another crack at her. As Jimbo said, once you've played these people they become your own.

The Armitages telephoned with news: St Clair was to be married. Caroline was already married, to Jonathan Spencer, in Godmersham Church, where the vicar was almost the same age as the building and had forgotten to say the exact part of the service which means you are married. The congregation agreed it didn't matter a jot, a string quartet had played beautifully and the day had been full of flowers and festivity and charm. St Clair's wedding was to be in Dawlish in Devon. Tony and Celia suggested that I caught a train down and, after the wedding, stayed with them in a caravan. I love long train journeys and read a book straight through, glancing up to notice the changing scenery, and the sun shining on the sea. At the station, Tony and Celia were waiting. 'We're going straight to the church first,' they said. 'There's some problem about Zadok the Priest.' At the church was St Clair, now a naval man, grinning from ear to ear. 'Music missing,' he said, leading me inside where the organ was thundering. 'Come and meet Barlow.' Sitting at the organ, slamming sheet music about, white-faced and black-haired, scowling like a storm cloud, sat Stephen Barlow, the boy-wonder musician of St Clair's schooldays. 'We've come to help look for Zadok the Priest,' said Celia and we fell on to piles of music, shuffling and sifting, while Barlow played 'Oh I do like to be beside the seaside' in the manner of a cinema organist. I don't think Zadok surfaced: but I remember holding my knuckles to my chest to stop my heart crashing in such an extraordinarily thumping way, which was as mysterious as it was uncomfortable.

The wedding was delightful: brother officers lofted swords, apricot-clad bridesmaids fluttered around, speeches and toasts, telegrams and the cake. That evening there was a discotheque 'for the youngs'. Tony, Celia and I went, intent on leaving early so the youngs, of which I was no member, could do their own thing. Distinctly young was Barlow, to whom I spoke briefly. In that wedding-y way one does, we agreed to meet at some time in London, ostensibly to go to Ronnie Scott's, although we both knew we wouldn't do anything about it. When I got back to London the next day, I sat in the kitchen with Janie and John Caird.

'I met an extraordinary musician,' I began.

'Oh, I know who that will be,' said Caird, fast as a knife, 'Stephen Barlow: we were in a music and poetry group together called Circle of Muses. Yes, yes, brilliant. Invite him to the first night on Thursday.'

Jane was about to open in a play at the Warehouse, directed by John, or Jean-Caird as I now preferred to call him. The evening came and went. The play was good, the audience as theatrical as paint, the crush oppressive. We squished into some sort of hostelry and juggled spaghetti and wine over a plank. Sometimes I saw Stephen frowning slightly, dazed, and slightly appalled, by the whoops of 'Dahling!' and the screeches of intimacy that are so funny and homely to theatre people. He spent the night in the once-au pair's broom cupboard, and the next day he left, only this time neither of us said anything about meeting again. Pht! Who cares? He was much younger than me and in any case I was perfectly contentedly tied up with Michael Kitchen, whom I told about this dark young conductor, and the coincidence of his knowing John Caird. Barlow went from my mind, absolutely, at once and for ever, except for an odd sense of loss and disappointment whenever I thought about him, which was never, except when his white face and black hair appeared unexpectedly in my mind's eye. A year later, visiting the Armitages, I said, 'By the way, what became of Stephen Barlow?' 'Marvellous news,' said Celia, 'he has just married a talented young singer. We're so pleased for him, he's really settled down.' And that was that.

Chapter Eleven

wo *Pink Panther* films: but by now Peter Sellers was
dead. I met him a few times, most memorably with
Jeremy Lloyd, who, when he heard Peter had holed up in a
Kensington mews cottage in a fit of depression between wives,
took me and a dish of haddock cooked in milk to visit him.
Peter was gloomy and restless, filled with misgivings about his
abilities, the future, friends, death and the universe. We stayed
for three hours, during which time Peter ate the fish, cheered
up and gave me an armful of Dory Previn records. Months
later, he spotted Jane Carr and me eating spaghetti at the
Trattoo and sent over a bottle of champagne. We joined him
after supper. He was with Spike Milligan, sitting at the top
front part of the restaurant where Alan Clare was playing the
piano. They were in peak condition, and we all sat clutching
our sides and rocking with laughter.

Spike has always been one of my heroes, brimming with
concern for the welfare of animals, people, the planet and old
friends. I watched him signing autographs once, leaning on
one of Landseer's lions at Trafalgar Square. No slapdash
scribble or brusque brush-off: he wrote elaborately in Elizabethan italics, his name written as clearly as a schoolboy's, with
twirls and curlicues, so although he didn't manage to get many
done, each one was something special for the collector to
treasure. He walked off alone, perhaps to catch a bus or
Underground train, an extraordinary figure before whom the
crowds opened politely.

All this rushing about in darkened cars with sirens and
outriders is nonsense. The grandest people I know are to be

found travelling about normally, Julie Christie at Earls Court Tube, Margot Fonteyn walking like a sixteen year old through the middle of Covent Garden, Harold Macmillan strolling through St James's Park to the House of Commons, Meryl Streep, queuing with a piled luggage cart at Nairobi Airport. Sometimes, however, humble scuttling about can backfire. I was invited to switch on the Regent Street lights with David Essex: the ceremony was to be performed from a balcony in front of one of the big shops. I arrived in time, dressed to kill, and parking my Mini behind the Burlington Arcade, ran quickly to the main entrance of the shop in Regent Street. All the pavements had been cordoned off and a vast good-natured crowd had gathered, monitored by amiable ten-year-old policemen. I got bogged down at once, coming up against a barrier.

'I'm supposed to be in there!' I yelled over the din.

'Sorry, love, all full up,' beamed the boy P.C.

The crowd recognized me. 'Hallo Joanne! Come to see the lights?'

Struggling as if in a dream, making no headway, I saw David Essex stepping out on to the balcony. 'David!' I howled, 'I'm down here!'

But my cries were drowned by a far larger shout of 'David! Cooee, Dave! Hallo David!' from his fans in the street. The lights were switched on, the crowd dispersed and I slunk back to my car. ('Is this your car, Joanne? Stroll on!')

Hired cars, although luxurious, are wildly expensive, so when I was called down to Pinewood Studios to meet Blake Edwards I drove myself. Blake, as usual surrounded by what at first seemed to be the Mafia but later turned out to be producers, son and colleagues, sat at a desk with dark glasses on. He told me the story of *The Curse of the Pink Panther*: how Inspector Clouseau, with the fabled pink diamond, had entered a clinic in Majorca run by the Countess Chandra, and had undergone surgery so extensive that his head would remain bandaged for the whole film: how Herbert Lom, terrified that the world-wide search for Clouseau would unearth him, tampered with the computer selecting a super-sleuth to track down his old enemy, and how the computer thereby picked a complete klutz who wouldn't be able to find a hole in a colander: how the chase spread across Europe till Super Klutz lands (literally) on Chandra's clinic and unmasks Clouseau who has been changed into . . . Roger Moore! We slapped our legs with mirth at the sheer bad taste of the thing: I would play Chandra. 'And,' said Blake in a way that would become familiar, 'you might as well play the other part as well.'

When I got back to London, I found out from my agent Dennis Selinger that the other part was the lead in another film, *The Trail of the Pink Panther*, which would be shot simultaneously, or, as the business puts it, back to back. In this story, a French journalist (me), tries to discover why Clouseau had disappeared (because he was dead, people whispered, Sellers was dead: sssshhh). In my search I interviewed all the people who had been connected with him, from Lom and Bert Kwouk to Graham Stark, Capucine and David Niven. There was a brush with the Mafia (Robert Loggia) and an interview with his ancient father (Richard Mulligan). At each stage there was an opportunity for the interviewee to say, 'I remember when . . .' and then would appear footage from previous films; or, as the antagonists to this procedure called them, out-takes. (The storms over legal wrangles started before the first day of shooting and were to continue long after the film had been released, each party suing the other for hundreds of millions of dollars.)

Filming started at Pinewood Studios. My journalist character was called Marie Jouvet and was French: should I play her with a French accent? No, said Blake, she speaks just like you. Three days into filming, he wandered out into the corridor where I was sitting waiting for my car to take me home.

'It's not really right,' he said, sitting down beside me, his legs stretched out in front of him clothed in regimentally ironed blue jeans. The dark glasses were on again, assistants hovered discreetly in doorways, just within earshot. Like an emperor he was never alone, moving majestically in a scurrying wave of aides and lackeys.

'I 'ad 'oped zat I may 'ave a bash at a French accent,' I said, at which he turned on me, snatched off his shades, eyes alight with the prospect of an expensive palaver.

'That's it,' he cried, snapping his fingers at the shadowy cohort. 'We re-shoot! Everything!' and the ripple rustled through the studio like fire streaking along corn stubble. To my amazement, everyone was delighted at the prospect of the trouble and drama a re-shoot would cause. Like faithful retainers on a huge estate, they had grown to expect and love Blake's idiosyncratic behaviour, often recalling with affection the catastrophic occasion when film units were flying in and out of Hong Kong on a daily basis, while Blake searched for the perfect lift shaft in various hotels. 'You wait till he really gets going,' they chuckled fondly. Blake was clearly revving up for some typically Blake behaviour.

Next door to my dressing-room was Ted Wass, one of the actors from the American series *Soap*, who had been cast as Super-Klutz. He had had a pac-man machine installed and through the walls I could hear the beeps and jingles which denoted successful avoidance of bouncing bombs or munching crocodiles. The English weather depressed him and he didn't trust our drinking water. Majorca was our next location, where Countess Chandra's health spa and plastic surgery centre was perched on a cliff top.

I never got to Majorca. On the way down the news broke that Blake had suddenly tired of Majorca; the rumour had it that he had hired a yacht to use in the film and in which he would live. The crew had been audible, creeping about their duties and irritating Blake, who had ordered everyone off to Valencia, thereby notching up a few more tension points for everyone concerned. In Valencia we were joined by President Reagan's daughter, Patti Davis, who was playing another reporter (bear with me), and who was travelling with a retinue of secret police – Patti, not the reporter. There may have been as many as fourteen of these bodyguards, whose job it was to accompany Patti wherever she went. She had become a keen runner, never happy until she had covered at least five miles a day. Several men ran along behind her, jogging about the sand dunes outside Valencia, guns tucked discreetly in their armpits. When Blake took several of us out to dinner in the town, three extra tables were booked for Patti's men. From Valencia we went on to Nice and David Niven.

I think many people fell in love with Niven at first sight, and I was no exception. He was, by now, quite ill from the motor neurone disease which was to kill him, but he was as charming and funny as could be, although he was filled with drugs and feeling ghastly. As soon as we met at the millionaire's villa which was the location for his home, he drew me aside. 'The thing about this damn disease is that it makes me do everything in extremes. I can't smile, I have hysterics, I can't feel glum without howling.' He then proceeded to tell a wildly funny story about the clinic in America where he underwent tests and had to travel about the hospital holding glass pots of unmentionable lavatorial substances. We clutched each other and yowled with laughter. He tired easily, and was horribly conscious of losing his ability to enunciate clearly. 'G O R - I L L - A,' he would practise before the take. 'Dressed as a gor-ill-a,' but when he said, 'Golilla,' and everyone said, 'Doesn't matter,' it did matter, most dreadfully, to him. His own house on Cap Ferrat was beautifully positioned at the end of a promontory, with pine trees and statues overlooking the sea. Years before, I had whizzed past his house on a speedboat with friends and we had all waved and shouted and held up our champagne glasses like yahoo jet-setters, and the distant figure of Niven had waved back a benediction. Playing his wife in the film, Lady Litton, was Capucine, whose beauty could dislodge boulders. Like several leading ladies I know, she was practical and mothering. Often grand stars bake cakes for the crew and fuss about with glucose and scarves if someone falls ill. Flora Robson knitted socks, Julie Andrews, Blake's wife, fed me delicious little portions of cheese and fruit when she heard I was feeling off-colour. Stories abound of Marlene Dietrich scrubbing floors and Sophia Loren cooking spaghetti. Most leading ladies carry plasters and headache pills, spare hankies and cough drops, safety pins and the address of a man who'll fix your back.

All through the filming in every country ran a sense of unease. Blake was waging a separate gargantuan war with the American studio bosses, often so preoccupied with his next tactical move that scenes that should have been immensely funny went unrehearsed and under-shot. Richard Mulligan was cast as Clouseau's decaying father living in dotty splendour in his vineyards. Blake and his co-writer, his son Geoffrey, had written a scene involving an aged maid and a sheepdog. They had been convulsed in England by *One Man and His Dog* on television. Nowhere in America do they have sheepdogs, and the notion that a dog would respond to a series of whistles made them double up every time they mentioned it. Père Clouseau, whilst explaining to me how his son had been brought up, calls for a glass of wine. The retainer, bent double with age, shuffles on with a tray and glasses and is guided to the table by a sheepdog nipping her ankles in accordance with the whistled instructions from the old man. Blake was sobbing silently as the scene went on, biting his cashmere jersey and wiping his eyes. It was extremely difficult to stifle our own giggles; as soon as the clapper-board sounded, Blake would start writhing with mirth beside the camera, in full view of all the actors. Then suddenly the joke was over and he walked away from the scene, and away into a helicopter. Whispers said he flew back to Gstaad for tea.

There was the saga of the Fuller's Earth. In Countess Chandra's health spa was a mud bath the size of a small swimming pool. It was decided that the mud should be made of the finest Fuller's Earth, usually bought in minute quantities as face-packs. Several tons of the stuff was ordered and flown out to Majorca and, at the sudden change of events, flown back to Pinewood. The combined cost of the earth and the air freight would have financed a short film without difficulty.

Then there was the problem of the barge. Graham Stark played a policeman who had retired from the French Sûreté: my character hunted him down to his retirement home on a boat, and quizzed him about Clouseau. In the script, the barge was on the Seine in Paris, but it could of course be shot anywhere. I forget where it was first set up, but Blake didn't like the location. After Nice, the barge was dressed with window-boxes and fishing rods and set up on the Seine with the Eiffel Tower in the background. Graham and I were dressed and made-up, the lines bubbling out of our mouths. At eight-thirty a.m. Blake arrived in a darkened car, got out wearing sunglasses and walked with ominous speed to the barge. He peered through the viewfinder hanging round his neck, at the barge, at the river, and finally with disbelief at the Eiffel Tower. He strode back to the car looking grim, murmuring an apology and drove away. Stark and I exchanged glances and went to change out of our costumes, while the film crew struck camp and the barge was dismantled again. The third time it was set up was in a canal in Middlesex; a different barge, beautifully attired in pot plants, old bicycles, gang plank, fishing rods and Graham Stark. The unit had been set up, caravans, generators, lunch tents, lights and seventy people, all on their toes. I met Blake as he walked across the field towards the canal, on his face a perfectly inscrutable expression.

'It's wonderful,' I gasped, 'it's perfect! It seems so right, it's exactly how I imagined it.'

He gave me an old-fashioned look, and gazed reluctantly at the barge which sat there offering him untold chances of more

Blakery. Then a smile broke over his face like sunshine on the blade of the guillotine. 'Good,' he said, 'we'll shoot it right here,' and he made me a mock half-bow like a Ruritanian officer. Graham Stark, hearing the news, tottered visibly and for the third time we ran through our scene together.

It was all a strange experience for me. Having been brought up in the almost nursery conditions of previous films, good humour and comradeship at every level, this high-powered, high-financed game unnerved me completely and I felt the cold breeze of standing on the wrong side of the railway tracks. Still, I had the lasting pleasure of being in a fight with Cato, as I crept round Clouseau's flat in search of clues. Bert Kwouk, elegance personified, assumes the role of the manic single-minded manservant like a jacket, facing the fame this part has brought him with amused raised eyebrows. Of theatre, films and television, films are far and away the leaders in madness and fantasy life, wastefulness and ephemeral glory. Small wonder that so many people involved in them seem to be several sandwiches short of a picnic.

Flattered and greedy for free books, I accepted immediately an invitation to become one of the judges of the Booker Prize. ('Has accepted already with unseemly haste,' as one Sunday newspaper put it, rather churlishly I thought.) The other judges were to be professionals: the novelists Nina Bawden and Marina Warner, the critic Jack Lambert and our chairman, Norman St John Stevas. I was there as a lay person, the man in the street, a book buyer and keen reader. As I had been writing regularly for *The Times*, reviewing books for *Punch* and contributing to the *Listener*, as I had already been a judge twice in Monte Carlo (of television film), at Ely (of dogs and babies), for two newspapers (of school magazines and amateur film scripts), at Ramsgate (of beauty queens) and of first novels (the Sinclair Prize for Fiction, chaired by Fay Weldon), I didn't think I was too unlikely a candidate. One daily paper, however, wrote a leader guffawing at the incongruity of my appointment. An actress! Reading books! They just stopped short of writing 'worrying her pretty little head about it!' Norman St John Stevas came in for a bit of stick, too: after all he was only Minister for the Arts.

It's always rather dismal to find how many people are suspicious if you show an interest in more than one thing at a time. Sarah Bernhardt was an accomplished sculptress, Winston Churchill wrote and painted, Bill Oddie is a distinguished ornithologist, actors Callow and Sher write like dreams, and yet here was a national newspaper doubting my ability to read and decide if one book was better written than another, when an actor's life is largely made up of decisions about writing. Heigh ho.

We met for lunch for the first time at Book House in Wandsworth on a swelteringly hot summer day. Martyn Goff was there to steer and guide us and lie doggo. Norman St John Stevas arrived late: somehow the explanation for the delay involved the nearby Huguenot graveyard. 'Are you a Huguenot?' I asked him inanely. Some people are famously Catholic and he is one of them. Why do I feel compelled to make small talk without thinking first? It shouldn't have mattered (I wouldn't mind someone asking me if I were a Buddhist) and I got the religion right, after all. He quite rightly ignored the remark.

We decided we would be an exemplary panel. Martyn Goff warned us of publishers' wiles. Each publisher could submit three books, and later slyly send in a list of more books that may be 'called in'. As this last list had their juiciest authors and the most keenly awaited books on it, there seemed no alternative but to call them in and watch the pile of books mount. The books came at first in dribs and drabs, a fat package with four, then six a week later, then two a day later. Those mornings were thrilling: brand new glossy books, each one potentially *Madame Bovary*. Wherever I went, books came too.

I read in the bath and at the table, putting on make-up, all through the night and in traffic jams. Just as you came to the end of a clutch, another parcel would arrive with ten, with twelve, with sixteen novels spilling out, brilliant dust jackets and intriguing blurbs, errata slips here and there and the odd uncorrected proof. There were, I think, 112 books in all, each clamouring for attention. There were huge generation-spanning sagas and dry, wry, slim, snappy glimpses of senility, Islington dramas, spoofs and spin-offs, dull books, over-written books, taut plots which went plonk when plucked, misty reminiscences and furious marital tiffs – in short, we read a bookshop from wall to wall. When pictures are chosen for the Royal Academy Summer Exhibition, we are led to believe that the selectors spend a full three seconds on each painting. Poor painters! for we were far more generous (I was: but if, after thirty pages and a middle dip and an end read, it hadn't absolutely seized me, I would lay that book aside for later perusal).

We met again with the purpose of establishing a longish short list of about twelve titles, to be shrivelled to six. Only six! Good grief. And of these only one would win. It is of course very difficult to judge one work against another. Is *Nicholas Nickleby* a 'better' book than *Cold Comfort Farm*? Or *Franny and Zooey* superior to *Decline and Fall*? What struck me as excellent about the Booker Prize was that it encouraged the discussion and purchase of books: for a few weeks there was wild speculation, as alternative short-lists were proposed by the literary sections of the papers, and solemn prognoses appeared suggesting probable winners. When our short-list appeared officially (the books' covers photographed hastily on the pavement outside Book House), all hell broke loose. We had actually come up with a very quaint list, yawning with serious omissions which set the literary critics snarling and whining.

Melvyn Bragg collared me at London Weekend Television,

where we were both audience guests in *An Audience with Billy Connolly* (and during which show I nearly had to be dragged out unconscious, I laughed so much).

'What about *Hawksmoor*?' he said irritably. 'How can it not be on your short-list – it's incredible.'

Incredible indeed: and bad luck for Bragg who had prepared a programme about Peter Ackroyd, *Hawksmoor*'s author, so confident was he that the book would win the prize.

In our finite wisdom, and acting as a committee, we had done what any panel has to do to agree; compromised. I'm not sure that the book which won was top of anyone's list: *The Bone People* by Keri Hulme. Books are a matter of taste, and discussing them can be uncomfortable if you disagree. It's hard to go on protecting a book which everyone is mocking, and hard to go on attacking a book which your colleagues are championing as the probable winner. Long before the final showdown (our chairman didn't know that I'd be on stage the night of the prize-giving in a play, and threatened to discount my vote), I had grown sick of the whole thing. The so-called bitchy world of acting was a Brownie's tea party compared with the piranha-infested waters of publishing. I wrote an impassioned letter to plead my case against the winning book, and that night on stage paced about distractedly waiting for the phone calls which would keep me abreast of the final moments of deliberation – none came: and I was told which book had won by a newspaper reporter, in a telephone call asking for my reaction to the winner. The book was an unpopular choice and with the smarting slap of fate that can sting you as you pass, I attracted a lot of the blame ('What can you expect of non-professional critics', etc.). I packaged all the books up, sold them to a second-hand dealer and gave the money to a splendid cause called Books for Development, which supplies textbooks and reference books to the enthusiastic and needy schools of Third World countries.

Chapter Twelve

From Rawalpindi to Gilgit, by road, took two days. ('Can't be true,' said my mother before we left England: 'Jimmy, Rawalpindi to Gilgit, what ... three weeks?' From inside a book my father answered, 'Maybe two and a half weeks. Incredibly tough country.' 'But we rode,' said my mother doubtfully, 'how will you drive? What will you drive on?') The Karakorum Highway, or KKH, was built as a Sino-Pakistan venture, with Chinese workers crossing the borders carrying their Little Red Books, not mingling with the local people, just working all day on the construction of this fantastic road and sleeping at night in separate Chinese compounds. The old route, a faint scar, a rough track in my parents' youth, had been enlarged and made of tarmacadam. In places it had been re-sited, sometimes travelling along the other side of a river or delving through solid rock where before a steep climb and descent was necessary. The land it travelled through had to be seen to be believed; bleak, hostile, rocky, shaly, precipitous, unstable, tree-less and more than once looking like photographs of the moon's surface.

This was the land of the North West Frontier, where as a twenty-one year old my father and his Gurkha soldiers set up pickets. All mahogany-coloured men, my father too, toasted black by relentless wind and sun; all granite men, from nipping up and down several hundred feet twice a day to occupy positions from which they could defend the columns marching far below, living off chapattis and a tot of rum. This was the land of Sir Henry Newbolt's 'He fell among thieves':

He did not hear the monotonous roar that fills
   The ravine where the Yasîn river sullenly flows;
He did not see the starlight on the Laspur hills,
   Or the far Afghan snows.

The Karakorum Highway was the old Silk Road, curving up through the most northern region of Pakistan called Hunza (but the Hunzakuts view themselves as separate from Pakistan), over the Chinese border and curling on round, due east, until finally, thousands of kilometres later, it arrives at Beijing, or Peking. Hunza is surrounded by four different, sometimes sparring, countries: Afghanistan, the USSR, Chinese Turkestan and India. It is marched through by the Karakorum Range, which boasts more high mountains than the Himalayas, into which the Karakorums collide at their south-eastern end. It is wild, wild country and I was there by the purest and most unexpected good fortune.

One of the charities with which I was connected was called GAP – Gap Activity Projects. This was an organization which arranged for school-leavers to do something interesting and useful in the year before they went on to further training or university. Hatched at Wellington College and headed by Wellington's Senior English Master, Peter Willey, one of the expeditions was to discover the effects of the Ismaili religion on the remote valleys of Hunza. Eleven of us made up the group: Willey, Margaret Hutton, an Australian nurse, Barbara Kleiner, a photographer and I were the grown-ups (as it were). The youthful members were four ex-Wellington boys: David Nicholas, Jan Altink, Gordon Hogarth and Richard Winstanley. Two young men from quite different backgrounds, suggested to GAP by Operation Drake and coming from Plaistow, were Ray Oram and Steve Hennessy; and Jamie, my own Jamie came too, at fourteen easily the youngest of the party. We all travelled separately in small groups to Pakistan, and Jan, Barbara, Dave and Gordon went on ahead to the Swat Valley. The rest of us converged on the Hamid household in Rawalpindi. Hassan Hamid had been at Wellington and his parents, General and the Begum Hamid, housed four of us with the greatest hospitality and kindness for two nights when we arrived. Their garden had guava, pistachio and avocado trees, tuberoses and jasmine, zinnias, roses, mynah birds and hoopoes.

We ate and slept and sat for several hours at the Pakistan Touring Development Corporation to see if we would be lucky enough to get permits to visit all our chosen valleys. I had never heard of Shimshal before I arrived in Rawalpindi. Even when we finally prised our permit out of the official's grasp it was just another name to add to the list of valleys: magical names of Chitral and Swat, Ishkoman, Yasîn and Hunza.

The official scratched his ribs and moved a 7-Up bottle on to another pile of papers which fluttered under the fan. 'You will see that you may not go beyond the Passu Bridge.' We nodded, looking intelligent; 'And you will see that you may visit Shimshal.' We nodded again like toy alsatians in rear windows.

Outside the temperature ticked over 120 degrees and sweat ran down my throat and chest into my baggy Pakistan breeks.

'Shimshal!' said Peter Willey. 'How splendid. Vair important that we go there. It was used by the former Mirs of Hunza as a prison settlement; too difficult for a man to escape on his own.' As the leader of our party, it was up to him to decide which of us would go where. At once, but silently, I earmarked Shimshal as my goal.

We set off early in the morning from Rawalpindi, piling our kit-bags and equipment on to the top of a minivan which was driven by a weary looking fellow called Ghulam Nabib, the slave of the prophet. Ray Oram at once nicknamed him Tom. Tom had a red beard and red hair, dyed with henna which signified that he had made his Hadj, had visited Mecca. He had pale eyes and only smiled once, when the vehicle got stuck in a flash flood, and we all got out to push. We suspected that he was sustaining himself on bhang, the marijuana that grew like wild nettles beside the road and upon which the cattle grazed most peacefully. Certainly his driving was hair-raising, as often the KKH could accommodate only one car, and we would reverse at tremendous speed round rocky corners, or worse still, inch past the oncoming car with our wheels scuttering on the loose shale which sprayed down the hundred-foot escarpments beside us.

We had lunch in Abbottabad, where Ælene was born. Monsoon rain poured down as we dashed into a restaurant called the Mona Lisa, where the lavatory chain didn't pull but water poured unexpectedly from another tap, sluicing the floor with all that had gone before. There was an English church, neat roads and well-made bungalows. Our guide book said, 'Abbottabad is full of soldiers,' and there were barracks everywhere. We had come through camel trains, Mogul ruins, an animal fair and vast poverty-stricken Afghan refugee settlements. Sometimes we would pass a local bus, squashed full with people, the bonnet and sides beautifully decorated with beaten silver and painted with vivid flowers.

After Abbottabad, the scenery changed to brilliant green paddy fields, high wooded hills and rushing mountain streams. The road grew steeper and steeper, the gorge grew narrower and suddenly the little tributary our road followed joined the huge grey Indus and we turned north to Besham. We reached the rest house at six-thirty in the evening, when a grey mist hung over the river and the air was filled with the soft roar of the slate-filled Indus. Tom the driver slept like a dead man on a charpoy on the veranda, waking in a vengeful mood the next day. We hurtled onwards through monsoon rain, which brought down rockfalls (landslides are an everyday event out there), and searing heat, collecting at an arranged meeting-point the four members of our party who had returned from

Swat and Chitral. Jan was running a high temperature and was the first to succumb to the various illnesses which were to smite us all (except Jamie). We reached Gilgit late at night, screeching into the town on three wheels, and kicking up gravel in front of the Chinar Inn (chinar means plane tree). Those of us well enough ate a good rice-based supper in a lofty fan-cooled dining-room; we would spend two days in Gilgit before journeying on to Upper Hunza.

When the day came, the sky was so brilliantly blue and the mountains so blazingly close and the flowers so searingly bright, it was as though we were peering into a furnace, or somehow seeing with a new kind of three-D vision. Gilgit, which once had a British Residency, had a polo ground (polo started somewhere nearby, with severed heads being whacked about, or goats, or something equally ghastly – as players the Pakistanis are lethally good), a Government school, library, banks, shops and bazaars where I bought metres of cream-coloured silk. It also has an airport, but the small airplanes experience extreme difficulty in navigating the mountain ranges, and flights are sometimes delayed for a week. We completed our research as far as it went: how many teachers, what subjects, what medical facilities, noting down everything piously in exercise books. We were shown round by Group Captain Shah Khan whose son Asif was to continue with us on our journey as a guide and interpreter.

We set off for our main camp at Aliabad, feeling that until we were actually sleeping under canvas we weren't on a proper expedition. At every mile signs of civilization died away. We nicknamed the road to Aliabad the Valley of Death, falling silent as Asif pointed out Blood Rock where on the old Silk Road camel trains (which had taken the golden road from Samarkand) were regularly swept to their death as gales howled down rocky valleys gathering speed at every twist and turn. In a flat stony valley the two jeeps which now transported us stopped. We all got out. 'Your first view of Rakaposhi,' said

Asif and there she was, white snow against a navy blue sky, 25,500 feet high with elevations racing straight to the summit from the side of the road. Aliabad was the other side of the mountain, and we began to notice how the moonscape was scarred with neat terraces and irrigation canals, bringing water from the glaciers to the garden valleys of Hunza.

There were apples and apricots, mulberries, vines, fields of peas and beans, wheat swaying in stone-walled fields, hollyhocks and daisies. Exactly where water was came greenery and life, softening the scabby hillsides and providing food and shade for the people; and where water stopped, the wilderness was an inch away. Our camp site was in an apple orchard, neat grey tents already erected with charpoys inside, wooden campbeds slatted with canvas and infested with fleas. There was a brick cookhouse which smelt of kerosene, a wash-house with a row of basins leaking grey water and some lavatories which defy description. But across the valley was Rakaposhi, and at night you could hear apples plopping down into the grass under the bright stars.

The drinking of alcohol is not permitted in Pakistan, being a strict Muslim country, but in Hunza they consider themselves apart from such laws. Hunza pani, which means Hunza water, is a sort of 120° proof white spirit, based on mulberries. It is brewed in secret and drunk in stealth. When we first arrived in Aliabad, I begged Asif to track some down, but every source had dried up, or the brewer was away in the pastures. Finally, one evening, as I drove back to Gilgit in the jeep with Asif, he said, 'What good fortune! Here's my friend: we'll give him a lift.' The friend was walking jauntily, swinging a petrol can in the twilight. After exchanging pleasantries, I saw the friend pat his petrol can and they both laughed. Asif's eyes glittered. 'We'll have a drink with this good man. His home is not far from here; the road goes right by his land.' We drank Hunza pani in a house in a valley, with a hurricane lamp and a large dish of walnuts, which contained just as many cockroaches as it did nuts. Our driver sat in the corner with a glass of water, occasionally peeping through the shutters as our behaviour grew livelier and voices louder. The hangover I had the next day weakens me just to remember it.

Wherever you go in the Indian sub-continent the first question you ask is, 'What is the water like?' In Aliabad, I must report, the water was not good. Despite our sterilizing tablets and the camouflage of orange-tasting powder and boiling, the water began to take its toll. It was greyish-green and had flowed in open canals or drains through two villages before it reached our water supply. By day we would continue with our research (how many goats and chickens? how many people? how old?), by night we clutched our stomachs and sweated through minor forms of dysentery, with hepatitis waiting to pounce. Peter Willey was ill, Richard was ill, Dave and Jan were losing weight and running high temperatures. 'What do we do, Asif?' I said, sitting pastily at the table near an old chapatti and a bottle of Dettol. None of our English drugs seemed to work. He disappeared and returned fifteen minutes later with two dark green lumpy pills, each the size of a marrow-fat pea. I ate them both: they were gritty and spinachy and tasted of the smell of dead chrysanthemum vase-water. 'Further up the valley the water is clean,' said Asif. 'There is a small village fed by a fresh spring, and the village has a hotel.' (He pronounced it 'hotle'.) 'I think you must leave here.' Babs Kleiner and I decided to see the village the next day, leaving behind our frail team to measure the forts at Baltit and Altit, and to pick up garnets which appeared in the dust like pebbles.

Gulmit was extraordinary, even by Hunza's standards. The village was so small you hardly knew you had arrived. The hotel was a low white stone building with wooden verandas and a charming garden filled with fruit trees. It had once been a private house (Asif's family house, although he was too modest to tell us straight away). There were empty little square rooms with charpoys, a cold-water shower and sweet crystal clear water in the taps. I knew we would get well there. In the garden, taking tea, were two middle-aged English women, schoolteachers from London, in stout walking shoes and travel-battered clothes. There was the sound of distant harvesting, wheat being scythed and stacked, ready to be trodden down by oxen harnessed to a beam, who would trundle slowly round a central pivot, tramping the grain from the chaff. We moved camp a day later.

'I thought you were joking,' said Ray Oram, 'when you showed us your drawing of the mountains here,' and they did indeed look like a cartoon picture. They were the Passu Cathedrals, a fantastic jagged pile of pinnacles and towers, each needle-sharp against the sky, changing colour and contour as the light moved from east to west. Beneath them lay the forbidden Passu bridge and beyond them the frontier with China, still closed and impassable.

'Do people climb the Cathedrals?' I asked Asif and he laughed in amazement.

'They are just tiny hills, no one bothers with them.'

Asif's elder brother, Shere Khan (like the tiger), was a climber and accompanied Reinhold Messner in expeditions of blood-chilling daring. The Khan family was of royal blood. They were cousins of the Mir of Hunza, who had entertained us all in his palace at Karimabad, a town re-named to honour the Aga Khan, the spiritual leader of the Ismaili community.

In Gulmit, we found our strength and health, walking each day to tiny villages to ask our questions. (What do you eat? How old is the head villager? Where is the dispensary?) People were extraordinarily polite and hospitable, often begging us to come in and honour their homes, insisting we share with them some porridge or bread. It was so different from faraway Rawalpindi and Karachi, where women were veiled and ignored. Here they wore bright clothes, small embroidered pillbox hats, and the veils they wore hung down behind, never obscuring their faces. They all seemed to be grinning at us, infectious laughter bubbling out, and their behaviour was affectionate and forward. I had brought out all sorts of small presents, hair clips and jewellery and coins commemorating the Prince and Princess of Wales's wedding. One village woman, to whom I had given a butterfly pendant, pinched my arm. 'Too fat,' she said, then looking at the pendant. 'When I look at this, I shall see you; I will wear it when I die,' and roared with laughter, as her words were translated for me. The women examined my hands with interest, patting and stroking them. 'So soft! So white!' and in comparison with their calloused hard-working farmers' paws, my hands looked pappy-soft and useless. But in their brown sunburnt faces often shone bright green or blue eyes, and the skin of the arms which had been covered was often as pale as ours and often freckled. There were everyday stories of the fairy folk, who had blonde hair and blue eyes, who had lived in the high summer pastures and stole away young goatherds, keeping them for a year and feeding them on milk. The fairies spoke in the rustling poplar trees, and the local soothsayer, crazed with smoke from juniper twigs, would gibber in fairy language and relay fairy messages. Alexander the Great's armies had moved through these regions thousands of years ago – were these the pale-skinned, blue-eyed descendants of those men?

In each valley they spoke an entirely different unconnected language, as different as Danish, Spanish and English. Wakhan was spoken in Gulmit; two miles away at Shishkat, the language was Burushaski. Raja Bahadur Khan, Raja Sahib, took me with him to visit his lands of Shishkat. A few years before a massive avalanche of rocks and ice had sliced through the village and destroyed part of the KKH and the treasured Friendship Bridge which signified unity between China and Pakistan. Raja Sahib had tried to construct a temporary bridge but that too had been swept away, and the approach to the village was over a mile-long tumble of stones and rubble, under which lay the bodies of a man and two young girls who had been tending cattle.

Shishkat used to be called Nazimabad after Raja Sahib's grandfather, a former Mir of Hunza. We sat together on the veranda of his old house, on the square wooden seat where he had sat as a boy beside his father and listened to the villagers' problems. Sweet green apples hung on the trees, and the flat roofs and the village houses were orange with drying apricots. Apricots, which have to be eaten with their kernels, form the staple diet of Hunzakuts, eaten fresh in season, and in winter dried and pounded into a sort of flour mixed with wheat. They are famed for their size and taste but most of them are exported to the Chinese. Shishkat was less slapdash than Gulmit, each house having a carefully tended garden filled with flowers, string beans, cucumbers and tomatoes. The wind always blows; the white seams in the surrounding hills are filled with aquamarines.

A yak hair rug was spread out beside a stream and we were given tea, very strong and sweet. I told Raja Sahib of my desire to go to Shimshal. He paled and clutched my arm. 'I beg you not to go, you will die.'

'Asif says I will be able to manage the journey.'

He rubbed his plump hands over his face, and addressed me earnestly. 'I walked to Shimshal once. As you know, I collect precious and semi-precious stones and there are emeralds in those dreadful valleys. We stumbled and crawled – there were bridges I can't describe – it never ended, there was no way back. When we got to Shimshal I sent a message to the Mir asking him for his helicopter to collect me. The messenger was gone two, three days, and each night I dreamed of those paths, those bridges. I beg you, do not go to Shimshal.' He looked at me imploringly, but our plans had been decided; we were to set off in two days' time.

Preparations were made. Peter Willey was not well enough, and in any case, he walked with a limp from a war wound: the fifty-two-mile journey to Shimshal was, in the most optimistic expectations, perilous. Babs Kleiner was still not strong enough, and it was decided that only three of us would attempt the week-long trip – Gordon Hogarth, Ray Oram and I. Asif would lead us, and we would have four porters, Shimshali men who made the journey regularly. First we had to pass the 'Shimshal Bridge' test, as Asif put it. Not far from Gulmit, a tiny weedy strand-of-wire bridge stretched a hundred yards across a wide gorge. At every large pace, a piece of wood had been stuck into the wire to make treads – thin wobbly wires were handrails. We must go across it twice. We did, and I thought of Raja Sahib all the way. It was not too bad, it was O K, it was actually pretty safe! We clapped each other on the back: Shimshal would be a piece of cake.

At the hotel was a fourteen-year-old boy, Ghulam Shah, the slave of Shah, who worked for the Shah family. He had been brought over from Shimshal when he was nine to go into service, and had never returned. His nickname was Shimshali, and he was wicked. 'Hey! Shcmz!' he would call to Jamie, buzzing an apple at him. 'Shcmz!' He was bright and sulky, inquisitive and elusive. It was agreed that Shimshali would come with us to visit his mother and his brothers and sisters.

'You look a scruff, Shimshali, you need a haircut. You must make your mother proud of you.' I was the company hair-dresser and we managed to trap Shimshali on the veranda, me brandishing scissors and Babs holding the tilly lamp. He became quite serious at once: he wanted it to look – so – not like Ray's (too short, ugh!), not long there, but this bit off and these bits left longish – in fact, behaving just like every man whose hair I have cut. We gave him a handmirror and he watched every snip, crooning with mock-anguish and making monkey noises. When I had finished, he peered at his reflection with a furious smile and rushed away into the darkness, making sounds like a motorbike.

I went round to see Raja Sahib the night before we left. He was sitting on the balcony with gemstones on the table in front of him. ' "In such a night as this when the sweet wind did gently kiss the trees and they did make no noise",' he said, putting down his magnifying glass. 'So you have decided to go. I love Shakespeare. I used to be able to quote long passages but it is a long time since I've seen it written down. Don't be afraid to call for the Mir's helicopter. The bridges: the bridges.'

He had made me feel very uneasy about the whole venture, particularly when there was talk that we should have to spend the whole journey roped together for fear of losing anyone who stumbled.

'What *is* it like, Asif?'

'It's fine, not hard. You walk well, there is no problem.'

We would set off at four o'clock in the morning so we could get many miles behind us before the heat and wind exhausted us. We had a farewell supper all together the night before, all feeling extra fond of each other, everyone giving advice. I was rather fierce with Jamie about leaving his watch out on the veranda where the dew would get it; better fierce than howling, as I suddenly thought I may never see him again. At the last minute, the hotel cook Karim decided he couldn't do without Shimshali, who would have to stay behind doing menial tasks instead of seeing his mother for the first time in five years. Shimshali disappeared and refused to come to say goodbye. Asif hunted him down outside the back of the kitchen; when he returned, he was carrying a little bundle. 'Sweets,' he said, 'from Shimshali for his mother.'

'A mile in Shimshal is three miles anywhere else,' goes the saying. We crossed a metal bridge, which would carry vehicles if there had been a surface on the steel crossbars, and set off due east into the rising run. At once we started to climb, very steeply it seemed to me. 'Ho!' I called out to the porters, 'slowly,' and I patted my chest to show how quickly I became breathless, and pointed at my legs to show how unfit I was compared with them. They laughed and nodded: from then on, although the pace seemed relentless, it was obvious that they were holding back for the Memsahib (who refused to carry a rucksack. I don't think I could have made the first hill with so much as an extra handkerchief). We were travelling as light as possible: no spare clothes, just a toothbrush, comb, tin of Vaseline, Deep Heat treatment for sprains, a pot of Marmite, and a bottle of Rive Gauche (for me). Notebooks, cameras, torches, sleeping bags, penknives, sewing kit (for me), and a jersey for the glacier. The porters carried the world: cooking utensils and provisions, water (we each had a bottle at our waist), firewood.

'We carry firewood? And water?'

'No wood, no water on the way to Shimshal,' said Hyder Ali, the cook. He wore a western T-shirt advertising some rum night-club and had a face like an apprentice Walter Matthau. Our porters were so lean and tough that they did the whole journey like a stroll through Kensington Gardens, in hopeless plastic shoes with flapping soles and no bootlaces. I had got hold of some very good Austrian boots, and I wore two pairs of socks with powder in between each to stop blisters. Gordon had come to grips with a pair of Army boots, so gnarled and wooden looking you couldn't tell if his feet were in them or not. He was going to join the Army: Ray was too. Potential officer and tough squaddy, chalk and cheese they were and both nineteen, watching each other with critical eyes.

The path, sometimes three feet wide, sometimes non-exist-ent, was appalling. You could never take your eyes off your feet, as a false step could send you hurtling down to the sullen Shimshal river; loose scree and stones turned into vast boulders; huge rocks overhung the track forcing you to step along the edge of precipices, or inch your way, face inwards, crab-like to the next corner. On each side the mountains reared up and we were walking down a steep, ever-narrowing gorge, which twisted its bony way ahead of us, treeless, grassless, with the wind hurling down, and hot dust cracking our lips. Sometimes we had to climb down to the river's edge, searching out footholds and handholds; and no sooner had we got down than we started up again, eyes screwed up to try and see the path. Sometimes we took an hour to travel only a short distance, hauling ourselves up sheer walls and creeping across loose rocks. We stopped now and then for water, and occasionally a brew of chai, tea made with powdered milk, sugar and tea leaves boiled together in a tin can, dark brown and delicious. By midday, a tight pain came across my chest and down my left arm. My left hand swelled up like a rubber glove and I felt dreadful.

'Not far to go,' said Asif, 'soon we shall stop.'

'Asif, you have been on this terrible path before. How did you think I would find it easy?'

A faraway look came into his eyes. 'I have never been to Shimshal,' he said.

One of Raja Sahib's bridges appeared. It was two planks wide and about twenty feet long. Rough bolts winched it together and the many gaps had been stuffed with small stones and flat rocks. It tilted to one side, ready to throw you sixty feet down to the river. There were no handrails. I sat down. 'I can't go over that.' My arm hurt and my head was swimming. Hyder Ali took my hand, indicating that I should put my feet where he had put his; rather like leading a hooded horse into the starting gate, he took me carefully across the bridge and patted my hand. The boys were braver and didn't seem to care. By now I thought I had had a heart attack. 'Will you know what to do,' I said, 'banging the chest and mouth-to-mouth?' But we had reached Shams and the walking part of the day was over.

Shams was a square stone hut about five feet high, with one door, no windows and a hole in the roof to let the smoke out. We would all sleep together in there like cattle, huddled round the embers of the fire where our soup had been cooked. I lay on a sleeping bag till my feeling of death passed, then joined the others outside, sitting on the ground, whittling away at sticks, sometimes singing as the afternoon heat died down. We would all be asleep at eight as we must always beat the sunrise. That night, packed like sardines on the floor, I could feel a fever getting hold of me, I was on fire. Hearing me thrashing about, Asif said, 'Take your sleeping bag outside and cool down.' So I slept on the bare stony ground beside the hut, with the wind blowing round me and the stars shining, nine thousand feet up on the backbone of the earth. By the time Hyder Ali got up to put the can of water on the fire for tea at four-thirty, the fever had gone.

How soon normality melts away, and new normality replaces it! Cleaning teeth and washing in half a mug of water, spreading a few drops over your face and hands, scrubbing paler patches in dark grimy sweaty foreheads; rubbing Vaseline on eyes and lips and, most important, on boots to keep them supple; shaking out and tidying your bedroll or rucksack, folding filthy socks neatly at the end of the day. I carefully stitched on buttons and darned rips in shirts. Weeny quantities of Marmite were spread on chapattis (good flour going: but the Shimshal flour on our return journey was full of earth and tasted horrible). We talked about love, death and the universe, and how much we would like to drink some cold lager (ice-cold in Alex was right). We thought of things we'd most like to eat, our ideas growing less and less ambitious until we agreed that the favourite was cold baked beans straight from the tin. When you walk on and on, left, right, left, right, songs and sayings joggle and jingle in your brain, meaningless phrases become catchwords. If one of us called out, 'Quite frankly m'dear . . .' another must respond, 'Ah don't G I V E a damn.'

On the second day the chai stop was beside a small clear spring, trickling into a basin-sized puddle which was as clear and bright as ice. We lay on our stomachs and drank like dogs. Beside the spring grew a small industrious wild rose, its pink flowers nodding in the dusty air, all on its own. We saw three huge crows or ravens, which uttered strangled croaks before they wheeled away with motionless wings, carried on thermals ahead of us to Shimshal. We turned a corner and came to a strange sight – no path, just a huge grey slope of scree like a vast slag-heap. By now, we were all well-practised in using our sticks or staves. 'In Shimshal,' goes the saying, 'a man's staff is his brother.' We never took a step without the help of the stick; it propelled you, balanced you, tested the ground for you. On the slag-heap slope we leaned inwards towards the hill, the stick angled at ninety degrees. Each step you took sank and slipped. We looked like ants. Although it was easier to walk on than on boulders, a stumble would have meant a headlong hurtle gathering impetus to the precipice at the bottom. At the end of the scree slope, two miles further on, we descended one at a time, leaning right back across our staff, taking huge leaping steps, each of which slid another four foot, so each pace was about fifteen foot at twenty miles an hour. Like being on a big dipper, you had to yell. Even the porters yelled, and everyone applauded each other at the bottom. That night was at Ziarat, the shrine, where prayer flags fluttered above bones of sacrificed hens and goats. Both boys looked ill and were getting thinner each minute.

On the third day we crossed a glacier, blue ice in impossible crevices, at the top of a two-hour climb straight upwards, rising two feet every step like crawling up the Empire State Building. The glacier was cool, the air was fresh and the sun scorched down and Hyder Ali did a dance which looked like a Highland Reel while we clapped time. When he stopped, he coughed dreadfully. His thumb, which he had cut almost to the bone on the first day, had gone septic. He had rubbed the open gash in earth and now it was hugely swollen and so gruesome that I couldn't get it properly clean. We only had Germolene; on it went, bandaged up, hope for the best. One of our young porters was a Shimshal schoolmaster; on top of all the things he was carrying he had tied a mattress which he was taking home. Everything that goes in or out of Shimshal goes on a man's back. He smiled ceaselessly, never complaining about his burden.

One last hill and we saw Shimshal: a long broad valley, full of crops and grass, the village on two levels, above and below a cliff, painted stone houses, a handsome Jamat Khana, the mosque, with coloured glass windows and an arched gateway. No roads; there are no wheeled vehicles in Shimshal, not even wagons. We plodded down from the mountains, speechless with fatigue, almost unable to celebrate. An advance party had been sent to meet Asif, a prince of royal blood, the first member of royalty to visit the village for many years.

We were led with some ceremony to the schoolteacher's cottage where we would stay. There were two rooms only, each about ten foot square. Asif was led ahead into one room and sat on the bed, cross-legged, so he would be above the villagers who came to pay their respects and tell him Shimshal's news and problems. The room filled up, the windows were black with jostling faces. A sort of porridge was brought, tremendously slimy with unidentifiable gobbets in it. The boys were white and waved it away, and I only managed one mouthful. The villagers sang a song. 'They want you to sing back, as visitors,' said Asif, so I sang it back, a lovely verse and chorus, rather like 'Molly Malone'. They listened with rapt attention, and at the end they went, 'A-aaah!' and smiled and nodded. That night as I got into bed, the village stood at the door and window and watched my every move.

Next day, the only day in Shimshal, a message was brought to say Hyder Ali had pneumonia and would I go and cure him. I took the Deep Heat ointment and a couple of aspirin, and was led to his house. Larger than Sham's but built in the same way, it was a square around a fire, with the cooking pots stashed neatly, the raised dais where visitors would sit, the part where the animals would live in the winter, the centre roof hole instead of chimney. It was very dark, and kippered with smoke of ages. Hyder Ali's wife was making bread, the children playing round her skirts. Hyder Ali looked ghastly, greyish in colour and with a rumbling rattling wheeze when he breathed. He was gloomy and didn't even try to pretend to be his clownish self. I gave him the pills and, putting him by the fire, rubbed Deep Heat into his back and chest, saying confidently, 'You're getting better now.' The house had filled with silent onlookers, the fire crackled, there was the slap and pat of the wife making dough, and the wind above us whined and whistled. Time stood still just then, and we had always been there, watching and rubbing, playing and cooking, wheezing and murmuring. Then it was all over, and Hyder Ali beamed at me, looking like a villain again. I think it was his faith that made him whole.

We did our research: a hundred houses, a thousand cows, seven hundred yaks and five chickens. Five! No explanation was given for the lack of chickens. No shops, no roads, two schools, no instances of cancer, no drinking of tea or Hunza pani, the local mulberry gin, no smoking. No police; any disputes were settled by the village council. There was a chronic shortage of books in the school, only a few magazines and pamphlets, but they were kept like treasures.

Shimshali's mother was not here. She had gone with his sisters to the high pastures for the yaks' summer grazing. The sweets were delivered to an elder brother, who looked as though he had forgotten Ghulam Shah's name altogether. When we left early in the morning, the head man brought his favourite yak, Yashgar, to carry the Memsahib the seven miles along the valley to the foot of the glacier. When I dismounted he fed us on the cold goat and chapattis he had tied to Yashgar's shoulders. As we walked away, he stood in a position of salute; behind him, twin rainbows soared into the stormy sky above Shimshal, and rain pelted down. 'Shimshal weeps to see you go,' said Hyder Ali.

*

The journey back was, of course, easier. We could recognize different parts of the route, the climbs seemed easier. Ray had got a new song, 'The sun always shi-ines down in my rainbow valley', and we strode along. I crossed the bridges without help, we ran out of sugar which Ray had been devouring to keep up his energy; Gordon again refused to be carried over part of the river to keep his boots dry. Leather boots were a luxury, it was the boots the men respected, but Hogarth strode into the swirling rapids like St Christopher, muttering, 'Damned if I'll be carried across like a woman.'

'Suits me,' said Ray Oram, Oram-Sahib. Like Gareth Hunt he made up his own language. '*Katanga guana*, woman sahib!' and he folded his arms like an emperor and pretended to whip the porters. 'Get on, toe rags.' They had got the measure of Ray and they were always fooling about, racing each other up and down rocks, shooing him away from the sugar. We had run out of powdered coffee on the journey out, but now Ray took a sachet from his hatband that he had saved specially for me. '*Katanga guana*, woman sahib, who says I'm not a gentleman.' Ray was the squaddy for whom Kipling wrote 'Gunga Din'. Two hundred miles due south, beyond the great mass of Distaghil, looming at 27,000 feet, was Srinagar. It was all Kashmir, now irrevocably divided between Pakistan and India. It was all my home.

Back at Gulmit, we tottered into the hotel to be greeted by the others. Hassam Shah, the cook who enjoyed his Hunza pani, grudgingly boiled me a bucket of water. I put the bucket of hot water on the duckboards in the bathroom: through the window I could see two tiny children dawdling through the orchard, tending seven docile cows. It was the best bath of my life. First, hair and face, sweat and dust sluiced out, then the same water for the body and finally, when the water was Limpopo-coloured, feet.

There was great excitement. The next morning the frontier

between China and Pakistan was to be opened at the Khunjerab Pass, and we were doubling and trebling up in bedrooms to make room for all the officials who had travelled up from Islamabad. No foreigners would be allowed to watch this historic event. Asif, knowing how keen I was to go, introduced me to the customs men, who had made their camp in the dining-room, with a signpost on a stand saying, CUSTOMS – THIS WAY in English. They were in a quandary: they had got uniforms but the gold braid and medals were not attached. I took my sewing kit and sat on the floor, sewing on epaulettes and badges by candlelight, a humble supplicant. They produced a bottle of whisky that they had confiscated at the airport, and we drank it out of mugs. 'Prove you are a journalist,' said the senior officer. 'Show us your card.' I trotted off to collect my Equity card, as I didn't belong to any press union. 'This means I'm allowed to act as a journalist: I write for *The Times*. It will be big news in one of the world's greatest papers.' But it didn't work. We heard them leaving at five o'clock the next morning as we started to pack to return to Rawalpindi and Karachi and, finally, England.

Chapter Thirteen

That Christmas, the Christmas after Hunza, there was a card with writing which I recognized immediately, although I had only seen it once before. 'How are you?' it said inside. It was from Stephen Barlow. Janie Carr and I were sitting at the kitchen table, undoing the mail, and she said, 'That marriage must be on the rocks. You mark my words, something will come of this.'

'What nonsense,' I said, 'don't be silly.' But I was absurdly pleased that he had bothered to write.

Dear Janie: as wise and as loyal a friend as anyone could hope to have. I have ended up not writing at all about my nearest and dearest. It is as if they are too important to be included in anything as ordinary as a series of recollections. I don't know how to describe my parents, my sister, my son. If I did, I would fudge it; but it's also rather comforting to know that probably we all feel like that, which is why there are a thousand records each year dedicated to 'the best mum in the world', the words hardly ever changing, and why obituaries use the adjective 'beloved', which we all recognize, respect and understand. People glimpsed or met once are easier to describe, like a painting seen in a gallery, and the impression lasts vividly over the years, occasionally taken down from the shelf and handed round for general inspection before being put back carefully in its place.

As I write, the Archbishop of Canterbury's special envoy, Terry Waite, is still in captivity; but he was there at the drinks party in London, held to wish us well on our trip to Hunza. Very tall and bearded, he was an impressive figure, the words 'gentle giant' immediately springing to mind. He wandered about talking to everyone; when he came to me, we discussed travel in general and the proposed trip in particular. 'When you come back, would you like to meet the Archbishop? We shall arrange a lunch,' he said; but although I have since met the Archbishop several times, I never saw Terry Waite again.

Very different and equally disturbing was the unfinished story of Lord Lucan. I sat next to him at a dinner party and he talked a great deal about my son Jamie and his education. Two or three weeks later, three of us dined together: Dominic Elwes, 'Lucky' Lucan and I. It was a casual occasion, arranged at the last minute. 'Are you doing anything for supper tonight?' and we booked a table at the Rib Room in the Carlton Towers Hotel on Sloane Street. We were all in rather high spirits. Dominic, a very funny man at the best of times, was in towering good humour and we spent the meal deciding who should be what in a hastily proposed pantomime to be held for charity. Lucky was assigned the task of asking Princess Margaret to play the lead role, a job which he accepted with confidence, and, just as quickly as we had pounced on the whole idea at the beginning of the evening, we dropped it at the end.

A week later, flying in from Bonn, I read, 'Lucan nanny murdered' in the evening papers. That night, I was woken by the telephone at about two o'clock. Still half asleep, I couldn't find the light switch in the drawing-room. I stood shivering in the dark, listening in terror to Dominic who was weeping and incoherent. It seemed that he had been taken by the police to the scene of the murder and made to look at the gruesome evidence, enough to unhinge anyone's mind. No one knew where Lucan had gone or quite what had happened. Only a few months later, bowed down by the dreadful aftermath, Dominic took his own life, leaving me to keep bright the memory of at least one immensely happy evening, when death and destruction were still strangers.

Grasping Mohammed Ali's arm for a photograph and finding his biceps were the size of a whole human being; steering my car down Holland Park Avenue with Sir Robin Day singing 'My Old Man said follow the Van' beside me; putting elastic bands round George Michael's elbows before a Wogan show, so that his sleeves wouldn't descend when he danced; rushing to say to Cliff Richard, 'I think you're marvellous,' only to hear him say it first to me (and I didn't have time to tell him about the tennis racket and 'Livin' Doll'); and hearing Frank Sinatra sing! Not at a concert; at a private party. Soon after we had finished filming the Bond film, Cubby Broccoli threw a party to celebrate one of Sinatra's visits. It was held at Tiberio's, a restaurant in Mayfair with crisp little bay trees outside and opulent luxury inside of high-class Italian elegance. The downstairs had been cordoned off and we were scrutinized discreetly as we were allowed in. I can't think how many people were there, but Sinatra siphoned one's attention away from everything else, a magnetic field of aura and charisma; wherever he was, was a knot of attention and energy. I suppose we ate a buffet supper and drank delicious wine; at any rate, at some stage someone was brave enough to say, 'Will you sing for us, Frank?' At once, there was a clamour, swelling to a roar when he shook his head and put up protesting hands. 'Oh, Frank, P L E A S E! Frank *do*!' until, motioning us to pipe down, he said, 'Well, I just happen to have my pianist here, so if there's a piano . . .' There was, and there was a microphone like magic, just as he liked it, and there was sheet music in his pianist's case; we pulled up chairs and pushed back tables, cramming ourselves in like cubs around a campfire. He poured a whisky (no, he didn't: he put out his hand and a drink appeared, just as he liked it; and a cigarette arrived lit and just so between his fingers), and half sipping, half smoking, he began, 'It's quarter to three, there's no one in the place 'cept you and me . . .' The extreme familiarity of his voice and the electric focus of his face loaded the room with brilliance, leaving me with the sharpest memory of that haze, that half light, those rapt faces, that night when Sinatra sang.

Sheridan Morley is not strictly speaking a relation of mine, but as his father Robert is a cousin of my cousins, the Neale twins, we claim kinship whenever it suits us. He wrote to me in February 1983, starting the letter, 'Now is the time for our family to stick together,' so I knew something good was brewing. He enclosed a script, 'not exactly a musical or a play', which he had assembled and written, which was a compilation of songs and two-handed scenes from Noël Coward's plays. It was called *Noël and Gertie*; there were to be two Noëls and two Gerties; one singing and one acting each character. Dan Crawford, who ran the King's Head in Islington, wanted to put it on for the month of May. Would I play the acting Gertie?

If I was to find out whether the demon stage fright had left me, there was no better place to discover than at the King's Head. Being a pub theatre, it held only about 150 people, so if I went wildly wrong or started to howl like a wolf, I could afford to buy them all a drink (and pay in pounds, shillings and pence, as Dan had a lofty disregard for decimal coinage). Simon Cadell would act Noël Coward; the singing parts would be taken by David McAlister and Gillian Bevan, with the legendary William Blezard at the piano. The narration would be spoken by Sheridan, and, occasionally, Martin Tickner. I said yes (and felt my pulse as I said it; quite quiet and normal).

We rehearsed in an upstairs room of a disused pub not far from Sadler's Wells. Whoever arrived first lit the coal fire, shovelling out nuggets with a tablespoon from a plastic bucket. The windows were huge and extremely grimy, from coal dust within and the lorries hurtling past outside. The piano was see-through, all the panels having disappeared, and one of the pedals lay limply on the floor like a dead leaf on an African violet. There was a lavatory far away across the back-yard, approached through a deep puddle and unlocked with an iron key. Alan Strachan, directing us, wore a thick scarf up to his chin; everything we touched was cold and dusty.

How I loved it all! The demon had gone from me, which left me free to concentrate on the deceptively easy text of Coward's *Private Lives, Blithe Spirit, Brief Encounter, Tonight at Eight Thirty*, letters and telegrams, woven together with his songs, telling the story of the relationship between Noël and Gertrude Lawrence. David Shilling, best known for his attention-grabbing hats, made me a white brocade dress, with a low back and floating shoulder panels, cut on the cross, with a skirt gored with silk chiffon and studded with silver bows. There were virtually no props: a glass, a cigarette, and two wooden boxes which could be put together to make a bench or be separated like two chairs. Our three-week rehearsal period drew to a close and we moved to the King's Head to run through it on the tiny stage before we opened for the first of our four previews.

It was mid-afternoon, we were half-way through the dress rehearsal and our public performance was only four hours away. For some reason, I thought Simon had placed the box he had just moved wrongly. 'Not there surely: *there*,' and I picked it up and plonked it down six inches further forward. Exactly then, I slipped a disc in my lower neck.

As swiftly as a self-inflated dinghy, my left shoulder rose in a muscular spasm, moving my neck sideways and downwards until I looked as though I was doing a feeble imitation of the hunchback of Notre Dame. I couldn't turn my head at all, not a centimetre either way, and to compensate for my uneven shoulders, my hips re-arranged themselves into their own version of levelness.

Barry Robertson, the osteopath, who had un-crocked me (and most performers in London) for the past eight years was out of the country. It was five o'clock when our choreographer Kenn Oldfield put me face-down on the floor and walked anxiously up and down my spine, and six-thirty when they found a doctor in Wimpole Street, who pushed a long needle into my hump and wrote a prescription for quadruple strength pain-killers. We did the show but it was a blur in my memory, my mouth thick from the drugs which didn't get to the pain as much as slow down my reactions. I was beyond it all, out of it: not so the rest of the cast, who had to work like fiends to get the audience to believe that Gertie Lawrence as I portrayed her was a magical captivating performer. Three, four days in bed; then the first night and on with the show.

Part of the reason for not being afraid was our dressing-room. Behind the black-painted stage, raised to about table level, was a corridor leading to a lavatory. It was where we all changed every night. It was half the width of a railway carriage, with shelves above us and hooks behind us on which our glamorous evening clothes hung. Under these conditions you must brush aside normal feelings of modesty. McAlister had a colourful line in underpants and was nicknamed 'Unterhosen'. Bevan and I sausaged away our hair like Hilda Ogdens and squeezed into wigs. Sheridan or Tickner were allotted the lavatory position and had to be climbed over by us all as they struggled in a tight corner between door and chair into immaculate dinner jackets. Simon would start, 'M-yee, m-yee, m-yah m-yah papalaka papalaka papalaka *poo*,' and we all gargled and sprayed and combed and prinked in front of lighted mirrors. Blezard liked to eat before the show.

'What did you have tonight, Blez?'

'A goodish piece of cod, jam sponge and custard.' Blez almost always had fish. Outside, people would be finishing their food, tables were being cleared. 'What was on the menu tonight? Oh dear.' The audience reacted predictably to the food; some dishes made them uneasy for the rest of the evening. They were allowed wine and coffee during the show, and seemed to like being able to sit with their elbows on a table. Then Blez would start playing, to warm them up and quieten them down, and his music at once soothed and excited them. Soon came the familiar bars which meant prepare, get ready, positions please, and then stepping out into the spot-lights.

There was something about the King's Head, with the pub behind the room where we performed, something about the leaking roof and lack of ventilation, about the audience being on top of you, about Dan Crawford stuffing an extra £10 note into our tiny pay packets ('What's this, Dan?' 'Oh, the show's going well, you know, why not') that made it the happiest place to be on a May evening in 1983.

I love short runs: no time to get bored (or even to get it right, often), only concentration, packed houses and regret when it ends. My life seemed to be getting fuller and fuller; trips to the USA to promote the *Pink Panther* films, a visit to India, a test-drive of a Mercedes in Siena, a directorship of Capital Radio, journeys to Egypt, Norway and the Masai Mara in Kenya; switching on the Blackpool lights and sitting in for David Frost on his Sunday morning show on TV A.M. Television shows – *The Weather in the Streets*, *The Glory Boys* and *Mistral's Daughter* – enabled me to take stage jobs which couldn't offer much money. Would I play Hedda Gabler at the Dundee Repertory Theatre? I packed my bags and left for Scot-land.

Dundee Rep was everything a small provincial theatre should be: professional, poor-ish, ambitious and user-friendly, in that the public used the restaurant in the daytime and packed the auditorium at night. Wonderful, open Scotland; it was just the place to perform Ibsen's claustrophobic play. Translated by Christopher Hampton, it was both formal and funny, and the story came as a shock every night. Robert Robertson, who directed it, said this about making a fluff or mistake: 'Forgive yourself at once.' Forgive yourself at once! What a terrific, invigorating idea! Not just for actors, but for everyone who has gone wrong and must continue as best they may. Guilt is a ball and chain: if you can't change what has happened, put it behind you and just concentrate on the future.

I used to walk along the beach by Broughty Ferry in the afternoon before going to the theatre. One day, when the sun was particularly bright and the Tay's waves extra sparkling and the beach as empty as the desert, I said out loud to myself, 'I wish I had a dog.' Immediately, by my right side was a black mongrel dog. I was far from the road and the row of small houses, I was right by the water's edge and yet suddenly there was this dog. He was holding a stick in his mouth, which I threw and he fetched. He barked at the waves, raced round me in mad circles, put his nose in my hand and trotted along beside me. After quarter of an hour, I said, 'Well, I've got to go to the theatre now, dog,' and he put the stick down at my feet, turned and ran flat out, away, up the beach, never stopping or turning, until he was a black dot in the distance, and then he was gone.

Jamie came to see me in Dundee, travelling up on a train, nursing a bout of flu during school half-term. Something rather marvellous happens to children: they start off being small with a prodigious amount of luggage, and suddenly they've grown-up and carry your suitcases as well as their own. He is an excellent critic, generous, observant, open-minded and articulate. I love it when he's in the audience, knowing I'll get a fair appraisal of the play.

It was quite a thrill, some months later when we were back in London, to find an invitation from Stephen Barlow asking us both down to Glyndebourne to see Oliver Knussen's double bill, 'Higglety Pigglety Pop' and 'Where the Wild Things Are'. Stephen was conducting one half of the show. We packed up a picnic supper, Jamie put on his dinner jacket and I dug out my old white Mexicana dress, all layers of cotton and flounces and grand enough to go to Glyndebourne. Forgetting to pack the champagne, we drove down to Sussex, following the instructions given to us by Stephen over the telephone, and parked in the mud on a mizzly English summer evening. After the first half, we walked out to the lawns and spread out the cloth, putting out bits and pieces and sharing the supper which Jonathan and Elizabeth Groves had brought. Jonathan was Stephen's agent. The drizzle had stopped and it became a long pale English dusk. We all talked and ate, except Stephen, who was ticking slightly as the time grew nearer to the second half. ('One down, one to go,' I had heard a man remark as he wrestled his way towards the bar.)

'I'll take a picture of you,' said Jamie, so we stood up, dusting away the grass and crumbs, and I politely took Stephen's arm and there we were, in front of the house, wreathed in smiles, me clothed all in white, the wind blowing our hair. When people see it now, they say, 'Is that your wedding photograph?' It wasn't, of course: all that would come much later. This was just a run-through with photo-call, arranged by fate: a dress-rehearsal: this was just a photograph of the future.